THE EXTRAORDINARY FIXER

THE EXTRAORDINARY FIXER

THE UNCONVENTIONAL AGENT BEAUFONT™ BOOK 1

SARAH NOFFKE

MICHAEL ANDERLE

DISRUPTIVE IMAGINATION

LMBPN Publishing
PMB 196, 2540 South Maryland Pkwy
Las Vegas, NV 89109

Version 1.00, February 2022
eBook ISBN: 978-1-68500-533-7
Print ISBN: 978-1-68500-534-4

THE EXTRAORDINARY FIXER TEAM

Thanks to the JIT Readers

Dave Hicks
Deb Mader
Veronica Stephan-Miller
Dorothy Lloyd
Christopher Gilliard
Debi Sateren
Angel LaVey

If we've missed anyone, please let us know!

Editor
The Skyfyre Editing Team

For, Craig, my rockstar. I'd always be front row at all your shows.

— Sarah

To Family, Friends and
Those Who Love
to Read.
May We All Enjoy Grace
to Live the Life We Are
Called.

— Michael

CHAPTER ONE

Recording Studio, Rooster Records, Hollywood, California

The padded walls inside the large recording studio absorbed the guttural screams full of a unique pain. The band members of Punch Line, the hottest rock band in the world, were used to loud noises. However, all of them still winced from the screams as they watched the needle penetrate the lead singer's arm as if it were them getting the tattoo and not Archer Finch.

"This isn't right," the keyboardist implored, running his hands through his dark brown hair. His gaze reflected tension as he watched the scene before them.

"It's necessary," Archer stated through clenched teeth, tears spilling over his cheeks from his bloodshot red eyes.

"Is it, though?" The drummer looked between the tattoo artist and the lead singer.

The tattooist simply shrugged and glanced at the man standing on his right. His attire was much more formal than the rest, a starched black suit and a bowler hat that shielded his eyes. He'd introduced himself simply as Mr. J, and that's how he'd signed the contract he held in his hand, as well.

Mr. J nodded sternly. "The ink is full of powerful magic.

Unfortunately, that's going to make the process of tattooing much more painful than usual."

The tattooist nodded as if this was a sufficient answer and continued his work. Archer screamed as soon as the needle touched his skin, but he remained still, and the words etched on his skin began to glow—imbued with magic unlike any other.

"Maybe we don't have to do this," the bassist offered, but there was no conviction in his voice as he slumped on a stool in the corner.

"I do." Archer kept his eyes pressed shut tightly, and his head back like the pain would soon make him pass out. His long black hair had come loose from its usual ponytail and matted to his sweaty face. The many other tattoos on his arm appeared ordinary alongside the new one full of lyrics from the band's soon-to-be latest song.

"I don't have to do this," the keyboardist argued, shaking his head in disgust. "Look what this is doing to you. It's breaking you."

Archer's eyes flashed open, sudden soberness in them as he stared at the other man. "No, don't you get it? I was already broken. *She* did that to me when she dumped me. Since I'll never feel love again, no one else will either. I want everyone who listens to our music to know the same heartbreak as me."

"That's wrong." The drummer's voice suddenly grew uncharacteristically loud.

"It's the way of the world," the guitarist stated matter-of-factly, leaning against the wall in the corner.

"Heartbreak sells." Mr. J lifted his chin and flashed a convincing look at the drummer.

"So did our other songs that were about love." The keyboardist braced his shoulders like he was about to fight over the matter, although he wasn't the type.

"I can't write love songs anymore." Archer closed his eyes. He seemed calmer now, like he'd gotten used to the pain—assimilated it with the other wounds he harbored.

"This new song is a killer." The tattooist leaned forward to study his work, a series of lines surrounded by musical notes. "It's going to be your biggest hit yet."

"This magic will make it break people's hearts who are in love," the drummer argued.

"That will make them come back for more and more music." Mr. J's voice was quiet but commanding. "Those who are broken always want a song that drives the dagger deeper into their wounds."

The keyboardist shook his head. "That's sick, man."

"It's the way of the world," Mr. J said coldly.

"We don't need the money that badly," the drummer insisted, starting to pace, his head down like he was brainstorming. "I can write a song. We all can."

"You all are shit at writing songs. I'm the writer in the group, and you all know it." Archer's eyes were still closed.

"I *do* need the money," the bassist insisted. "I burned through the money from the last tour."

"Me too." The guitarist nodded.

"Then you sing this song, and it will make millions." None saw the wicked smile Mr. J hid with his chin tucked and his bowler hat low. "Then you write other songs, we'll do the same thing, and you continue to break hearts and rise higher than ever. You'll be the greatest rock band in history."

The drummer halted his pacing and threw up his arms. "But we'll have hurt so many to do it. Everyone who hears this song with lyrics we've charmed will have their hearts broken."

"Do you think The Rolling Stones, The Doors, or Pink Floyd became legends singing love ballads?" Mr. J spoke like he was asking about that day's weather.

"What about the Beatles?" the keyboardist countered. "They wrote about love."

SARAH NOFFKE & MICHAEL ANDERLE

"They also wrote about death, loneliness, conflict, and heartache," the bassist declared.

The drummer spun to face his band member, his face red with surprise. "Whose side are you on?"

He shrugged. "I'm on the side that gets us money. Lots of it. Quick and easy."

"I second that." The guitarist nodded.

Mr. J folded the contract that Archer had signed on behalf of the band. "I assure you that this song and the ones that follow will make you richer than ever before."

The drummer turned to face the lead singer. "How are we supposed to believe this guy? He shows up and gives you some magic ink that's supposed to make our song resonate stronger with fans, and we just take his word for it?"

"The magic ink will work, I assure you. It will make the song a hit, much bigger than it could have been on its own. I'll also handle all the distribution of the new record," Mr. J interrupted. "Sing the songs, and I'll take care of the rest. It makes it all quite simple for you."

"It sounds fishy to me." The keyboardist shook his head, his eyes hooded.

"You said you wanted to play music and drop all the bureaucracy that went with our last label," the bassist stated. "This is our chance. If this is a home run and all we have to do is sing this song, why not do it, take the money and run?"

Mr. J nodded approvingly. "When you have another song, I'll supply the ink. Then we do it all again."

"You said that once we broke hearts, the fans would line up for the next songs," the drummer argued. "Why would we need to keep putting Archer through this?"

The man in the suit tilted his head back and forth. "You don't, but you'll make more this way."

"I'm fine with it," Archer grunted.

"Then I am too," the bassist said. The guitarist nodded in agreement beside him.

"You need to get over her," the keyboardist argued, giving the lead singer a meaningful look.

Archer flashed him a murderous glare, his eyes sharp. "There is no getting over Ella. That's impossible. Don't you see, that's why I'm doing this."

"Arch." The keyboardist softened a little. "It takes time."

Archer shook his head. "You don't get over the love of your life. You simply write songs that hopefully break the rest of the world so they don't get to have the love you lost."

"This is the song that will do it." The tattooist slid back and appraised his work, a scroll of words that ran down Archer's bicep. "I'm all done."

Without hesitation, Archer Finch rose to his feet and looked each one of his band members in the eyes. "Then we play the song. We find out if this works. If it does, we record it and release it worldwide."

The bassist and guitarist didn't need more encouragement to pick up their nearby instruments. However, the drummer and keyboardist stood frozen.

It was the tattooist who asked the question they must have been thinking. "If you all play this song with magical lyrics and we hear it, won't we all feel sad?"

Mr. J lifted his chin so everyone could better see his face and flashed a rare smile for them all to witness. "I think we can all agree that the seven of us in this room are already broken. It's the lovers of the world who are at risk. It's their hearts that will shatter when they hear this song. They'll line up to pay top dollar for concert tickets and merchandise and buy every record you ever release."

"Amen to that." The bassist strummed his strings, his expression hungry.

Archer took his place in front of the microphone, grabbing it with the arm that wasn't red from magical ink. He glanced back at his band members, the keyboardist and drummer finally having caved and taken their spots. "Are you all ready to break some hearts?"

They all nodded, some more enthused than others. When the band started playing, the music that followed created red notes in the air that looked like dust particles in the wind as they swirled and crashed into the studio's padded walls. Mr. J smiled with a knowing look.

"Is that what's supposed to happen?" The tattooist watched as musical notes soared off the instruments and flew around the recording studio like ghosts haunting the space.

"Yes," Mr. J answered before Archer opened his mouth and sang words that sounded much more painful than his earlier screams. The lyrics of his heartbreak song were beautiful. They were poetry. When broadcast worldwide, they'd tear lovers apart.

CHAPTER TWO

Little Pleasures Farmhouse, Outskirts of Boulder, Colorado

Love was the confluence of two things. It was that simple. Most overcomplicated it, but not Guinevere Paris Beaufont. She knew from an early age that true love was a union. One of two people. One of two elements. The flowing together of respect and passion. Without both the people and the elements, love simply didn't work. Paris understood that better than most because she was unlike anyone on the planet—due to her very composition.

"Do I look like an agent for the Casual Love department at Fairy Godmother Agency?" Paris peered at her image in the mirror that hung over the hostess stand of Little Pleasures restaurant. It was currently closed, but the preparations for that night's dinner service were audible in the distance.

Faraday, a squirrel unlike any other, glanced up from a strange device he'd been tinkering with on a sideboard and snickered, flicking his bushy tail. "You look like a motorcycle cop."

Paris sighed, blowing an errant strand of blonde hair away from her heart-shaped face. She whipped off the reflective sunglasses she'd been wearing and held them up. "I'm an agent. What do agents wear?"

"Suits, usually." Faraday returned his attention to the device. When fixed, it would either neutralize radioactive particles or blow something up. With the strange scientific squirrel, it was hard to know how his clever experiments would turn out.

Paris grunted, turning back to her reflection. She glanced at the new leather jacket her parents had bought her to replace the ripped one she used to covet. This one had more buttons and straps and was much nicer.

Although she was an adult, she rarely felt like one, but the leather jacket made her feel young and old at the same time. "I'm not wearing that suit the FGA sent, citing some bologna that it's an agent's uniform. I think it was a men's suit anyway, so I'll tell them it didn't fit, the zipper was on the wrong side, and therefore, I'd never figure it out."

"I don't think that excuse will fly," Faraday muttered, his focus mostly on the device as he picked up a tiny screwdriver and went to work.

"I'm about to make you fly, squirrel."

"Oh, your threats always make this feel like a real home," Faraday said, mock sentiment in his tone. "You never wore the pale blue gown they issued you at fairy godmother college, so I don't think anyone will be surprised when you show up on your first day as an agent at FGA dressed like a biker's girlfriend."

Paris scoffed, turning again and brandishing a punishing glare. "As if I need to ride on the back of some guy's hog. I would have my own and make my boyfriend ride behind me."

"You wouldn't be caught dead on a motorcycle," Faraday countered matter-of-factly.

"Well, of course not. They're death traps. Speaking of which, did you know that there's a vat of some green glowing sludge in the basement downstairs?"

Faraday looked up suddenly, tensed, and gulped. "Oh, you found that, did you?"

"It's yours, isn't it, squirrel? What is it?"

"It's nothing," he chirped uncomfortably, his eyes skirting to the side.

"By nothing, do you mean that it's probably plutonium?"

He laughed nervously. "Plutonium. Oh, Pare. You're so cute. I'd never store plutonium under your restaurant and home. If I did, I'd ensure that it was in a very safe and magically sealed container that only the most experienced scientist could open and only under the most stringent of circumstances when needed for experimental purposes, of course."

"Don't blow this place up, Fare, or we're putting squirrel on the menu here."

He nodded, returning to his work. "I promise that when I test this new device, I'll do it far from the property. I might need your help carting that silly and very safe container to a deserted section of the Mojave Desert for me, hundreds of miles from human life."

She rolled her eyes. "I'm an agent for FGA, the magical organization that's in charge of creating, monitoring, protecting, and furthering love in this world so the Earth remains a mostly happy and healthy place. My job is *not* to be your lab assistant."

"Science makes the world a better place too," he argued, shaking his shoulders and obviously offended.

"Oh, for the love of the angels, the things I have to deal with," Paris complained as the head chef for Little Pleasures restaurant strode in from the back, absentmindedly reading that night's menu.

"I told them to take parsnips off the appetizers." Clark Beaufont shook his head.

"Is everything okay, Uncle Clark?" Paris gave the man with slicked-back blond hair and a worried expression a thoughtful look.

The head chef wasn't only Paris' uncle or the one who ran the kitchen for the farm-to-table restaurant she owned. He was also a Councilor for the House of Fourteen—the organization that governed magic in the world. The man didn't like to sleep or socialize, so for him, working two full-time jobs wasn't that big of a deal.

Clark glanced up, saw his niece, and smiled. "Nothing for you to worry about, Pare. Your concern should be getting ready for your first day as an agent. Go ahead and get dressed, and I'll put together some lunch for you to take."

Paris grunted, glancing at Faraday and then her uncle. "I am ready. This is what I'm wearing."

The squirrel and the man exchanged looks before running their eyes over Paris' black leather pants and boots that matched her jacket and the reflective glasses in her hand. Finally, Faraday shook his head and smirked at her. "I told you that you look like a motorcycle cop."

She shook her head dismissively and returned her attention to Clark. "What's wrong with the menu for tonight?"

"Nothing," Clark lied. Then he caught the challenging look in her eyes, deflated, and admitted, "Well, it's just that the front of the house put parsnips on the appetizers menu and the crop didn't yield enough for tonight's booking. Reservations are full."

"Don't worry, no one will order the parsnips," Faraday offered.

Paris nodded. "Yeah, even the squirrel won't eat those things."

Clark frowned. "I happen to like parsnips."

"Well, then don't worry if we don't have enough," Paris began. "I'm sure they will turnip."

Faraday groaned, set down the device in his paws, and shook his head. "Oh, wow. You didn't just make that joke...not that I'd classify it as such."

"I did, and it was brilliant," Paris stated proudly.

"On that note, I'm going to go and get some equipment before we head out to FGA Tower for our big day." Faraday scurried off the table and up the stairs that led to the farmhouse's living area.

"*My* big day," Paris called after him. "Don't forget that you're my sidekick and simply accompany me, who is the agent and totally looks like one."

Hemingway, the groundskeeper for the farm and Paris' boyfriend, snickered as he entered from the back. He carried two brown paper sacks. "Yeah, no better way than to be taken seriously as an agent at FGA than to bring a squirrel to work."

"A talking squirrel," Paris argued, smiling at him. "He knows science too. And can get into small places."

Hemingway winked. He hadn't been out to the field yet because dirt didn't cake his jeans and flannel shirt, but it would soon. His roguish dark brown hair was still in place, but by the end of the day, it would be windswept. His handsome, bright blue eyes would still be buzzing with delight after all the hard work. "I feel better knowing that genius is with you at all times."

"*Most* times," she amended. "If he follows me to the bathroom, he's getting nailed to the wall."

Clark and Hemingway laughed.

"So we didn't get a full harvest of parsnips this season?" Paris asked her boyfriend.

He nodded. "It appears so. The crops are still young. I'm sure next year they'll yield more."

Little Pleasures farm and restaurant was young at barely a year old. It had been part of Paris' graduation project from Happily Ever After College, the place that trained fairy godmothers. The students were assigned to create a business that promoted love to graduate. Many went small or safe. Not Paris Beaufont, though.

She'd created a huge farm with animals, a farmhouse, and grounds that provided everything Little Pleasures restaurant served. The place produced dishes using magical ingredients and experiences that left their patrons feeling intoxicated, satisfied, and comforted. Its purpose was in its name: to give their guests little pleasures. In doing so, hopefully, the patrons left and created more love in their world, thereby creating a domino effect on the planet.

The graduation project had been an enormous success. That was chiefly why Paris had achieved her promotion to an agent at FGA instead of being assigned a role as a fairy godmother for one of its many departments.

In truth, Paris never wanted to be a fairy godmother and had told the leader of FGA as much, none other than Saint Valentine himself. She wasn't like the others in her class at Happily Ever After College.

First, she hadn't wanted to attend the place to begin with. It had been a way to keep her out of jail—a second chance effort to erase her long rap sheet. Once the love-jaded young woman started at the college, she liked creating love in the world, but not as a fairy godmother.

Paris was different from her peers in other ways too. The rebel wasn't only a fairy like them. She was that, but she was also something else. Paris Beaufont was and remained the only half-fairy and half-magician in the world.

She was a product of a genie's wish, one her mother had made to ensure that Paris wasn't born a demon since her father had been bitten by one. The whole thing was very complicated, and it only got more so.

You see, Paris was also part-demon. So she was more than a halfling. She was unique. Irreplaceable. A person who it was impossible to replicate...ever again. Her mixed blood made her sensitive like a fairy, analytical like a magician, and powerful like a demon. That was chiefly why Saint Valentine made her the very first female agent for FGA, giving her the Casual Love department to manage.

The wise leader knew that Paris didn't fit as a fairy godmother. However, he couldn't deny that the agency needed her. In her short time at Happily Ever After College, she'd already proven to have a unique way of dealing with the old problems related to love and the world. Saint Valentine was an aging man forced into a modern world where love was evolving. He might not be changing with the times, but he knew enough to employ those who could better tackle the challenges that the new generations would encounter when it came to love.

So although FGA historically had male agents who led the departments and female fairy godmothers who took their orders, things were about to change. A new halfling was about to set foot into FGA Tower and do things the only way she knew how —her way.

CHAPTER THREE

Little Pleasures Farmhouse, Outskirts of Boulder, Colorado

Paris gave her Uncle Clark an apologetic look. "Well, take the parsnips off the menu. It sounds like on the rare occasion that someone might order them, we'll disappoint since we don't have enough. The last thing Little Pleasure does is disappoint."

Clark frowned, shaking his head. "Parsnips are delicious, especially how I make them."

"I love everything you make. However, when given the option between sweet potato taquitos, mozzarella sticks with marinara, or pureed parsnips, I'm not ordering the latter."

"Hey, my crop of parsnips are delicious," Hemingway said proudly.

Paris rolled her eyes. "So now I've offended both the grower and the chef. Cool. I've got a question for you then. Either can answer. What's the difference between parsnips and boogers?"

Hemingway and Clark exchanged looks of confusion. Finally, the head chef shrugged and said, "I don't know. What's the difference between parsnips and boogers?"

"Children will eat boogers." Paris winked and smiled at her uncle.

Neither of the men laughed.

"So you might want to lay off the jokes on the first day," Hemingway offered casually.

"Or the first week," Clark added.

"Or the first year," Hemingway tacked on.

Paris shook her head, returned her attention to Clark, and ignored their advice. "Are you all set otherwise for tonight? I don't know when I'll be back. Traffic could be a mess."

Hemingway chuckled. "You're portaling to work."

"Well, you know how the portaling channels can get congested during peak times. I mean, it will be rush hour," she argued.

Clark's lips pursed as his expression turned confused. "I'm not aware of portaling channels or any—"

"She's making it up," Hemingway interrupted.

Clark nodded. "Of course. I should have realized."

"Anyway." Paris continued to stare at her uncle. "It's booked tonight. Is the kitchen prepped? The waitstaff lined up? How about the grounds?"

"Pare, everything is under control," Clark answered calmly. "None of this should be your concern. You turned over the restaurant's operation to Hemingway and me, and we're perfectly capable of taking charge of things. Your job is at FGA. Now, I'll go and get your lunch together. Who knows what kind of sugary snacks they'll have in the break room at that place. You'll crash by mid-day if you eat too much fairy food. I swear those fairies survive off cane sugar alone."

"They do, I can attest from my time at Happily Ever After College," Hemingway offered, holding up the two brown sacks in his hands. "I already got Paris' and Faraday's lunches and snacks together."

Before becoming the groundskeeper for Little Pleasures, Hemingway had worked at the fairy godmother college. That's where he and Paris had met and fallen in love. Together they'd left it behind. Now they were starting a new chapter of their lives.

A chapter that left Paris feeling very nervous. She was setting off to a strange new place with stuffy agents and rule-abiding fairy godmothers. Even more stressful was that she was leaving Hemingway behind at Little Pleasures.

Sure, she'd see him later, but she didn't know when that would be or what her days would be like. Paris didn't know what her life was about to look like. She did know that there was no turning back. She was an agent now.

She tilted her head and gave Hemingway a sweet smile. "You made our lunch? Thank you. That's very sweet."

He gave her a coy look. "You're welcome. Don't get yours mixed up with Faraday's. Otherwise, he'll get the wrong impression if he reads the note in the bag for you."

Paris paused as she was reaching for the brown bags. "You included a love note in my lunch?"

He nodded.

She didn't take the sacks despite her outstretched hand. "It sounds like you put a note in Faraday's too?"

He nodded again.

"What does his say?"

"I told him to be a good squirrel and keep an eye on you."

Paris laughed. "You have met Faraday, right? He's curious by nature and is always getting himself into trouble, which in turn means he's always getting me in trouble."

Hemingway nodded. "Yes, but you two take care of each other at the end of the day."

"Well, thank you for lunch." Paris eyed the brown bags. "However, is it okay if I don't bring those today? I'm not sure the other agents will take me seriously if I show up with a packed lunch."

Hemingway nodded, sticking the bags on the hostess stand. "Sure, but do you think they'll take you seriously wearing those sunglasses?" He pointed at the reflective shades in her hand.

She gawked at him. "Of course. Have you seen *Men in Black?*"

Clark and Hemingway exchanged nods.

"Yeah, they wear black suits like the one FGA sent you," Hemingway answered.

Paris rolled her eyes. "Yes, but the important takeaway is that they have those cool shades. Just like these." She held up her sunglasses.

Hemingway pulled his mouth to the side with a speculative look. "I don't think that's the takeaway for most."

Chuckling, Clark strode over, kissed Paris on the cheek, and smiled down at her. "Regardless of what you wear, you're going to impress everyone. Have a great first day, Pare. I know you'll do wonderfully."

"Thanks, Uncle Clark. I hope so." Paris smiled up at him. "If you need anything with the restaurant, I'll have my phone—"

Clark shook his head, striding back for the kitchen. "I'll be fine. Don't worry. Focus on you. And be safe."

"I create love, not fight pirates," she called after him. "How dangerous will it be?"

Clark turned at the dining room with a challenging look. "You're a Beaufont. Danger will find you, regardless of what you do. It's inevitable."

She sighed. "You see why I'm worried about you here."

"Pare, you're a young halfling who will probably be in the field. However, I'm an experienced magician who runs a restaurant protected by powerful wards," he argued. "I'll be fine. If I'm not, I've fought my way out of more battles than most. Not your mother or your aunt, but still. I'll be fine."

Paris nodded. Liv Beaufont, her mother, was a Warrior for the House of Fourteen and the most formidable force on the planet. Liv was the very reason Earth was still spinning on its axis. Her Aunt Sophia was a dragonrider and pretty much kept mortals from warring on a daily basis. To say the very least, Paris had big shoes to fill. She came from the stuff of legend.

Hemingway must have sensed that the stress of the first day had crept back into Paris' head because when Uncle Clark vanished into the back, he stepped forward and put both of his hands on her shoulders. He leaned his forehead against hers and smiled into her eyes. "You're going to be great. Better than great. You're going to set a new standard because...well..."

"I'm a Beaufont," Paris supplied.

He shook his head. "No, being a Beaufont makes you great, for sure. You come from one of the first magical families on this planet. The magic that runs in you and your relatives is stronger than most. Your mother, your sister, and Clark are the most honorable, bravest people I've had the pleasure to meet. However, you're going to be amazing because no one understands love better than you, Pare. I know that firsthand, better than most. You're the protector of love. It's what you were born to do, and you'll never let anything threaten it because it's what makes this world go 'round."

There was no response Paris could give to this, so she simply leaned into the man before her and pressed her lips against his— her kiss, her way of saying, "thank you."

After the tender moment had come to a natural end, Paris and Hemingway pulled apart. He looked her over once more. "Okay, you don't need a lunch. You have your trusty leather jacket and your cool shades. Need anything else?"

"My squirrel," she supplied.

He nodded. "That's what all the girls say. None can leave the house without one."

"I'm here," Faraday squeaked, hurrying down the stairs. "I had to check my catalytic-hydro-filter-permeator to ensure it was on a low setting. We wouldn't want it overheating."

Paris growled, stepping away from Hemingway. "If you want to destroy the squirrel's lodging area while we're gone, you're welcome to. You might be saving all of us from being launched into the sky while we sleep."

Hemingway laughed. "I'm sure Faraday was joking. I don't think there's such a thing as a catalyst-blankety-permanent-thing. Right?" He gave the squirrel a pointed look.

"That's right." Faraday paused beside Paris. "I was telling one of my usual jokes."

Paris shook her head, offering Hemingway a smile. "Well, I'm off."

"I'll see you both for dinner." Hemingway leaned down and kissed Paris discreetly on the cheek.

She suddenly hugged him tightly, pulling him to her for an extra bit of comfort. He was more than happy to oblige and wrapped his arms around the tiny halfling. Like her mother and aunt, she was short and petite but all muscle. Unlike them, Paris had wings, but like most fairies, glamoured them away. They were too much of a nuisance and not at all useful. Wings were mostly for show, which was why only the fae brandished them.

Pulling away once more, Paris straightened, trying to bolster her confidence.

"As I said, you'll be great," Hemingway encouraged with a twinkle in his eyes. Once more he pressed his lips to Paris', and that kiss was enough to give her the hope that her first day would go smoothly. It simply had to. Saint Valentine and so many others had wagered their reputations on her. She couldn't let them down.

Hemingway looked at Faraday and squatted so he was closer to his height. "And you, little guy, will do great too. Now, do you want a goodbye kiss also?"

"Do you want me to bite your jugular?" Faraday asked simply.

Hemingway thought about it and shook his head. "I like the way my jugular is currently. You know, all intact and stuff."

"Then keep your lips to yourself."

Hemingway nodded and settled for reaching out and patting the talking squirrel on the head. "Good luck, Faraday. Look out for my girl."

"Consider it done."

Although they didn't say it, one could see the mutual respect Paris' two best friends shared for each other.

"Okay, well, I don't want to be late for my first day, so we better head out." Paris strode toward the farmhouse's front door.

"Have a good day." Hemingway waved.

"We will." Faraday scurried after Paris as she opened the door. The early morning sunlight streamed across the large porch.

The mountains and farmland were always beautiful. She sucked in the sight, knowing that after they stepped through the portal to FGA Tower, the landscape would change greatly.

CHAPTER FOUR

FGA Tower Plaza, New York City, New York

The polluted air and loud noise were the first indications that Paris and Faraday had entered a new world, unlike the one they'd come from. In contrast to the farm in Colorado, where the temperatures were brisk but manageable, the air was biting in New York City—adding insult to injury as Paris pinched her nose from the chemical smells. The sounds of car horns, screeching tires, and engines were also a stark contrast to the quiet expanse on the farm where only the songbirds and crickets interrupted the silence.

"We're not in Kansas anymore," Paris said as she closed the portal behind her and took in the many sights demanding her attention.

Faraday rolled his small dark eyes, studying the area too. "Colorado. Little Pleasures is in Colorado." The squirrel shook his head. "We have to work on your geography knowledge."

Paris held up a fist and brandished it at the squirrel. "I'll show you some geography."

He sighed with disappointment. "Again, I think you're confused. Your hand and its appendages are better known as anatomy. I get that science is hard for you. We'll keep working on it."

"I've got something for you to work on," Paris muttered, too distracted by their surroundings to volley a better insult or threat.

The portal had taken them straight to the large plaza around FGA Tower, as Paris had been informed prior to her start date. Her instructions further stated to find the "large" fountain at the front of the fifty-floor skyscraper and wait for her tour guide, which would start her orientation.

The bricked plaza was bustling with fairy godmothers in the pale blue silk gowns with large pink ribbons tied around the collar, signifying they were graduates of Happily Ever After College. The magic of the gowns made the women's hair all a soft grayish-blue, which contrasted with their young faces. The idea was that the Cinderellas and Prince Charmings they matched were more trusting of grandmother-type figures. Paris thought it was a poor attempt at conformity and refused to put the gown on when at the fairy godmother college.

That's why Faraday was correct, and no one should be surprised that she hadn't worn the agent uniform that FGA had sent for her. Mae Ling, Paris' mentor at the college, had encouraged Paris not to conform from the beginning. The mysterious fairy godmother didn't wear the gown either, did things her way, and no one seemed to mind. She had further told Paris that her rebellious ways would save the fairy godmothers one day, but how remained a mystery. That was how Mae Ling worked, often talking in riddles.

Paris' Aunt Sophia had echoed this advice about conformity but then complicated it when she gave her a pep talk the night before her first day. Last night she'd told Paris not to conform but to kind of conform. Talk about confounding. Sophia had then told Paris that she and Mae Ling would further explain the night of her first day when they had a little "field trip" to take her on with them.

In contrast to the fairy godmothers, agents arrived in their starched black or dark navy blue suits through portals—all showing up for a day of work at FGA. Apparently, the plaza around the shiny skyscraper was a portal zone. Inside the building, wards would prevent anyone from arriving that way, which was consistent with most magical places. There were usually barriers in place that stopped entry from those not invited and also portal blockers. The plaza seemed to be an open spot, but Paris suspected it had further protections from the rest of the buzzing city around it.

The agents couldn't have looked more different from the fairy godmothers they managed. The women who went out into the field to create love in the various departments were whimsical, full of smiles, and probably giggled with their manicured hands over their mouths. They held wands and didn't hurt their tiny brains with complex things like working out the solutions to matchmaking. That all was for the agents to do.

The agents for FGA were all men in dark suits who didn't carry wands. Instead, they usually wore sullen expressions, a lack of humor, and a magical instrument that directed their powers. Unlike magicians, fairies usually needed a tool of sorts to channel their powers.

Fairy godmothers used wands. Agents often had small things like pens, tie clips, or a piece of jewelry. Saint Valentine carried an elegant silver cane that was his. All of the objects held a gem, which identified the agent and became their name.

Paris briefly recalled the agents she'd met: Agent Opal, Agent Topaz, and Agent Ruby. Bitterly she remembered the latter who'd been all about preserving the old ways at the expense of the current institution's integrity. Paris had to bring that man down before he brought down Saint Valentine.

It had been then and only then that Paris had visited FGA to rid it of the demons that Agent Ruby had allowed to infiltrate the place. She'd done that alongside her father, Stefan Ludwig, the famous demon hunter for the House of Fourteen.

Of course, the prospects of death had preoccupied Paris too much to take in many of the sights. That's what was currently soaking up her attention since she wasn't worried about her survival, although after her Uncle Clark's warning, she realized that she should be. Beaufonts were never safe. They seemed to be danger magnets. That was because their charge was to uphold justice, which usually put them in evil's path.

Paris didn't feel invisible as she and Faraday stood watching portals open all over the plaza and fairy godmothers and agents file through and head for the tall mirrored building ahead of them. She realized that many were gawking at her as they passed, although they kept their expressions politely neutral.

Word would have gotten out about the halfling with demon blood who would be the first female agent at FGA. Paris had prepared for the whispers. Since starting at Happily Ever After College, she'd gotten used to being the subject of gossip.

"Wow, look at all the weary commuters," Paris joked as all the shimmering blue portals opened, blue- or black-dressed women and men spilled out, and strode ahead.

"I'm not sure if the people here will get your sarcasm," Faraday offered, intently watching the passersby too.

"By here, do you mean 'Earth?'"

"Something like that." He hid a grin. "There's the fountain over there." He pointed.

The squirrel was getting about as many looks as Paris in her leather jacket with her messy blonde shoulder-length hair. She looked in that direction and realized it had to be the meeting spot. The fountain was round and came straight out of the ground with spigots that shot water straight into the air in patterns. For a solid ten seconds, Paris watched as the alternating streams of water went on and off together, then took turns. She realized she could stick around most of the day and watch it but figured that would get her fired.

Best to not get fired on one's first day at a job, she thought. That was better on the second day, which would probably be the case knowing her track record. She'd gotten kicked out of Happily Ever After College on her first day, so that set her expectations.

In the distance around the skyscraper, Paris saw other areas of the plaza that had bronze statues of winged creatures like Pegasi and other regal-seeming animals like centaurs and dragons.

None of those magical animals were as majestic as people made them out to be. Pegasi were exceptionally naughty, which was why on Roya Lane, the area in London where magical centers were, there was a corrections office dedicated to the creatures.

Centaurs were notorious for getting offended. They could have a conversation alone and insult themselves. Dragons, well, they either took themselves too seriously all the time or cracked bad jokes. There wasn't a middle ground with the animals. Aunt Sophia's dragon Lunis was the best because he refused to be serious. You could find him eating Doritos and marathoning Netflix shows most days while the crusty old dragons recounted the days of yore.

Paris checked her phone for the time. "We're about six minutes early."

"Punctuality is the magical ingredient to success," Faraday chirped.

"Remind me never to let you make me a cake," Paris stated. "The magical ingredient is mischief."

"I think a good cake needs a leavening agent," Faraday said as Paris strode for the outskirts of the barrier around the plaza.

"Get a life, squirrel. How about we check out what this place looks like from the outside?"

"Well, but we have orientation in six minutes." Faraday ran after her. "I'm sure it looks about how we see it."

Paris spun, glancing at the high-rise coated in magic that made it appear so abnormal, it couldn't pass for a sprinkled donut in a pastry shop. This place looked like something right out of a fantasy adventure with all the magic swirling around it and stuffy agents and fairy godmothers. No, Paris was sure a glamour covered it, and her curiosity wanted to see what mortals saw when they glanced at the structure. So she knew the level of deception that she was entering.

"You're usually the curious one." She peered down at the squirrel, who had stopped in his tracks to stare up at her.

He gulped and nodded, his paws held in prayer as if asking her to return to the fountain. "Yes, that's true."

"You have that strange little lens of yours?"

He nodded, pulling out the glamour-off lens attached to a rope around his neck like a necklace so she could see it. "Of course. I always try to bring it on adventures."

Paris grinned. "Good. I want to be the curious one and see what this place looks like from the other side of the block."

Faraday glanced in that direction. Then at Paris. Then again before looking her straight in the eyes. "That's the other side of the block."

She sighed. "That's what I said. Maybe we need to get you memory lessons."

Not hearing her, he said, "That's the mortal side. Those types will be over there."

Paris leaned forward and whispered, "I'm not afraid if you're not."

He straightened. "I'm not afraid. It's just that we're supposed to be reporting to FGA as agents and not socializing with mortals."

"I'm supposed to be reporting to FGA as an agent. I think you're supposed to be hibernating."

He huffed and crossed his arms.

Paris sighed. "I want to see what this place looks like from the outside. That way I know what I'm dealing with in a way. Also, we have like six minutes to spare, and I'd prefer not to be stared at by polite fairy godmothers and stuffy agents who wonder why I'm wearing leather and carrying around a rodent."

"We have five minutes," Faraday corrected. "Don't you think they're wondering why I'm naked and carting around a badly dressed human?"

"No," Paris said simply.

The two had a short staring contest before the squirrel acquiesced and hopped in her direction. "Fine, we'll check out the other side of the barrier, but I'm sure it doesn't look much different. Then we can get to the fountain and find out where they keep the paperclips in this place."

Paris laughed, following the squirrel across the busy intersection. "An entire skyscraper full of the magic that runs the world of love and my sidekick wants paperclips."

"They make genius devices for all sorts of experiments," he chirped and added, "I'm your partner. No sidekick business. I get fifty-fifty."

"You get a shoebox to sleep in, and you'll like it."

CHAPTER FIVE

Fifth Avenue, New York City, New York

"Okay, I was a touch wrong on the way this place appears to outsiders," Faraday admitted from the other side of the intersection.

"A touch?" Paris challenged, staring at the dilapidated warehouse that stood where she knew the FGA Tower and plaza was on the other side of Fifth Avenue in New York City.

Faraday held up the monocle-like device tied around his neck to his eye and peered through. It was a glamour-off lens the nerdy squirrel had created—it saw through the magic that disguised things. Glamour was what Paris used to hide her wings. It also made magical buildings like the House of Fourteen look like a palm reading shop in Santa Monica instead of a vast mansion.

Glamour often hid places from mortal peering eyes or kept unwanted people out of locations. In the case of FGA Tower, powerful glamour was in use to disguise the fifty-story skyscraper.

Faraday's head swiveled as he studied the area.

"Anything of great interest?" Paris stared around as people jostled around them to cross the street, catch the bus, or make their way into the shops at their backs.

"There's a barrier around the plaza's block that appears to keep out those not invited to FGA Tower," Faraday explained.

Paris glanced back at the rundown warehouse and noticed that no one walked on that side of the street. She checked around her as people queued at the intersection when the light turned red. No one noticed the old warehouse with a rusted roof and surrounded by a chain-link fence. She guessed that FGA Tower maintained further wards to be of no interest, which probably made it so developers and real estate investors didn't pry into the location. Otherwise, it seemed obvious that someone would be interested in a huge lot located in a prime area of Fifth Avenue in Manhattan.

"Hey, that's mine!" an old woman's voice yelled from the cluster of people gathered around the corner, waiting to cross the street.

Paris and Faraday both glanced in that direction as a man in all black yanked a large purse from a woman. Then he darted for the road, but a car going too fast bumped into him, making him roll over the hood. Unscathed by the collision, the thief rolled off the car and stood in the middle of the street, seemingly dazed by surviving the incident, the woman's purse still clutched in his hands.

The older woman shook as she yelled and pointed at the man who stood in the road. The lights still said it was unsafe to cross. Beside her, mortals simply stared or protested about the incident, but no one did anything.

"Stop!" Paris yelled, springing into action and running after the man. She peeled around the crowd, having to jump into the road to get around them. For a moment, she thought the mugger would simply stand there until she apprehended him. However, he came to as she ran straight for him. Waking to his reality, about to be assaulted by a tiny woman dressed in black leather, the man spun to the side and ran straight for his best option for escaping—the abandoned warehouse on the other side of the avenue.

CHAPTER SIX

Fifth Avenue, New York City, New York

The thief, probably used to running and more importantly outrunning people, was fast. He would've been able to get away from most. No doubt with his longer and more muscular legs he could outrun most women. However, Paris Beaufont wasn't most women or like any people. Her demon blood made her stronger and faster than ninety percent of those on the planet.

Realizing that Paris was easily about to catch him, the man cut across the busy street and straight for the chain-link fence. His arms pumped and he leaned forward, willing his legs to move faster as he hopped onto the empty sidewalk.

Fear radiated from the mugger's eyes as he glanced over his shoulder and saw Paris speeding up beside him. She extended her arm, reaching for the purse. The man didn't slow or drop the bag. He simply continued to flee like somehow his fate would change, and Paris wasn't about to stop him and smash his face.

With a swift jerk, Paris yanked the woman's purse toward herself. The thief wasn't letting go, though. The desperation in his eyes told her that he wasn't giving up.

Gritting her teeth, Paris grabbed tighter to the bag and pulled her weight back, stopping dead on her heels. The action was enough to halt the man's progress. It was also enough to tear the purse from his grasp.

However, the unrelenting mugger dove for Paris, knocking into her as he tried to snatch the purse yet again. Unfortunately, their altercation was also enough to throw Paris off-balance, making her tumble through the barrier and into the plaza of FGA Tower with the thief in tow.

CHAPTER SEVEN

FGA Tower Plaza, New York City, New York

Paris knew as soon as she and the thief tumbled through the barrier and into a seemingly new world that she'd made a huge mistake. In essence, she'd invited this mortal into FGA Tower, where he wasn't allowed.

Having rolled to the bricks of the plaza, the thief jumped to his feet, shock covering his face. Then he looked at Paris, and the purse clutched in her hands, still deciding whether it was worth going after again.

Many of the agents and fairy godmothers coming through portals around the plaza noticed the disturbance. In the distance, a set of FGA guards were hurrying over. The man stared all around, trying to figure out where he was and how. Now that Paris was looking at FGA Tower through the eyes of the mortal, she realized it looked quite strange and magical.

Then fear finally got the best of him, and the mugger sprang into a run, careening straight into a horde of confused fairy godmothers. They screamed, many falling over from the assault. Unconcerned, the intruder continued through the plaza, weaving in and around scared fairies who all jumped away as he shot past them.

"Grab that criminal!" Paris yelled as the man streaked by a set of guards.

Not only did the men dressed in black with batons on their hips not apprehend the man, they simply watched as he sprinted in the opposite direction, finally cutting through the other side of the plaza and to the road where he was outside the barrier once more.

Glancing over his shoulder to check if anyone had followed him, the thief halted, apparently seeing the abandoned warehouse once more. Confusion briefly covered his face before a car blared its horn, alerting him that he was partially in the road and about to get hit.

The man yelled at the car, pulling his attention away from the glamoured sight of FGA Tower. Then he continued on the path, away from the strange place he'd entered, constantly looking over his shoulder as he disappeared on the other side of the street and away for good.

Paris sighed with defeat, realizing that now everyone in the plaza was staring straight at her. Before, the fairy godmothers were politely gawking at her. Now they were making no mistake about their curiosity, looking her over with disapproving glares.

"Did you bring that mortal through the barrier?" one of the security guards asked, a rather grumpy looking guy, his baton in his hands now, which Paris sensed served as his magical instrument of sorts. Fairy men never used wands for the most part. Usually, it was an object specific to them and their roles.

Paris held up the older woman's handbag. "I was getting this from the criminal. He stole it from a lady across the street."

The security guard gave his partner beside him a confused look. "Why would you do that?"

Paris rolled her eyes. "Why help an old woman and stop a

thief? Is that a serious question coming from two security guards who are supposed to keep this place safe?"

"We protect FGA Tower," the other guy said. "What were you doing outside the barrier? You're new to FGA, right?"

"Because I wanted to know what the Tower looked like from outside."

"Why?" He was obviously confused.

Paris sighed again. "Because I'm curious by nature. If you're supposed to protect this place, why didn't you stop that guy?"

"Because..." The security guard looked at the other guy, hoping he had an answer. He appeared to have swallowed a canary.

"Because then you'd get your hands dirty," Paris supplied.

"Again, why did you pull that mortal through the barrier?" the security guard questioned.

"I was grabbing the woman's purse, and when I did, it pulled us both through. I didn't mean to, obviously."

"Mortals aren't allowed in here." The other guy had fully swallowed the canary and found his voice.

Paris rolled her eyes again. "I know that. I didn't invite him in here. We weren't going to have tea on the tenth floor or anything."

"There's no tea room on the tenth floor," The guy sounded confused.

A loud sigh fell from Paris' mouth. "I get that you two don't have much to do here, but when there is a threat to security, I think you might think about stepping into action."

"What department are you working in?" The security guard was offended. "We'll need to report this to your supervisor."

"I'm the agent in charge of the Casual Romance department," Paris answered proudly.

The men exchanged more confused looks. "That's impossible. Agents are—"

"Usually men," a melodic voice said at Paris' back. She recognized it immediately and instantly felt a surge of excitement, relief, and tension.

Paris spun and found the man she expected. None other than the leader of FGA—Saint Valentine.

CHAPTER EIGHT

"S-S-Sir!" one of the security guards stuttered, rushing around Paris to Saint Valentine's side, bowing clumsily.

"We can explain the disturbance that's transpired," the other security guard said, now on the other side of Saint Valentine. He pointed at Paris. "It was all her fault. She brought a mortal through the barrier, putting FGA Tower in danger."

Saint Valentine looked as handsome and distinguished as the last time Paris saw him. He wore a sharp black pinstriped suit with a bright red rose pinned in the lapel. His salt-and-pepper hair bespoke his age, but his twinkling blue eyes made him seem younger somehow.

"I'm glad you're giving Agent Beaufont full credit for the incident." Saint Valentine's focus centered entirely upon her. In his hand, he held his ornately engraved silver cane, also his magical instrument, and gestured at Paris.

"Sir, I can explain," Paris began, but the pleasant expression on Saint Valentine's face made her pause. He seemed to be brimming with pride as he regarded her.

"Oh, but Agent Beaufont, you don't have to unless you want to," he explained. "I witnessed the whole thing, and you were very brave. It was noble of you to go after that mugger and retrieve the mortal woman's purse."

"But sir, she brought a criminal into the plaza," one of the security guards protested.

When Saint Valentine focused on the security guards, he didn't have as pleasant an expression as before. "I don't see how she could've avoided that. Paris grabbed the woman's purse. The assailant wasn't willing to let it go. When Paris pulled it from his clutches, the effort sent them sailing through the barrier."

He glanced back at Paris. "It was a true act of courage. I dare say, if we had more people like you on the streets of New York, it would be a safer place."

"But she brought one of those unsafe people into the plaza," the other security guard argued. "He could've harmed someone."

"Then you would keep us safe from him, wouldn't you?" Saint Valentine questioned. "That is your job, correct? To keep FGA Tower and plaza safe, right?"

The guy appeared to have eaten another bird. He gulped, looked at his partner, and nodded dumbly.

"Well, thankfully the incident is over, and none came to harm," Saint Valentine said proudly.

"Almost over." Paris held up the purse. "Would one of you be a dear and return this to the mortal it belongs to? I'm sure you can find some identification inside it."

Neither security guard answered. Instead, they looked at Paris like she'd asked them to add the purse to their ensemble permanently.

Saint Valentine nodded. "Yes, that's a good task for you two since Agent Beaufont's tour and orientation is about to begin, and she'll be too busy for such things."

She smiled slightly, looking straight at the guards. "You can even take full credit and tell the woman that you retrieved her purse."

"Why would we do that?" one of the security guards asked.

Paris couldn't help herself. She chuckled. "So you appear to be somewhat useful."

CHAPTER NINE

FGA Tower Plaza, New York City, New York

If Saint Valentine was offended by Paris' remark to the security guards, he didn't show it. Instead, he gave the two men a look that meant, "You're dismissed," and turned his attention fully on Paris Beaufont.

"I see that you're already off to an entertaining start." He sounded amused.

"I'm sorry for pulling that thief through the barrier," she began. "I shouldn't have left the plaza. It was just that I had some extra time and Faraday and I wanted to see what the FGA Tower's glamour looked like from the other side."

"You are quite the curious type, aren't you?" He looked around. "Your friend Faraday has accompanied you today. How very lovely."

"Is that okay?" she asked. "I told him that it might not be a good idea because it's my first day and he's a talking squirrel and all."

Saint Valentine chuckled good-naturedly. "I think a talking squirrel is exactly what we've been missing at this place."

"Oh, how very specific…"

The leader of FGA turned and appraised the tall skyscraper in front of them, looking up at the fifty-story building proudly. "FGA has been my life for the better part of a century."

As Paris had suspected, Saint Valentine was old, even by fairy standards. She didn't say a word and didn't follow his line of sight. Instead, she studied the man before her, recognizing that there was something different about him than the last time they'd met. He seemed tired. Not as full of his usual spark. Maybe paler too.

"I love what this organization represents," Saint Valentine went on, looking around the plaza. "Our mission is to create love and monitor it. Nurture it in unique ways. And to ensure that it's always protected. However, over the decades that I've led FGA, things have changed. They've evolved."

He sighed, and Paris saw his fatigue. "I'm not the young man I once was. I fear that in my old age, things in my organization have changed that I wouldn't have allowed before." Another sigh. "Honestly, I don't know what I don't know. All I do know is that there's something not quite right inside the ranks of this place. However, I'm not in the place to pinpoint it."

"But you're the leader," Paris argued at once, realizing that many in the plaza were staring at them. She must have been of great interest to those around who saw the rebel speaking to the illustrious leader of FGA and dearly wished to eavesdrop on their conversation.

Saint Valentine's voice was low when he replied. "Most think that a leader is in the perfect position to see. However, from on top of the mountain, usually one is stuck in the clouds. It is those on the ground who see the army approaching. They see the whites of the enemy's eyes, whereas the general only sees the troops after they stormed his army."

Paris held her breath, aware that Saint Valentine was confiding something very important to her, but not sure exactly why, and more importantly, what. He seemed to be telling her that something was amiss at FGA. Furthermore, he seemed to be implying that he didn't know what it was. Was he saying that she could see it?

Turning to face her directly, he offered a warm smile. "Agent Beaufont, I put you in the position that you're about to start because I firmly believe you're the change we need here. I might be resistant to change, but I'm not against it. The modern world means we need to adapt. I believe that you can help us see things that we couldn't before.

"You've already helped the fairy godmothers so much during your time at Happily Ever After College. Whether it's because you're a halfling or have demon blood or a Beaufont, you understand love better than most. You're willing to do something that none of my fairies have ever been willing to do, and that's risking your safety for others.

"By nature, fairies are selfish and self-preserving. We need someone like you. I'm counting on you to take this place to new heights. I fear that before you can do that, we'll have to fix underlying problems inside our organization. I hope you'll help me and my office, Matters of the Heart, to find those."

"You've been trying to find these problems?" she asked.

He nodded. "Yes, but old eyes only see what they've always seen. New eyes—fresh eyes—those that aren't afraid to find problems and run after thieves, well, they see what has escaped the rest of us."

"Okay, well, I'll do whatever I can to help."

"I know you will." Saint Valentine smiled with a twinkle in his eyes. "Your job now is to learn about this place. That's where things will start. I have every hope that it will lead to many discoveries for you, then for me as well."

Saint Valentine was speaking in riddles, much like Mae Ling. Paris respected and understood that he couldn't come out and say precisely what he was thinking. There were problems inside

FGA. Traitors, possibly. She needed to keep her eyes open and her instinct for finding evil honed.

In the past, some of his agents had attempted to assassinate Saint Valentine. The board, which was full of old fairies with financial interests in FGA and outdated ways of thinking, was constantly causing problems for the leader. The organization was huge, with tons of departments and hundreds of employees.

The places where dissension was rife inside FGA were confounding and overwhelming. Still, if anyone could find them, it had to be Paris Beaufont. She believed that this was one of the main reasons Saint Valentine had elected her as an agent. The last thing she wanted to do was let him down.

CHAPTER TEN

FGA Tower Plaza, New York City, New York

Realizing that her orientation must have started, Paris glanced around, finding the large fountain in the distance. A group of fairy godmothers who she thought were newbies were gathered beside it.

Paris recognized two of her friends from Happily Ever After College in the group. One of the funniest fairies she knew, Christine Welsh, was assigned to the fashion department. Beside her was Penny Pullman, who was much less extroverted and would be working in the Practical Love department.

"I guess I should go and join the group." Paris pointed at the large fountain in front of the entrance.

Saint Valentine shook his head and smiled down at the bricks as Faraday joined them. "I see you were able to get through the barrier just fine. I requested that you have access to FGA Tower and plaza since I suspected you'd accompany Paris to work."

"Thanks, Saint Valentine." Faraday bowed slightly.

The leader of FGA returned his attention to Paris. "Since you're the only new agent starting today, you'll get a personal tour tailored specifically for what you'll need to know. The fairy godmothers there won't need as comprehensive a briefing as you." Saint Valentine indicated the newbie fairies by the fountain.

"Oh, more comprehensive," Faraday squeaked, obviously excited to explore FGA Tower. Usually if not allowed to explore an area, that's exactly where the scientific squirrel wanted to be.

"Yes." Saint Valentine smiled. "I've arranged for our resident expert to give you the entire tour. He has the most extensive information about this place, although there will be gaps in his knowledge."

"Gaps?" Paris wondered who this expert would be. *Probably an uptight and disapproving agent or security guard,* she thought.

"Well, I've allowed departments to have their own security," Saint Valentine explained. "You see, I recognize there is industry-specific information within certain ones that they can't disclose."

"So one reason you wouldn't know everything that's happening at FGA is because of these individual security measures," Paris guessed, noticing this statement pique Faraday's interests. She'd have to fill him in later on what Saint Valentine said to her in so many words.

"Yes, that's correct. Alfred will know more than anyone else, but he still doesn't have access to all areas of FGA or all departmental areas. However, he will be a wealth of information for you. I dare say you are already familiar with him."

"Alfred?" Paris questioned. "I don't think we've met."

Saint Valentine's blue eyes twinkled with delight. "In so many ways, you have." He cleared his throat and held his chin up. "Alfred, will you please join us?"

From seemingly nowhere, a hologram of an English butler in a gray, three-piece suit with a bow tie materialized. At first, he was transparent, then became so solid that Paris knew she could reach out and touch him.

The man before her looked exactly like the AI magitech butler with slicked-back gray hair and a regal expression who tended to Happily Ever After College. However, Paris' instinct told her that this one was much different than her Wilfred—who'd endeared himself to her during her time there.

Wilfred had been more than a vast source of knowledge and assistance while at the college. He'd become her friend. She hoped that Alfred would too, because more than anything, Paris knew that she needed friends at FGA to succeed.

CHAPTER ELEVEN

FGA Tower Plaza, New York City, New York

Extending her hand, Paris smiled at the man who looked exactly like Wilfred but wasn't—not entirely. "Nice to meet you, Alfred."

"You as well, Agent Paris Beaufont," he answered in the same voice she associated with her friend Wilfred, his tone distinguished and his accent a posh English one. "However, you will find that I know you very well."

Paris blinked at the AI magitech butler in confusion, then at Saint Valentine. He understood her baffled expression at once.

"Alfred received a full update from Wilfred, complete with all of your interactions and your background according to the butler at Happily Ever After College."

"Oh," Paris squeaked. "Well, that makes it easy. So you know I made Wilfred laugh and that I take my coffee black and prefer not to have my leather jacket laundered."

"And that the squirrel prefers cheese sandwiches and is allergic to nuts," Alfred stated quite seriously. "But I do believe it was the dragon, Lunis who made Wilfred laugh."

Paris rolled her eyes. "Whatever. I wore him down."

"Honestly, I believe it must have been a fluke of his programming," Alfred said matter-of-factly. "I do hope you won't waste your efforts with a similar endeavor here."

Saint Valentine flashed Paris a caring smile. "Alfred is a newer model and is probably right. Although I appreciate the sentiment, I'm not sure you'll have any luck with getting any rogue emotions from him, especially laughter. He was programmed to be FGA Tower's resident expert and assistant."

Paris nodded, familiar with how the AI magitech butlers worked. They were impressive pieces of technology that could provide information readily, tended to the location, and had multiple forms that could be in many different places at once. "Well, if I happen to tell a joke and you happen to laugh, I won't tell anyone." She winked at Alfred.

"If you do laugh at one of her jokes, you will be the first." Faraday chuckled.

Paris glanced down at the squirrel, giving him a threatening look.

Saint Valentine laughed too, bringing her attention back to the man. "Well, I think you're in good hands for now. Alfred will give you the complete tour, which should take most of the day. Then I'd like you to cap off your day by visiting your department, Casual Romance. Your employees have been alerted to your arrival, and I do hope that you all get on well."

Paris' chest tightened at the idea that she had employees. Fairy godmothers, to be exact. She knew that being an agent in charge of a department meant she'd have employees, but the idea hadn't landed quite yet. Not like it just did.

Hiding her nervousness, Paris feigned a smile and nodded. "Thank you. I promise to stay vigilant and report to you anything of use."

Saint Valentine backed away, holding up his cane and smiling gently at her. "I think you realize that I'm counting on your report to save this very place. It's a lot of pressure to get on your first day here, but it's best if you know what's at stake and why you're in such a unique position."

"Okay, I appreciate your candor."

"Also, Agent Beaufont," Saint Valentine continued with a thoughtful expression. "I think if the stakes weren't high and the challenges here weren't great, well, we wouldn't put your talents to good use here."

CHAPTER TWELVE

FGA Tower Plaza, New York City, New York

"So." Paris drew the word out as she focused her attention on the AI magitech butler. "Where should we start? With the bowling alley or the stables?"

Alfred frowned. She was used to that expression from Wilfred. He knew so much about everything, yet jokes, humor, and playfulness were foreign to the servant meant to assist and not be a companion. However, the magitech part of the AI gave Paris hope that it could adapt, learn, and have a personality separate from its programming.

"There is no bowling alley or stables that I'm aware of at FGA Tower." Alfred didn't sense that Paris was joking.

"Good, because she can't bowl," Faraday chirped.

Paris nodded. "And I scare the daylights out of horses with my demon blood."

"Why don't we start with the plaza." Alfred held out his white-gloved hand in a presenting manner, welcoming the pair toward the building. "Each brick was delivered as a gift to FGA from the gnomes with whom we created an alliance several centuries ago."

Although Paris was interested in the history of FGA Tower

and the fairy godmothers in general, a figure who stood beside the giant Pegasus on the far side of the fountain stole her attention. The man resembled all the other agents around the plaza with his dark black suit and pursed expression. However, where the others were undoubtedly discreetly watching her, this man was staring intently. Paris could tell that he studied her every move even though a bowler hat partially covered his face.

Faraday followed her line of sight, catching the man staring. When the halfling and the squirrel caught him spying, the man narrowed his eyes and charged toward the building's entrance. The way he walked held authority—like he thought he owned the building. As if he thought he was Saint Valentine himself.

Paris almost ran straight into the back of Alfred when he halted suddenly, looking up at the tall building. The AI had no idea that Paris hadn't been listening to the last few things he'd mentioned. She hoped there wouldn't be a test.

"FGA Tower is composed of fifty stories and a five-level basement." Alfred squinted as he pointed at the rectangular building's top floor. "The top level is Saint Valentine's office, Matters of the Heart. Only he and his closest cabinet members can enter the fiftieth floor so that won't be on our tour."

"I've already been there," Paris interrupted. "My father and I fought a demon who was hiding out there, leeching emotions from fairies here."

Alfred's eyes went dull before he sparked to life again. "Of course, I have that history in my database. Many felt indebted to you and Stefan Ludwig for ridding FGA Tower of those two demons."

"Some wanted to kill me," Paris joked, thinking of Agent Ruby, who was trying to destroy Saint Valentine and his fairy godmothers. It was one of those "if I can't win, no one will" situations. Agent Ruby wanted to do things his way or not at all.

Paris didn't know if she'd meet others like that evil agent set in the old ways, but she suspected that she'd find similar mind-sets, and that's what Saint Valentine had warned her about. An old organization such as FGA had to be full of many types. Since it had been slow to change with modern times, there would be many who weren't playing by the rules, afraid of being deemed irrelevant in the new world of love.

"The forty-ninth floor is also off-limits," Alfred continued. "It is where the FGA board meets. Only those members are allowed entry there."

"Who wants to hang out with a bunch of old grumps anyway?" Paris muttered, thinking of all the trouble she'd heard about caused by the FGA board. They were always creating problems for Saint Valentine or the headmistress at Happily Ever After College, Willow Starr.

It appeared that the board was composed of fairies afraid of change. They had their interests, and they didn't seem as aligned with the mission of creating and protecting love so much as creating opportunities for the old fairy families that composed the board and protecting their egos.

"The forty-eighth floor is solely for the Finance department." Alfred either hadn't heard Paris' remark or chose to ignore it. Wilfred often did the same—so well-mannered.

"That's a lot of people counting peanuts." Paris looked down at Faraday.

The squirrel scrunched up his brow and studied the building. "I wouldn't think that the third most important level in an organization devoted to creating love would be finance."

"As the agent who serves as the director for finance says often, 'Love makes the world go 'round, but it's money that makes the world,'" Alfred imparted in a demure voice.

Paris narrowed her gaze, looking up at the top of the skyscraper. "I'm sure I'll enjoy meeting this agent and learning more about his philosophies related to love and money. What's his name, Agent Diamond?"

Paris knew that the agents usually had gems for names that

were the same as those attached to their magical instruments. It was a title and also a way of tracking magic. It had been Agent Ruby's gem that linked him to the crimes he'd created. That was fitting since he'd framed other agents by stealing and using their magical instruments.

"Agent Jackson Zelle prefers to go by his name rather than electing a gem name like most," Alfred informed her.

"Good to know that's an option," Paris said, mostly to herself.

"The majority of FGA Tower is divided between three main branches," Alfred explained. "There's IT, Basic Love, and Advanced Love, with further divisions into multiple departments. Agent Beaufont, as you're aware, you're in charge of the Casual Romance department inside the Basic Love branch."

Paris' stomach tightened. Along with the strange notion that she was in charge of her very own department at FGA and being the first female agent, she was leading the department for casual romance. Those kinds of relationships seemed cheap, silly, and meaningless.

However, when Paris had expressed this concern to Mae Ling, her fairy godmother of sorts had stated that all types of love were important because they could always lead to something meaningful. She'd encouraged Paris to push her cases so her Cinderellas and Prince Charmings went past surface-level relationships and created something more substantial. Paris had promised to keep an open mind about the whole thing. Mae Ling stated that if she approached her department with a holistic and creative outlook, she might revolutionize it.

"The twenty-seventh through the forty-seventh floors are for the various IT departments," Alfred went on, probably not sensing that Paris was bouncing back and forth with internal doubt and hardly listening to his tour information. "The third through the twenty-fifth floor is for all the Basic Love departments. The first and second floors are for stores, shops, and other businesses that serve FGA employees. For instance, on the first floor—"

"What about the twenty-sixth floor?" Faraday interrupted.

Alfred halted, blinked, and looked down at the squirrel, like he was suddenly surprised he could talk. "Now what was that?"

"The twenty-sixth floor?" Faraday repeated. "You didn't include it when listing the others."

"Oh, true, I didn't." The dull expression in Alfred's eyes returned. Paris had seen that look on Wilfred's face when he was computing something or searching his database for answers. A moment later, Alfred surfaced, his eyes bright once more. "There is no information on the twenty-sixth floor."

"How is that possible?" Faraday's eyes went wide with alarm.

"I simply don't have any information about it."

"Surely you've been there, or someone has, or someone has asked about it," Faraday urged.

Alfred shook his head. "No one asks about the twenty-sixth floor."

Paris gave Faraday a stern look. "Stay away from it."

"Pare, there's a mystery there. You know how I can't stand not knowing something."

She shook her head with an adamant look. "We'll look into it, but not yet. It's our first day. At least wait until I've been here for a week until you unleash old ghosts or secrets or whatever storm is waiting on the twenty-sixth floor."

Faraday huffed. "Fine, but I'm going to find out why no one asks about that floor."

"Yes, but not today," Paris stated with determination, turning her attention to Alfred. "The Advanced Love branch? Where is that?"

"It's in the basement of FGA Tower," he answered.

"You said that was composed of five levels," Faraday chirped. "Why do the IT and Basic Love branches get so many more floors?"

"And ones with windows?" Paris added.

Alfred thought for a moment and shrugged. "The Advanced Love department doesn't require much space, it seems."

Paris glanced sideways at Faraday, the two exchanging a knowing look. Something wasn't right with this set. She suddenly had a lot more questions than she had answers. However, she would keep collecting information and slowly uncover the secrets she knew lay buried inside this skyscraper.

CHAPTER THIRTEEN

Lobby, FGA Tower, New York City, New York

A wave of familiarity swept over Paris as she entered the building's spacious lobby. Instantly, she remembered being there with her father, fighting demons. However, the space seemed different because of all the various people in the lobby.

When Paris and her father had been there before, the FGA Tower was mostly empty. Many fairies had left, afraid of being leeched by the demons. Currently, there were dozens of chatty fairy godmothers and discerning agents standing or milling about. Many of their gazes skipped to Paris and Faraday before pretending to be uninterested and looking away.

Much like the FGA agents, the lobby was all sleek black, reminding Paris of the suits they all wore. The walls were all black marble, which didn't contrast against the black granite floors. Hanging overhead was a huge and modern black glass chandelier.

In contrast to the rich, warm wood all around the mansion at Happy Ever After college, the lobby of FGA was ultra-modern with straight lines and lots of sharp corners. The couches in front of the bank of elevators at the back of the room didn't look comfortable.

"The lobby is my main station," Alfred said over the echoing chatter. The lobby had active acoustics thanks to all the cold stone walls, ceilings, and floors. "However, you can also page me by calling for me with a request, similar to how you summoned Wilfred."

"Yeah, he only responded to his full name and not Will or Willy," Paris remarked to Faraday, who snickered in response. Paris glanced at Alfred with a serious expression. "How about you? Do you think you'll materialize if I say, 'Hey, Al, I need some schooling?'"

"I can program that into my response functions if you so desire, Agent Beaufont," Alfred answered in a robotic voice.

Paris' mouth fell open with surprise. "Are you serious? Will would never do such a thing for me. I asked. You're way cooler."

Alfred almost blushed, looking around like he was suddenly self-conscious. "Well, I'm guessing that way cool is a compliment, but I don't deserve it. You're simply granted more privileges as an agent than you had as a student at Happily Ever After College. If Wilfred didn't add your commands to his functions, it was because you weren't in a position of authority."

"Oh, so agents can do that, huh?" Paris mused.

"Yes."

"And fairy godmothers?" Faraday asked.

Alfred shook his head.

"Very curious," Faraday muttered, combing his paws over his furry chin.

"The security guard station is also in the lobby." Alfred pointed at an area in the corner where several disinterested and lackluster guards had gathered.

"I say we put a frozen yogurt shop there instead," Paris muttered.

"If you have a sweet tooth, you might try the coffee shop on the first floor," Alfred stated. "Fairy Grounds serves scones that many find very tasty. Apparently, it makes up for the bland and often burned coffee."

Paris blinked at him. "Shouldn't a coffee shop have great coffee?"

"Fairies don't like the stuff," Alfred explained. "It's too bitter for most of their tastes. They feel obligated to have it since most of the rest of the world desires the drink."

"Fairies are so weird," Paris joked, shaking her head.

"You're talking about yourself," Faraday reminded her.

"I'm only half-fairy, and I happen to love coffee."

"Probably because magicians love things that are bitter and biting and make them alert and jittery," the squirrel retorted.

"All the reasons I like you," she teased, and turned back to Alfred. "I was saying to replace the security guard station with frozen yogurt because that would be more useful than a bunch of dimwits who seem to have a head full of froyo."

His eyes dulled for a moment. "I see that froyo is a slang term for frozen yogurt on the world wide web. However, I don't think the FGA has security guards with frozen yogurt in their heads, although I realize that fairies do consume more sugar than anyone else in the world."

Paris groaned and rolled her eyes. "Yet again, I have to teach an AI butler about sarcasm and when I'm joking."

"Oh, that was a joke?" Alfred looked rather confused.

Faraday nodded. "I hardly know when she's joking either. It's because Pare doesn't get that the key is they need to be funny to give it away."

"I'm about to give you away," Paris threatened her squirrel.

"If you'd like to continue the tour, I'll take you to the second floor." Alfred held his arm out to the bank of elevators at the back of the lobby. "Although I do have a disclaimer to make about FGA's elevators."

Paris gave him a reluctant look. "They don't work, and I risk getting stuck in there with the squirrel and therefore having to resort to eating him?"

"I'm right here," Faraday complained.

Alfred shook his head. "No, the elevators work just fine. Well, mostly. It's that they're magitech-laced."

"What does that mean?" Paris asked.

"It means that many times, if you're alone in the compartment, it will take you to where it thinks you need to be, rather than where you want to go. For that reason, it is always advisable to travel on the elevator in pairs at least. That way it doesn't have a choice but to take you to the floor you've chosen."

Paris shook her head, realizing that she'd entered another strange and wonderful world where nothing was what it seemed, and there would be a surprise around every corner. Oddly enough, she felt very much at home in a place like this.

CHAPTER FOURTEEN

Second Floor, FGA Tower, New York City, New York

The aroma of curry and spices was enticing and perplexing when Paris stepped onto the second floor—the elevator thankfully delivering her and Faraday to the correct one alongside Alfred. According to the AI magitech butler, that was because the elevator only chose for someone if they were alone. Otherwise, it would be hard to do with multiple people in the compartment.

"Wow, that smell is intoxicating." Paris noticed that the hallway on the second floor was similar to the first with black marble walls and floors. It was also bristling with fairy godmothers in blue gowns or agents in black suits. This made it so that she, Alfred, and Faraday stuck out from the rest of the crowd quite easily.

"What you're smelling is FGA's main restaurant, Curry-Osities," Alfred explained, leading the way down the hallway lined with people.

"Oh, so it's an Indian restaurant," Faraday guessed.

Alfred held up a single white-gloved finger. "Not just any ordinary Indian restaurant. Curry-Osities serves dishes that bring on different states of being. Patrons choose experiences over curries for the most part."

"So does the masala make one playful and the korma causes intrigue?" Paris joked. The air was rich with warm spices as they progressed toward the sounds of forks scraping plates and diners talking excitedly.

"Yes, something like that." Alfred was serious. "The samosas are pretty good for causing focus and the pakora is conversely sleep-inducing."

"Wait, the curries at this restaurant are magical?" Paris asked as they paused in front of the entrance for Curry-Osities. Colorful fabrics hung from the walls and over the ceiling draped the place. Firelight illuminated the many tables where fairies dined, chatting excitedly as shiny covered dishes were served to them. Steam wafted in the air, making Paris feel overwhelmed with so many competing emotions. She wondered if smell alone would cause someone to feel the dishes' effects.

"Yes, but if you don't want any extra emotions or altered state, they suggest to stick with the soup or rice," Alfred stated.

"So Fairy Grounds serves to die for scones and bad coffee, and Curry-Osities serves emotion-altering dishes." Paris tried to wrap her mind around all this. "Is there anywhere that someone can get a plain sandwich?"

Alfred thought for a moment. "You could bring a lunch."

Faraday laughed and climbed onto a pedestal next to the restaurant's entrance to get a better view of the place. "Seems that you probably should've taken the brown bag lunches Hemingway made for us."

Paris nodded. "I will tomorrow."

"Ummm, I'm going to need to cut ahead of you in line," a man's voice said behind Paris.

She turned to find an agent standing a few feet away. Like the other agents, he wore a black suit, but the jacket appeared to be working to stretch around his round belly. The guy was only a few inches taller than her and at least three times her width. He didn't look like he'd missed many meals but appeared anxious not to. Nearly obstructing his double chins was a thick goatee and in his fidgeting hand was a small screwdriver with a green gem at its end.

"Oh, are you in a hurry?" Paris looked the man up and down. "We're not in line."

The man narrowed his pale brown eyes at her—they matched his dull hair that he'd swept back in an attempt to cover his obvious early stages of balding. "I don't have to be in a hurry to cut ahead of you or anyone else. Do you know who I am?"

Paris glanced at the screwdriver that was for small electronic devices. She'd seen Faraday use them loads of times on tiny little gadgets. The guy was spinning the small tool around his fingers as one did with a ballpoint pen. Her eyes landed on the green gem, and she smiled up at the man. "I don't know who you are, but I'm guessing that you go by Agent Emerald and that you're in charge of the IT department."

He narrowed his eyes, apparently not impressed with her detective skills. Or maybe it was that she'd stolen his opportunity to reveal the information. Either way, she was right based on the steaming expression on his face. "You're the new fairy for the Casual Romance department."

"Halfling," Paris corrected. "And agent in charge of the department."

The guy didn't appear amused by the correction. "Well, if you need a computer, you'll have to put in a ticket. My team probably can't get to it for a while."

"I'm good," Paris chirped, already having a strong distaste for this pompous director over all the IT departments.

"Well, there's the old agent's computer you can use, but it needs a system overhaul first, and there's no way we can get to it this week."

"I'll do it," Faraday sang from his place on the nearby pedestal.

Agent Emerald's nostrils flared as he eyed the talking squirrel before glancing at Paris. "What's wrong with that squirrel?"

"The list is long, but he can take care of my technology needs to relieve the IT departments from having to worry about it."

The guy blinked with annoyance. "I'm sure at Happily Ever After College, where you're used to rotary phones and dial-up Internet, the squirrel seems very competent. However, we don't allow animals to work on our technology here at FGA."

"Maybe that's why you sound so backlogged," Faraday squeaked. "You want me to look at some of your system processes? I can access your server room and see if there are inefficiencies."

"His size makes him ideal for such tasks," Paris added, watching as Agent Emerald turned a darker shade of red.

"I don't need a squirrel chewing through my wiring or interfering in my processes," he complained, spit flicking from his mouth. "We aren't backlogged. We just happen to have the most important departments at FGA, which are in great demand. Which brings me to your wand. That will go through one of my departments—"

"I don't need a wand," Paris interrupted.

Agent Emerald's eyes widened. "Well, of course, you do. All fairy godmothers have one."

"Again, not a fairy godmother." Paris pointed at her shoulder like there was an invisible name badge there. "Agent Beaufont in charge of the Casual Romance department. It's nice too."

He sighed, obviously not enjoying the meeting that much. "Well, then as an agent, you'll need a magical instrument." He eyed her dismissively. "I guess you'll want a nail file or a hairbrush or something like that."

"Because I'm a girl," she cut in.

Agent Emerald shrugged. "Anyway, those go through one of my departments too, and the waitlist is quite long. Probably be a few months. I hope that's not a problem."

"Not really," Paris sang, not deterred. "I don't need a magical instrument. Remember, I told you earlier that I'm a halfling."

"I don't remember." He sounded bored.

"Well, as a half-magician, I'm not like fairies and reliant on an instrument to channel my powers," she explained.

"Not to mention that as a magician and one from a founding family, your magic is much stronger than that of a fairy," Alfred stated robotically.

Paris hid her satisfied expression. "Oh, well, I forgot about that."

"So you don't need a magical instrument, then." Agent Emerald's small eyes narrowed further, becoming mere slits.

She smiled and shrugged. "Yeah, it appears that I don't need any help from any of your departments. Between my squirrel and my genetics, I think I'm covered."

He leaned down, trying to look down at her. Paris widened her eyes and didn't blink. A contest of wills between Agent Emerald and Paris began. They remained locked in an angry and challenging stare-off for a long moment until someone called at Agent Emerald's back.

"Josh, can I get your help with my laptop?" a man asked.

Paris and Agent Emerald turned to find another agent, dressed in all black and holding a small laptop.

"Gosh, Barry, did you break it again?" Agent Emerald glared at the other man.

"I don't know what happened."

"Give it to me." Agent Josh Emerald tugged the laptop out of Barry's hands. He glanced at it momentarily and rolled his eyes. "Oh, my. Even an infant could figure out what the problem is here. I can't believe you're wasting my time with it."

"B-B-But you can fix it?" Barry didn't notice Paris or Faraday but appeared ready to pee his pants as he begged for help from the head of the IT branch.

"Of course, I can." Agent Emerald stalked off into the restaurant, the sniveling other agent chasing him.

"Bye," Paris called after him. "It was so nice to meet you. Thanks for the warm welcome."

"Let me know if you want my expertise with things," Faraday added.

Both shared a discreet giggle when Agent Emerald cast an annoyed look over his shoulder as he disappeared into the restaurant.

Paris shook her head, smiling at her friend. "It appears we're already making friends."

"I don't think that guy has any friends, only people he picks on with what he thinks is his superior technological knowledge," Faraday stated.

"Yes, and we're already learning a great deal about this place and very quickly." Paris cataloged the interaction, wondering if the head of IT might be part of the problems Saint Valentine alluded to.

If nothing else, a guy like that led to morale problems at FGA. She'd have to stop by Human Resources for a visit. They should be intervening when it came to workplace bullying, but something told her that the HR department was probably run by little cherubs and in need of some help along with so many other places at FGA Tower.

CHAPTER FIFTEEN

Second Floor, FGA Tower, New York City, New York

"Do you want to make any more friends or should we continue the tour?" Alfred asked like he thought things had gone pleasantly with Agent Josh Emerald.

Paris shook her head. "Tour. I have enough friends. Why don't you show me where I can buy a candy bar or something to take the edge off after a long day."

"We don't have a shop that sells candy, but Sundry Charms does have convenient items. Follow me." Alfred led them down the busy corridor where they received many more glares from passersby.

Paris and Faraday followed the AI magitech butler, both exchanging knowing looks. The director of the IT department was more than a piece of work. He was a downright jerk. It wasn't like they were making him out to be mean. He was a villain of his own volition.

When they slowed, as they progressed through a bottleneck in the crowd, Paris whispered to her friend, "That guy is total SHIT."

Faraday gave her a punishing glare. "I get that he was

unpleasant to talk to...and look at...and is probably a horrid card player, but I think name-calling is beneath you."

Paris was grateful for the moment of levity and giggled as they moved through the jostling people. "No, I meant that Agent Emerald is the total Senior Head of IT. What did you think I meant, Fare?"

The squirrel, knowing full well what she meant and that she was playing him, flashed her a mischievous smile. "Oh, sorry, I must have misheard you. Josh is total SHIT."

Paris nodded appreciatively. "I thought you'd agree with me."

"I present to you, Sundry Charms." Alfred paused beside a small and humble storefront where people continued to come and go. Inside were rows of brightly colored items and a refrigerated aisle. Strange chiming noises emerged from the shop. There also appeared to be a food counter in the back and an area for practical items in the corner like cotton balls, antacids, and deodorant.

"Okay, so this is where we go when we need your flea spray." Paris glanced at Faraday beside her.

In return, the squirrel gave her a murderous look. She was pretty sure that if he had rabies, she'd get it in the night. Thankfully she was almost positive that he didn't.

"I don't have fleas...well, unless I got them from you," he answered smugly.

"You wouldn't be able to get flea spray at Sundry Charms," Alfred answered quite seriously. "You can come here if you want a juice drink or small snack."

Paris pursed her lips and nodded appreciatively. "Well, that's good. It's always good to have a place to get some apple juice or a bag of chips during the mid-afternoon slumps."

Alfred held up a single white-gloved finger, something she knew the AI magitech butlers liked to do, and she loathed seeing. "Sundry Charms doesn't serve apple juice."

"Orange then," Paris amended.

He shook his head.

"Grape," she offered.

Another head shake.

"What does Sundry Charms serve?" Faraday asked in a low tone like it was a conspiracy.

"They have a line of different herbal remedy kombucha teas laced with various secret ingredients that offer unique properties."

Paris turned and faced Faraday directly, her hands on her head suddenly. "Oh, angels. The worst types run Sundry Charms."

He nodded. "I think you're right. If we back up, maybe they won't have spotted us. We can get by without a lecture on a colon or other congested organs."

She returned the nod, looking around in a conspiratorial manner. "We will never speak of being here or tell any of my family about it. If we shower straight away, I think we can get that patchouli smell off us that's lingered from the shop."

Faraday sniffed. "I thought that was incense sticks burning. It's going to take forever to get that scent out of my fur."

"I bet you'll welcome a flea bath now," Paris remarked.

"I don't understand what you two are speaking of," Alfred intervened, confusion written on his face. "Who do you think runs Sundry Charms? Criminals?"

Paris sighed heavily. "Worse." She leaned forward. "It appears from what you've told us, and we've seen, that it's operated by...hippies."

Alfred blinked at her and pulled away. "Well, if my information is correct, you're right. The shop owners subscribe to outlooks congruent with the hippie mentality. They sell crystals that help with different ailments, concoctions that help various disorders, and mood rings."

"How about a bag of Doritos?" Paris asked.

"Or travel-sized packages of hummus with pita chips?" Faraday questioned, ever the practical type.

Alfred shook his head. "No, they have small travel mixes of nuts and dried fruit based on your astrological sign, though."

Paris groaned and rolled her eyes. "Great, so they are a bunch of hippies."

"Hemingway will pack our lunches," Faraday offered.

"He's going to have to pack me extra patience," Paris stated. "You know how I do when I interact with a hippie."

"You offend them," Faraday answered.

She huffed. "Well, they ask for it with their Zen bullshit."

"No question there," the squirrel agreed.

"I'm not sure I'm following this conversation," Alfred imparted. "Jenny, the shop owner of Sundry Charms, is very pleasant and agreeable to all of her customers. Barring that Mercury isn't in retrograde or there isn't a family spirit haunting you on the occasion that you enter her shop, she's always happy to help you find an essential oil that will fix your day."

Paris glanced sideways at Faraday. "It's like we're the only sane people on this planet called FGA."

He chuckled. "You called me people."

"Well, at this point, you're more normal than the rest." Paris glanced around. "Let's try to sneak away before some hippie wants to read our aura. The last thing I need on my first day is to punch a fairy in the face because they tell me that my chakras are out of alignment."

Paris marched forward, finally leading the way, and nearly ran into a guy who was standing in the middle of the hallway. He was staring down at his phone as he blocked the thoroughfare. Paris was about to say, "Hey, you don't own the space, move it, buddy," but instead decided it was best to skirt through the small space the selfish guy had left for others to pass him.

As she was moving around the man, Alfred said from behind her, "Oh, this would be a good opportunity to introduce you to your director, the department head in charge of the Basic Love branch."

Paris paused and let out a breath, thinking that her life couldn't be this torturous. Then she turned to find what she expected. Alfred was holding a presenting hand at the man blocking their path, who seemed not to have a concern for any other human on the planet.

CHAPTER SIXTEEN

Second Floor, FGA Tower, New York City, New York

"Oh, hi." Paris looked at the man wearing a black suit the same as all the other agents at FGA. He also had added to his ensemble a pursed expression as he glanced up from his phone, which a shiny jasper case covered. "I'm Agent Paris Beaufont, your new head for the Casual Romance department."

The guy was undoubtedly attractive, in the way that high school football players were good-looking with their chiseled jaws and neat short curly blond hair, but also equally revolting with his dismissive glance and off-putting demeanor. The man looked up at her briefly and back at his phone. "Put this intro-duction in an email. I'm in the middle of something."

"Excuse me." Paris pulled her hand back to her side. "Say what?"

The guy huffed and looked up from his phone where he'd been typing. "What I need you to do, is message me everything you're about to say out loud. Then I don't hear it, and you don't say it. We're all saved the interaction."

Paris looked at Alfred, then the guy who had returned his

attention to his phone in its case, and back at the AI magitech butler. "I'm sorry, you said you were going to introduce me to the guy in charge of the Basic Love branch, not a revolting piece of waste. Can you please do that?"

Alfred, who obviously didn't have many interactions of this sort or know what sarcasm was or how to deal with Paris, straightened. His eyes widened. His mouth fell open several times before he said, "This, Agent Paris Beaufont, is Agent Barney Jasper. He's the director in charge of the Basic Love departments."

The guy who wouldn't have known that a meteorite had landed at his feet unless he'd received a text on his phone didn't look up when introduced. That's why Paris bowed low, taking one knee and making a show of being bowled over by meeting her boss, who couldn't care less. "It's such a pleasure to meet you, Parney Bearl. You are the essence of what I want to be."

Agent Jasper looked up at Paris kneeling in front of him. She noticed this as he blinked around in confusion. "No, thanks. I'm good. I don't need a shoeshine today."

Paris shook her head, wondering how so many tools could work at this place. Finding the problems inside FGA might be tougher than she thought. How had Saint Valentine let it get to this point? She guessed that he'd been so removed from the inner workings of this place for so long that he didn't see how archaic it was.

Standing, Paris shook her head and stared directly at her director, although he was now typing on his phone again. "Hey there, I don't shine shoes. I'm a halfling who was elected by Saint Valentine himself to work as the first female to lead the Casual Romance department under you. My name is Paris Beaufont. Although I don't usually drop names, why yes, I'm a Beaufont and the first of the founding families in the magical races, and I'm pretty much connected to the coolest people on this planet like

Mother Nature and Father Time if you ever want to pull on my resources."

The guy sighed. Then he huffed. Then he looked up and blinked like he saw Paris for the first time. "Hey, Parry. Here's how we're going to go moving forward. When you need me, pull up your phone, go to call me, and think better of it. That's when you'll send me a text that I'll respond to in about a day or a week or whenever I see fit. Okay?"

Paris flexed her fist and thought about punching the guy. However, a glance at Faraday told her not to. The squirrel was shaking his head from the floor. So instead, Paris let out a steadying breath. "Did you hear that part where I said I work for you now, or did you mishear me and think I was asking where you wanted me to drop off your dry cleaning?"

Agent Jasper offered a disingenuous smile, slipped his phone into his pocket, and sighed again. He was good at that, Paris thought.

"Here's the thing, Polly—"

"Paris," she corrected. "And I prefer to go by Agent Beaufont."

"Whatever." He waved dismissively. "I don't care who you are or how you got your role. Your department means nothing to me or anyone. That's why Saint Valentine gave it to you. You can't do anything in that place, and more importantly, you can't screw anything up. That man is simply playing a political game by putting you, a Beaufont and a halfling, in that role. So let's get one thing straight. I'm going to ignore you until you go away, and you're going to go away, hopefully sooner rather than later. In the meantime, simply leave me alone. I'll do the same to you until you're gone. Got it?"

Paris blinked at the man, wondering if his nose would look better on the right side of his face or the left. Or maybe he'd look best with two black eyes and a fat lip. She didn't get a chance to make up her mind because he removed his revolting face by walking around her and away, pulling out his phone once more and going back to typing on it.

Faraday hopped up next to her, looking up at Paris. "Wow, you're making so many friends so fast."

"Shut it, squirrel," Paris seethed, realizing that her problems were growing by the minute.

CHAPTER SEVENTEEN

Second Floor, FGA Tower, New York City, New York

This time it was Paris who held out a presenting arm to Alfred. "Now, please show me the way to the next circus act. I simply can't wait."

He blinked at her, his programming struggling to understand what she was talking about. "Up ahead is the shoeshine shop called Dwyer's Polishes. It's the only thing left on the second level to show you. After that, I'll take you to your department on the third floor."

"Well, to demonstrate how excited I am to visit my department, Casual Romance, please lead me to the shoeshine place where I have no interest."

Alfred again blinked, his confusion seeming to make his head overheat. "Okay, please follow me."

Paris trudged on with Faraday hopping beside her. "Hey, did you hear that? Your department is on the third floor, Pare."

"I heard…"

"Well, then you know what that means," he stated.

"I'm closer to hell," she guessed, all emotion absent from her voice.

"Well, in a way," he chirped.

"Have I mentioned how happy I am to have you here?" Sarcasm oozed from her.

"Although it's true, from my preliminary calculations that the lower the level in FGA Tower, the lower its importance, which means you're considered pretty worthless based on your placement—"

"I mean, do you want chocolates as a thank you gift for being my rock support on this day of constant wins, or would you prefer cash?" Paris interrupted.

Faraday shook his head. "Stay with me, Pare. I swear, I'm going somewhere with this."

"Cool, because guess where my boot is about to go? It rhymes with 'lore ras—'"

"Pare, I'm telling you, we're in a good position," Faraday cut in.

She paused, studied the squirrel, let out a breath of anger she'd been harboring, and gave in. "Okay, tell me what you're thinking."

"Well, first I think that 'lore rass' isn't a real thing," he stated.

"That rhymes with kicking you in your—"

"I get where you were going with it," he interrupted. "It just doesn't work."

Paris sighed. "Fine, continue."

"I know that you have a lot of jerks batting against you, and they think you're in a bad department where they can boss you around and withhold support." Faraday spoke in a rush, looking around and keeping his voice down as people passed, although it wasn't as busy on this end of the second floor.

"Can you get to the part where I feel better?" Paris asked.

He nodded. "Yes, I think that they'll always underestimate you, and there's a lot of politics to cut through here. We have so much to uncover, but that's what I'm good at. Thankfully, you're good at distracting people with your bad attitude while I do my job."

"Thank you..." Paris drew out the words ironically.

"You're welcome," Faraday chirped. "Anyway, once we figure out exactly what's going on here, we can make changes *because* they aren't paying attention to us. It's better that they underestimate us.

"I saw that agent in the plaza. They're watching, but they don't expect us to know how to create real change. Not only are we going to figure out what's going on behind the scenes here, but we're going to figure out what's happening in all the departments. From there, we're going to make a real difference. At my core, that's what I sense this place is missing. Real love hasn't come from FGA in a very long time."

Paris was shocked and speechless. She blinked at her friend, wondering where the speech had come from.

Faraday shrugged and smiled at her with his tiny paws in the air.

Finally, she said, "So where do we start?"

"With the shoeshine guy," Faraday suggested. "No one gets more secrets than a guy in his position. People never think those who hang out below them know what they're saying. That's why being in our lowly department is for the best."

"Yeah?" Paris was curious.

"Yeah, from there we can learn everything. Then we need to turn everything around...then we can do the most important thing."

Paris blinked at her friend in confusion. "What's that?"

"Find out what's going on in this place and discover what's happened to the Advanced Love department."

CHAPTER EIGHTEEN

Second Floor, Dwyer's Polishes, FGA Tower, New York City, New York

If Alfred noticed the terse conversation between Paris and Agent Punk Face, as she'd already taken to calling him in her mind, he didn't give anything away. The AI magitech resident expert seemed to have less personality than Wilfred. The "bugs" in his programming, so to speak, must have been worked out since he was a newer model.

"The last place on your tour of the second floor is Dwyer's Polishes." Alfred paused in front of a shoe-shining station. It consisted of two raised regal chairs with elaborate armrests and soft cushions. In front of the chairs were stools for the patron's shoes. Beside that was a bucket of bottles with thick bright liquids and rags covered in the strange substances.

Standing next to the station was the first smiling person Paris had seen at FGA Tower. The man was young with bright eyes and a wide grin. His messy brown curly hair flopped down on his forehead, and he seemed about as out of place as Paris, wearing dark overalls over a red and black flannel shirt.

"Hi! You must be new here." The guy extended a welcoming

hand. "I'm Dwyer the Third. You can call me Dwyer, though. I don't do titles, unlike the rest of everyone here at FGA."

"Hi." Paris found the man's warm nature refreshing. It felt so good to have someone smile at her, she realized. She shook his hand, which was firm but gentle, his palm covered in calluses from his days working. "I'm Paris Beaufont, the new agent for the Casual Romance department, but like you, I don't care for titles, so call me Paris."

He nodded and smiled again before squatting and extending a hand to Faraday. "Who might you be, little fella?" He glanced up at Paris. "Is he your support squirrel? Hazel in the potions department has a support ferret, and she refuses to come to work without the little guy."

"She's more like my support human," Faraday answered, earning a shocked look from Dwyer.

He pointed at the talking squirrel and gawked at Paris, his eyes wide. "He spoke. Your squirrel speaks!"

She nodded. "Sometimes too much."

"Hazel's ferret doesn't speak. It just leaves 'gifts' behind." He put air quotes around gifts.

"Thankfully, my sidekick is house trained." Paris laughed, finally feeling sort of like herself with this guy.

"You mind me asking how you can talk, lil' buddy?" Dwyer asked. "I don't get out much and have never met an animal that can speak."

"I can introduce you to a cat who tells riddles and a dragon who tells bad jokes,' Paris teased, referring to her mother's and aunt's familiars.

"Wow, that would be exceptionally cool," Dwyer said enthusiastically. "I'm sure glad you're working here, Paris. You seem like a cool chick."

"I think that you and Saint Valentine are the only ones happy about me being here." Paris glanced over her shoulder to ensure there was no one around. "My boss definitely isn't happy about it."

"Your boss…" Dwyer combed his fingers over his chin, thinking. "That'd be Agent Jasper. I wouldn't worry about him. The only thing that makes him happy is if I compliment his designer loafers, and that's only if he hears me properly since he can't pull his attention away from his blasted phone."

Paris nodded. "Well, then I won't take it personally that he hardly looked at me when we just met."

"Yeah, don't let that guy get to you." Dwyer waved his large hand dismissively. "All he cares about is his own behind. I only see him smiling when he gets awarded a large budget for some project from the Finance department. Incidentally, he's been smiling a lot lately. Probably got an extra line item for some fancy equipment from the IT department. I swear those two directors are in cahoots."

Paris glanced sideways at Faraday, knowing that the squirrel was taking in all the information and storing it for later purposes. She wasn't sure what to make of everything that Dwyer was unknowingly disclosing but realized that Faraday had been right and he was in the best position to give them helpful insider information.

"Anyway, your squirrel," Dwyer said when the conversation suddenly ran quiet. "How did you get him to talk? Can I get a squirrel and have him talk?"

"Unfortunately, I don't think so," Paris answered. "Faraday is the result of a scientific experiment that went wrong…or rather right, leaving him in squirrel form. He was once a very clever magician, but now he's a very clever squirrel and my best friend."

"It's true," Faraday chirped, smiling fondly at her. "I'm much happier as a squirrel. Life is less complicated, which is good because physics is very overwhelming. If you need anything science-related, I'm your guy."

"Squirrel," Paris corrected.

"Right," Faraday stated. "One of my advanced degrees is in chemistry if you ever need tips on shoeshine chemicals." He indicated the bucket of bottles with bright liquids.

"Why, thank you very much, but all my shoeshine products are a family secret," Dwyer explained. "I make them myself every single night so they're fresh and I can offer a special."

"You make your chemicals?" Faraday asked, impressed.

Dwyer nodded proudly. "Yes, they're old family recipes. Top secret magical potions that we've handed down for generations."

"Oh, so this is a family business then?" Paris indicated the shoeshine station.

"Indeed." Dwyer grabbed the top of his overalls and grinned. "I shine shoes just like my daddy and my grandpappy before him. We've held onto our secrets and have been shining the shoes of agents and fairy godmothers at FGA for three generations in the way that only we can."

"Wow, I guess I didn't realize that others besides agents and fairy godmothers would work here. But it makes sense," Paris mused.

"Well, of course," Dwyer sang good-naturedly. "I mean, the Parvati family runs Curry-Osities. Be sure to try Gobi Manchurian but be warned that you'll have crazy dreams that night. Then there's Jenny, the owner of Sundry Charms. She makes great cold-pressed juices daily that are wonderfully fresh, but don't get the blue spirulina. It doesn't matter if she makes it blue to make you forget that it's algae or if it is fresh. There's simply no way to make that stuff taste good. The security team is usually retired officials from FLEA—the Fairy Law Enforcement Agency."

He leaned forward with a conspiratorial look. "If you ask me, they're pretty worthless. As a whole, the security department's been gunning for a raise from the higher-ups for ages, but they aren't getting one, methinks.

"The departments that get the money around here are the

SARAH NOFFKE & MICHAEL ANDERLE

ones that are deemed most important, and most know that security isn't that big a problem around here. I mean, there was that time when we had a couple of demons let loose in FGA Tower, but it wasn't the security team that saved us from them. It was some demon hunter and his daughter."

Paris smiled inwardly, careful to keep her eyes off Faraday. He might make her expression crack. She simply nodded, not taking credit for being a part of the team that rid the place of demons.

"Oh, and we have Fairy Grounds," Dwyer went on. "A bunch of cute pixies run it. Sweetest little fairies anyone ever saw, but they can't make a cup of coffee to save their pretty pink or blue hair. Thankfully, their scones are to die for."

Faraday pointed at a chalk sign that sat next to the first chair. "Today's special is Fancy Feet. What does that mean?"

Dwyer chuckled. "Every day at Dwyer's Polishes, I have a special. Sometimes they are FGA favorites like Double Time or Quiet Toes."

"Oh, so are those magical polishes you use on someone's shoes to make them faster or quieter when they walk?" Faraday asked.

Dwyer fired a finger gun at the squirrel. "Exactly, little friend. Really, the specials are always a surprise and whatever I feel like coming up with the day before. You never know what you're going to get, so stop by each day to see what I'm offering."

He glanced down at Paris' boots. "Those are some mighty fine leather shoes. How about a shine on the house since it's your first day? I'll give you the special, and you'll be dancing through this building."

Paris gave him a nervous albeit appreciative smile. "Thanks, but I'm already getting a lot of unwanted stares. I think I'd rather not attract any more attention to myself today."

He nodded in understanding. "Well, the offer stands for the next time you stop by. Your first shine at Dwyer's Polishes is on the house."

"Thanks, that's really nice of you," Paris replied. "I'll be back for a shine and more. You seem like a wealth of information on FGA and also a nice welcoming face. I think I could use both as the newbie here."

He nodded. "Yeah, you don't seem like the others. I mean, all the other agents are uptight in their suits and always so serious, talking about budgets and meetings and stuff. None of them would have let me talk on and on like this about things."

"Then there's the other obvious difference." Paris smirked at him.

He scratched his head in obvious confusion. "Is it because you're not wearing that suit or have some magical instrument with a gem?" Dwyer looked her over. "Well, maybe you do, and I just don't see it."

Paris shook her head. "I don't, and I'm not wearing a stupid suit. I was saying that the obvious difference is that I'm a woman and agents have always been men. It's just that Saint Valentine thought it was time for a change. Since I'm part magician, he believes I can offer a unique approach to creating love."

"You're a magician?" Dwyer was shocked. "That's so cool. I thought you were different, but just 'cause you're cool in your leather jacket and have a talking squirrel. It's awesome that you're a magician too."

"And a woman in an agent role," Faraday added.

Dwyer shrugged. "Not sure why that should matter. I'm not sure why they've always been men anyway. Or why the fairy godmothers are always women. I mean, it seems like either gender would have something to offer the roles. But that's why I shine shoes and don't run this place.

"Anyway, if Saint Valentine thought you'd make a good agent, then he's got to be right. I've always liked the current Saint Valentine. My daddy did too. He's much more progressive than the one he replaced who reigned when my grandpappy ran this shoeshine place. Anyway, I'm finding more and more reasons to like you, Paris."

"Thanks, Dwyer. Same to you. I think I'll be stopping by here regularly."

"Please do." He winked and pointed at Alfred. "The grumpy AI is giving that look when he dismisses me from a conversation, so I better let you be on your way."

Paris turned to find that Dwyer was right. Alfred did seem grumpy, like he was bored with the conversation. "Al has to learn to laugh at my jokes. Then he won't be grumpy anymore."

"I'm not programmed to laugh at your jokes or anyone else's," Alfred answered at once. "According to protocol, I think you've spent more than enough time talking to Dwyer in comparison to how much time you've spent at other locations on the tour. Also, I think you should spend the last part of your day with your department, which we won't have time for unless we move along."

Paris blinked at Dwyer, pursing her lips. "He thinks a lot of things for having no opinion and zero sense of humor."

Dwyer shared her smile and pointed at his bucket of magical polishes. "Maybe I can concoct a special that will make him laugh and fun to be around."

"If you do, let's put it on everyone's shoes in this place," Paris joked, waving goodbye to the shoeshine guy.

"Deal," Dwyer replied as Paris turned to follow Alfred back toward the elevators.

CHAPTER NINETEEN

Elevator, FGA Tower, New York City, New York

The lights of the various floors lit up on the buttons as the three progressed in the elevator compartment. Paris gave Alfred a sideways look.

"I thought you were taking me to my department?"

The AI nodded. "I will. I figured I'd show you a few other floors first. However, I would caution you to observe rather than interact."

Paris lowered her chin and huffed. "Why? Because when I open my mouth and interact, I create problems?"

"That's an astute observation, Alfred," Faraday sang. He'd opened a panel on the front section of the elevator under the floor buttons and was inspecting it.

"I simply have observed that when Agent Beaufont talks to people, their blood pressure increases," Alfred answered.

She held up her hand and started ticking off fingers as she began to list. "Well, so far you've seen me talk to incompetent security guards. Then there was Agent Emerald, aka Agent Head-Up-His-Butt, and since I didn't bow for his greatness, he didn't seem to like me. Oh, and there was Agent Punk Face, who is going to try to pretend I don't exist. So yeah, I guess I made those guys' blood pressure rise. Dwyer seemed fine enough. So did Saint Valentine."

Alfred nodded. "Yes, he was fine. If anything, he was more relaxed when you left. So one out of the six individuals you interacted with went ideally."

"Wait, you said six but only listed five people," Faraday interrupted as the elevator neared the forty-fifth floor and slowed.

"Well, yes," Alfred answered. "I didn't mention Saint Valentine since from my perspective there was no obvious conflict during that interaction with Agent Beaufont. Nevertheless, FGA's leader had elevated blood pressure."

Paris' and Faraday's gazes connected as the elevator paused on the forty-fifth floor and the doors slid open.

Alfred held out his white-gloved hand, welcoming them to the floor with his typical presentation. "May I present to you the forty-fifth floor, also the home of my creation. This level is devoted to magitech."

CHAPTER TWENTY

Forty-Fifth Floor, Magitech Departments, FGA Tower, New York City, New York

The bright white countertops, walls, and floors were a stark contrast to the black marble all over the first two levels of FGA Tower. Bustling around in white lab coats over their suits or blue gowns were various technicians. They were agents and fairy godmothers with goggles covering parts of their faces. Most of them were seemingly deep in thought as they worked on pieces of equipment.

"Everyone stays quite occupied on this level," Alfred explained in a low voice. "This department is always in high demand and usually under tight deadlines."

"Because magitech churns out AIs like you to support other areas of the world of love?" Faraday hurried along beside them but stood every so often to peek at what was on the countertops —the various experiments or products.

Alfred shook his head. His loafers made small slapping noises on the white tile, but no one paid it any notice. "No, there are no AIs under construction at the moment. From the small bits I'm privy to here in the magitech department, their three main products are related to making phones more intuitive to users, weighted blankets that sense how much pressure someone needs, and robotic vacuums that are more efficient."

"Wait, wasn't it phone addictions that recently created huge problems with love on the planet?" Paris questioned. "Why would FGA try to make phones more intuitive?"

Alfred blinked, accessing the information related to this subject from his database. "Yes, there was an incident where a rogue agent contracted an outside source to make phones addictive so in-person relationships deteriorated."

"Yeah, and I shot down the satellite broadcasting that signal," Faraday said proudly.

"I read the report." Alfred nodded, continuing to march them down the lab's center aisle. "This project with phones is different. It's intended to allow the device to sense what the user needs and supply that content. Similarly, the weighted blanket will be of the same intuitive nature, sensing what its user needs. The vacuum, well, it will sense where it's needed most."

"All that sounds great," Paris began in a low voice while studying the many people and things they passed. "However, not for an agency meant to create love. Shouldn't this department's efforts be solely about creating love using magitech and not convenience, which is what it sounds like?"

Alfred paused and regarded her like she was suddenly foreign and he didn't recognize her. Then he blinked. "True. But FGA convenience also lends itself to love. 'When people's lives are easier, they have more time for each other.' That's a quote from Agent Emerald from a meeting during the first quarter when he presented his yearly plan."

"When people's lives are easier, they usually spend more time getting fat and ignoring their loved ones," Paris observed, looking around and not seeing the enthusiasm she envisioned in a department meant to create technology that nurtured love.

"Also, please remember that FGA is a for-profit institution."

Alfred didn't respond to her protest about modern conveniences harming love. "It is through many of our inventions, deals, and partnerships connected to love that we remain in business and profitable."

It was Paris' turn to blink at the AI in confusion. "Say what? We're a for-profit institution? So we have to do what will keep us out of the red rather than what the red heart desires? Doesn't having financial interests skew our objectivity as matchmakers?"

Alfred stared back at her blankly, then shrugged, his white gloves in the air.

"Are you kidding me?" Paris turned to face Faraday. "You see the obvious problems here?"

He nodded, then shook his head. There was a warning in his eyes. Paris knew that he was silently trying to say, "Observe. Don't speak. Right now we study. Later plan. Then we act."

Paris knew her friend was right. She let out a steadying breath and forced a smile. "Well, this is very enlightening. Thanks, Al. Where's next on the tour?"

Seemingly grateful to be out of the line of questioning, the AI marched back toward the elevators. "Next we'll see the potions floor."

CHAPTER TWENTY-ONE

Thirty-Ninth Floor, Potions Departments, FGA Tower, New York City, New York

"You know, they call these lifts in the UK," Paris began, pointing at the doors of the elevator as they neared the thirty-ninth floor. "In the US, we call them elevators." She turned to Alfred and shrugged. "I guess it's just that we were raised differently."

"Oh, dear…" Faraday groaned.

Alfred suddenly looked down at the squirrel as if Faraday might be ill. "Are you okay?"

"Yeah, I get sick from her jokes." Faraday nodded at Paris.

Alfred turned back to Paris. "Oh, that was a joke? That's the kind of statement that's supposed to produce a laugh, then."

"That's how I feel." Faraday chuckled.

"Oh, never mind." Paris rolled her eyes. "My brilliance is lost on you lot."

"It's definitely lost," Faraday stated as the elevators paused on the thirty-ninth floor.

Alfred presented the way with one hand. "Here we have the Potions departments."

The many smells competing for Paris' olfactory senses were overwhelming when they stepped off the elevator. She instinctively covered her nose, thinking that she'd get intoxicated by the fumes. Thankfully Faraday did the same, making her feel less self-conscious.

Not noticing their concern, Alfred led the way down a similar floor to the forty-fifth for magitech. It was mostly white with lab stations. Instead of devices, there were tons of beakers with brightly colored substances, cauldrons bubbling with concoctions, and fairy godmothers and agents in rubber aprons. They all wore the same goggles as the scientists on the upper floor.

"The potions department is most known for its youth moisturizers, which are the top beauty care product in any market," Alfred began proudly. "They also produce elixirs that create a multitude of states such as being satiated or hunger or numbness."

"Wait, my head's about to explode." Paris sped up to Alfred. "Why would FGA want to make people feel full and also hungry at the same time?"

"It depends on what our third-party vendor would desire," he explained. "A food court at a mall would probably desire for their patrons to be hungry. The one who owns a spa and wants money spent on services rather than food will want their customers to have their hunger pangs gone."

"So FGA is catering to a private market?" Paris looked around. To her relief, no one was paying her any attention.

"Well, again, how does the company make money?"

"I don't know. Create love?"

"I don't think that love on its own is considered profitable," Alfred stated. "That's what I gather after perusing the minutes from the most recent board meetings."

"Wow, this place is…" Paris didn't finish that sentence based on Faraday's look, which verged on murderous. "Numbness?

SARAH NOFFKE & MICHAEL ANDERLE

Why is that a product that FGA is devoting time, energy, and resources to?"

"There are many vendors happy to pay for potions that elicit numbness," Alfred answered. "It creates a blank slate that makes ideal customers for video game companies, drug dealers, or many other distributors of various types."

Paris pivoted on her heels, marching back to the elevator. "Next floor. I must be off this one."

CHAPTER TWENTY-TWO

Elevator, FGA Tower, New York City, New York

"I recently developed a severe phobia of elevators," Paris said in a mock meek voice when the three of them were back in the compartment moving down in FGA Tower.

Alfred looked up suddenly with concern in his eyes. "Oh, no. Are you all right, Agent Beaufont?"

She nodded, hiding her grin. "I'm fine. I'm taking steps to avoid it."

Faraday shook his head. "It's not working, Pare. You're not going to make the AI laugh."

Alfred looked between Paris and Faraday, again confused. "I'm sorry, but that was another of those jokes meant to make me do this laughing thing?"

"It's not a good attempt, but yes, that was her intention," Faraday explained.

"Oh, shush it, squirrel, or I'm taking you back up to the Middle School Romance department and leaving you there," Paris threatened. "Then you'll have to listen to eleven-year-old children talk about cooties and pretend not to like each other and have to science your way out of those complex situations."

Faraday narrowed his eyes at her. "You wouldn't."

"Just try me," she warned. However, Paris had to admit that Casual Romance sounded as lame and annoying as the Middle School Romance department. On their way down from the elite IT departments, they'd visited ones in her branch run by Agent Punk Face, or rather Agent Jasper. Middle School Romance and Online Dating all were about what Paris expected with lots of shiny workstations and self-important employees who were all too busy to pay her any notice.

Gnome-Mance, which was right after Interspecies Love, was pretty bare-bones with hardly any staff. Apparently, it was pretty difficult for gnomes to find love, which was why they got their own department. Interspecies love used to be a big deal before treaties between different races came into place and elves were encouraged not to mix with magicians and so forth and so on. Paris knew from her halfling state that mixing the races was nearly impossible.

However, those departments' furnishings, setups, and employee roster seemed sad compared to the higher levels, which were all bright and fully staffed. This tour should've primed Paris. She shouldn't have been surprised when the doors opened on the third floor and it appeared to be a ghost town. Paris imagined that a tumbleweed passed in front of them as they stepped off the elevator.

Again, Alfred held out a presenting arm. "Welcome to your department, Agent Beaufont. This is the Casual Romance floor."

CHAPTER TWENTY-THREE

Third Floor, Casual Romance Department, FGA Tower, New York City, New York

"Is it just me or is it cold in here?" Faraday's teeth chattered as he held his paws to his mouth.

Paris glanced at him. "You have a winter coat. Suck it up. It does seem a little cooler here. What are we walking on? Is that shag carpet?"

Alfred glanced down. "Yes, that's from the last agent in charge. They liked a more retro look."

"What, were they from the seventies?" Paris joked, but when Alfred didn't answer, she realized she didn't want the real answer. It appeared that the department she'd inherited was more than behind the times.

"I think the employees on this floor appear to keep it cooler for efficiency reasons," Alfred explained, leading them down a dark hallway. Unlike the lab-oriented departments, this one had small rooms lining the hallway. There were lots of nooks with bean bags or small tables. The place wasn't totally atrocious, and Paris thought she could probably work with the space.

Sitting on a nearby pedestal was a large clear corked bottle with some glowing pink liquid in the very bottom. Paris was about to take a closer look when a thought occurred to her. She straightened, jolted by the notion.

Paris realized that if she had an entire floor, she was probably dealing with a lot of space. Her mind started to race with the possibilities. Then a sudden new realization immediately squashed any ideas related to opportunities.

"Why does Casual Romance have an entire floor?" Paris stopped cold in her tracks and stared at Alfred's back.

The AI turned and smiled at her. "Well, that was only recent."

"Yeah, because magitech takes up a few floors, and it appears to be doing something." Faraday looked around the dead and darkened space. "This place seems to lack any life."

"Again, your words fill me with optimism and hope," Paris said sarcastically before returning her attention to Alfred. "Why is it that only recently Casual Romance has occupied this floor alone?"

"Well, because Agent Jasper moved the other department sharing this floor to other ones, consolidating them," Alfred answered in a neutral voice.

Paris realized that there would be some stuff that the AI had seen and some stuff that he hadn't according to security measures. He probably wasn't allowed on particular floors where the technology needed to stay secret or conversations had to remain private. The AI was supposed to give knowledge to the public, so anyone trying to shield their secrets would keep him away. However, there would also be things he saw and could report that someone might not think to guard from him.

"Why did Agent Jasper remove the other departments from this floor?" Paris chose her words carefully, hoping this was a question that Alfred could and would answer.

He looked at her directly, tilted his head, and answered honestly, "I believe the director of Basic Love stated, 'The halfling shouldn't be able to influence and infect my other departments with her wrong way of doing things. She's going to take down only one department, but more importantly, herself. I'll give her enough space to create a bonfire where hopefully she'd roast herself.'"

Alfred finished with a small cough, looking very proud of himself. Then he added, "That's all Agent Jasper said about you and this floor. Would you like to meet your two employees? I believe they are currently at the barre."

Paris nodded. "Good, and to add fuel to the flames, Agent Punk Face gave me a couple of lushes as employees. This should be fun. What is it, noon and my staff is day drinking?"

"Incidentally, do you know what they call day drinking in Russia?" Faraday asked, not at all deterred by all the bad news they'd recently learned.

Paris paused and looked down at the squirrel, reading the unshakable look of perseverance on his face. He seemed to be saying, "Don't worry, we're going to beat this guy at his own game. Just stay the course."

"What do they call day drinking in Russia?" she asked.

"Just drinking." He winked at her and hurried after Alfred, who was halfway down the long, dark, shag-carpeted hallway.

CHAPTER TWENTY-FOUR

Third Floor, Barre Room, Casual Romance Department, FGA Tower, New York City, New York

Too preoccupied with taking in the mismatched furniture around the open office space, Paris was surprised when she heard a woman's voice around the corner. She still couldn't believe there was an actual bar inside her department. It appeared there were going to be a lot of immediate changes she'd be making, starting with not drinking at work.

"Now just hold plank," the woman's voice called, all bubbly and light. "This is so good for you. And it's so fun."

"You need a dictionary," another woman grumbled, her tone strained. "This isn't what you call fun."

"Oh, we're having a great time, but it's almost over in ten, nine, eight..."

Paris glanced down at Faraday, who shared her confusion. However, the scene they heard made more sense when they rounded the corner. Well, it made as much sense as anything in this strange place full of oddities.

Two women held plank positions on their forearms and toes in the middle of a room with mats and other small workout equipment like weights, balls, and resistance bars. Along the far wall were floor-to-ceiling mirrors and attached to it a wooden bar like one might find in a ballet studio.

"Come down in three, two, and one," the cheerful woman said and gracefully dropped to her torso. The side of her face pressed into the mat.

The other woman groaned again and fell flat with a *thud*.

"Now, didn't that feel good?" The first woman rose to her knees, still not seeing Paris and the others standing in the entrance of what Paris belatedly realized was a workout room of sorts. It occupied an alcove off the main work area, which held cubicles or open areas with small conference tables. The entire space didn't seem to know what it was for and had lost any organization along with the desire to do any real work.

"You're a sick and sadistic individual if you thought that felt good," the other woman complained, pushing back on her heels and taking a child pose, her head pressed into the mat.

"Okay, break's over," the other lady cheered, popping up to her feet. "Let's get this workout started."

She twirled, putting one hand on the ballet barre attached to the mirror. That's when she realized they weren't alone— Paris, Alfred, and a squirrel stood nearby, watching them.

"Oh, we have company," the woman said with surprise and strangely, delight. Since the fairy godmothers, as Paris guessed, weren't wearing their blue gowns, the woman's real hair color was visible. She had short dark hair that met her chin and light mocha skin. Her brown eyes were full of excitement, and the smile that popped onto her mouth was easy. Paris could see it being contagious.

Instead of the blue fairy godmother gown, the woman wore pastel workout clothes and leg warmers that looked right out of the nineteen-eighties.

The other woman rose to her knees without hurry and turned. She didn't seem as enthused to find the three spying on

SARAH NOFFKE & MICHAEL ANDERLE

them. In contrast, this fairy godmother had long blonde hair that Paris was sure wasn't all hers. She further concluded that based on the woman's fake eyelashes when she blinked at them, probably trying to clear her vision after being facedown.

The fairy godmother swept a strand of fake hair off her cheek with fake black pointy nails that reminded Paris of a cat. They matched her tight black yoga pants and hoodie. The only color on the woman was the pink lipstick on her oversized lips.

"Who is our special guest?" the other woman with dark hair asked, striding over.

"This is your new supervisor." Alfred extended a presenting hand to Paris. "I introduce you to Agent Beaufont and her sidekick Faraday, the talking squirrel."

"Wait, what?" The other woman protested. "We have a new supervisor?"

"She's a she." The other fairy godmother sounded on the verge of disbelief as she looked Paris up and down.

"She has a talking squirrel." The other one also studied Paris.

Deciding that she was tired of being talked about like she wasn't there, Paris offered a tame smile. "Hi. Yes, I'm the new head of the Casual Romance department. Agent Jasper would have told you about me."

They both exchanged looks, searching each other's faces for information.

"Did you get a memo on this?" the bubbly one asked the other.

She shook her head. "No, the other department just vacated. I thought my trick of wearing too much perfume and leaving nail polish remover bottles open on the other department's desks by accident had caused them to move out."

"Although the members of the Practical Love department didn't appreciate your unwillingness to share the space, that's not why they moved," Alfred explained.

"Yeah, apparently it was because Agent Jasper didn't want them influenced by my 'wrong' way of doing things," Paris muttered, putting air quotes on the word *wrong*. "Of course, that was before he met me or assessed my skills so obviously a real informed opinion."

"I'm sorry." The woman with short dark hair waved both hands. "I'm going to need you to slow down and repeat yourself." She looked directly at Alfred. "What exactly is going on here? We haven't had a supervisor in ages. And a woman."

"You say that like you aren't one." Paris wished the lighting was better in this place. She felt like they were in a funeral home, which she guessed made her the funeral director, and this seemingly useless pair in front of her were her corpses for entombing.

The dark-haired woman's hearing had apparently died with her manners. She continued to stare at Alfred, ignoring Paris. "Is this happening?"

"I can't vouch for what you're experiencing in your reality," Alfred answered quite seriously. "I can say that Saint Valentine has placed Agent Beaufont in charge of the Casual Romance department. Although it is unconventional, her being the first female to hold an agent role, it is true."

"Why didn't Agent Jasper tell us?" The woman with long blonde hair crossed her arms over her large chest.

"Because that would involve talking to us or acknowledging that we exist," the other one imparted.

"I think we should start over." Paris smiled, holding out her hand. "I'm Agent Paris Beaufont, and I look forward to working with you both."

The woman with dark hair glanced sideways at the other one, then down at Paris' outstretched hand. "Are you seeing what I'm seeing?"

The blonde nodded. "Her cuticles aren't pushed back."

"There's no nail polish either."

"I had heard there were women who didn't get manicures, but I didn't think they existed."

Paris lowered her hand and sighed, glancing down at Faraday.

"They're doing that thing again where they talk about me like I can't hear them."

"Maybe they sniffed too much nail polish remover, and they think they're hallucinating," he squeaked.

Both women jumped back a bit.

Dumb grabbed her chest while Dumber squealed with fright.

"The squirrel talks," Dumb said.

"Out loud," Dumber stated.

"Yes, usually that's how people talk...out loud. Or squirrels, in the case of Faraday. Alfred already informed you that the squirrel talks, so I'm not sure what the surprise is. It's like no one has seen a talking squirrel." Paris swung around to face the AI. "Can you tell me their names so I can refer to them as something rather than the names I'm using in my head?"

Alfred nodded and pointed at Dumb, the one with darker skin and short hair. "This is Isha Parvati. She has been a fairy godmother for three years in the Casual Romance department."

"Oh, so it's your family who runs Curry-Osities," Paris observed.

Isha glanced at Dumber. "How does she know that?"

"I'm a detective." Paris answered the question not asked of her.

Alfred nodded at Dumber. "This is Holly Sanderson, and she's been at FGA for almost a decade, half of that time being in the Casual Romance department."

Holly pointed at Isha. "She's the sunshine of this place. I'm the darkness."

Paris worked to keep her surprise off her face because the roles seemed reversed since Holly was the blonde baby doll and Isha was the dark practical-looking one.

"It's true," Isha said as if she sensed Paris' doubt. "I like everything and Holly loathes most things."

"We balance each other out like that." Holly laughed.

Paris nodded, feigning a smile. "Hey, ladies. Nice to meet you.

As I mentioned, I'm Agent Beaufont. You can call me Paris. Today is my first day on the job as you've now learned."

"This is your first day as an agent?" Isha asked.

Paris shook her head, then nodded. "Well, first day as an agent and first day at FGA."

"Wait, you just graduated?" Holly pursed her oversized lips. "How is it possible that you're an agent? I mean, how is it possible that you're an agent at all?"

Before Paris could answer, which she didn't know how to succinctly, Alfred took over for her.

"Agent Beaufont had a graduation project at Happily Ever After College that created love off the charts and nearly broke the love meter," the AI began. "Due to Agent Beaufont's unique talents as both a fairy and a magician with demon blood, she was best suited for this leadership role according to Saint Valentine."

Holly swung around to her friend, grabbing her arms. "I've heard of the halfling. She eats kittens for breakfast to quell her demon blood."

"I don't eat breakfast," Paris said dully to Faraday.

"I thought so and always bought that bit you said about inter-mittent fasting, but now I'm onto you." His tone had turned mock accusatory. "Have you been sneaking little kittens at dawn when no one is looking?"

"You figured me out," Paris said dryly.

"I heard that she comes from the oldest magician family and that they've preserved their lineage through incest," Isha said in a loud whisper to Holly.

Paris let out a steadying breath, still staring down at her squirrel. "Do you think anyone will notice if I kill them?"

"I'll help you hide the bodies," he chirped, not missing a beat.

"I'm required to report any acts of violence," Alfred stated.

"But you're not required to stop me, are you?" Paris noticed that the two women weren't unnerved by the threat of death. They looked quite amused.

"She doesn't have a wand," Isha said to her friend.

"And no magical instrument, I'm guessing, since she's going by that weird name," Holly stated. "What did Alfred call her?"

"It's that strange hairdo from the sixties, I think," Isha answered.

"Oh yeah, a Beaufont." Holly ran her gaze over Paris. "Speaking of hair, has she even brushed hers recently?"

Paris was also a bit amused by this interplay but reached the end of her patience. She lifted her hand. A stream of blue light shot from her fingertips. The blast hit the shag carpet right in front of where the women stood, singeing the fibers and making both fairies jump back onto the mats behind them.

Since it was a tiny bit of magic and only meant to shock Dumb and Dumber, the fire went out immediately as Paris had planned. She stuck her hands on her hips proudly and smiled at the two dumbstruck women.

Shock covered their faces as they looked between the smoldering carpet and Paris.

"You did magic," Isha said in awe.

"I'm a magician," Paris stated with confidence.

"You did magic without a wand," Holly nearly stuttered.

"She's a magician," Faraday repeated. "And as far as I'm aware, she hasn't had a kitten today, so she might be hungry."

Paris chuckled at her squirrel and returned her attention to the fairies after finally getting their attention. "Now, how about we start from the beginning."

CHAPTER TWENTY-FIVE

Third Floor, Casual Romance Department, FGA Tower, New York City, New York

Paris cleared her throat. "Hello, Isha and Holly. It's nice to meet you. Going forward, when I'm in your presence, I will require you to talk directly to me and not pretend I don't exist."

They both nodded, their gazes flicking down to the burned shag carpet.

"Furthermore, although I do have demon blood, that doesn't make me crave kittens or puppies," she went on. "I'm a vegetarian as of recently. My demon blood only makes me hyper-aware of the presence of evil and drives me to stamp it out at any cost, which is usually at the expense of my safety and wellbeing."

"She's kind of cool," Isha observed, looking Paris over.

With a loud sigh, Paris lifted her hand, pointing at the fairy. "Again, you're not to talk about me like I'm not here unless you want to practice some fire-walking."

"Sorry," Isha said in a rush, holding up her hands in surrender.

Paris nodded, lowering her hand. "As I was saying, I'm a halfling, but that's precisely why Saint Valentine put me in this role. I have the emotional sensitivity of a fairy mixed with the practical and intelligent problem-solving of a magician."

"Why isn't she…I mean, why aren't you wearing a suit like the other agents?" Holly's face flushed red from her near mistake.

Paris grinned, realizing that these two were trainable. "They aren't my style. I can't throw a roundhouse kick in slacks or chase after bullies in loafers. I prefer this as my uniform."

The women checked her out, giving her appreciative looks.

"You know how to do a roundhouse kick?" Isha asked.

"Yeah, I can teach you."

"We do them in our kickboxing class." Holly pointed over her shoulder at the workout area.

"What is it that you all do here?" Paris looked over their shoulders at the area with mirrors and a ballet barre.

"Well, we had a barre class," Isha began.

Paris turned to Alfred. "Barre…so they weren't day drinking then?"

"I never said they were," he answered quite seriously. "I said they were at the barre."

"Have you ever tried barre?" Isha asked Paris. "It's the best workout. And it's so much fun. It's like a party."

Holly rolled her eyes. "Ish has a bit of a problem with her vocabulary. She calls things that are painful and torturous fun when she means they're a punishment."

"Oh, it's not torture when you have a nice round butt." Isha playfully waved at Paris.

Holly blinked her long eyelashes at her friend. "Like magicians would care. I hear that types like her can eat whatever they want, do magic, and bam, they have a calorie deficit."

"I want to be her," Isha complained, suddenly grumpy.

"I'm right here, ladies!" Paris sighed, wondering how hard it would be to train these divas fully.

"So you have a squirrel." Holly pointed at Faraday. "Where did you get him?"

"He sort of got me," Paris admitted, thinking of that fateful day when she headed to Happily Ever After College for the first time, and Faraday popped into her life and accompanied her. He'd been by her side ever since.

"Can I get a dog?" Isha asked her, quite seriously.

"If she gets a dog, I'm getting a cat," Holly stated adamantly, the pair like two siblings gunning for rewards.

"Neither of you is getting any animals," Paris stated. "You can't even take care of what you have here."

She looked around at the disorganized place strewn with clothes and makeup. A yoga ball sat near a desk crowded with cold-pressed juice containers from Sundry Charms. Littering another desk were recipes for homemade face masks and fashion magazines. "This place is a wreck. You might have succeeded at getting it all to yourselves, but now you're going to have to take care of it, or I'm corralling you to a tiny corner of it and taking away your workout space."

"You wouldn't," Isha hissed.

"She's mean," Holly stated.

"I'm fair," Paris amended. "I'd like to work with you and not against you, but that means we have to turn this place around. Why don't you start by telling me what you're working on."

"Well, I'm currently doing keto, but I keep cheating, and that throws me out of ketosis, so my goal is to stay away from Fairy Grounds," Isha explained. "I can't resist those scones."

"Who can?" Holly asked. "Currently, I'm trying to decrease my time for running a mile. The goal is to be able—"

"Are you both talking about your fitness goals still?" Paris interrupted.

They both nodded.

Holly pointed at Isha. "She makes me do stupid barre stuff, but I prefer cardio. If I'm not sweating, it's not working."

Isha shook her head. "I've told you that it's about micro-movements."

SARAH NOFFKE & MICHAEL ANDERLE

Paris held up her hands, pausing them both. "As happy as I am that you care about your bodies, although it's starting to sound like you're bordering on obsessed, when I asked about what you were working on, I meant at work."

The two women both looked at each other, again confused.

"Do you mean as it relates to fairy godmother stuff?" Isha asked.

"Yeah, strange, I know," Paris remarked dryly. "I'd like to know what cases you've been working on."

"Well, we don't," Holly remarked. "I mean, we're in Casual Romance. It's not like what we do makes a difference. Oh, but the other day, I told the girl behind me at the smoothie place that cashier guy had been checking her out. He wasn't, probably because she was wearing last year's yoga pants, but still, it made her smile."

"So you two don't do anything to promote love here?" Paris asked. "How long has this been going on? Since you've been without a supervisor?"

"Oh, that's where it started," Isha explained. "Our last boss, Agent Crystal, didn't care what we did. He said that love had been on the decline since Woodstock and there was no point in trying to help it until another music festival of that level came along."

"What happened to this guy?" Paris asked.

The women glanced at each other, both hoping the other knew the right answer. Finally, Isha shrugged. "I think he took some mushrooms he got from Sundry Charms and has been sleeping them off ever since." She glanced around. "I think he's probably hanging out somewhere here."

"Wow," Paris said in disbelief. "So you two have been hanging out here all this time, working out, painting your nails, and braiding each other's hair."

"Well, and also making fun of the dweebs in the Practical Love department," Holly added. "But we ran them out of here."

108

"It sounds like my presence did that," Paris amended. "We have our work cut out for us at this point. We need to get this space functional, look at the state of casual romance, and start making some plans for how we can create positive effects on love."

"Ummm...that's starting to sound like you want us to do work." Holly grimaced at the idea.

"Oh, I don't only want you to work," Paris began. "I want you to push yourself to greater heights. I want us to turn this department around completely. We're going to make Casual Romance soar so high that it breaks the love meter and all the higher-ups see it."

"Does this involve us having to show up every day?" Holly asked.

"Every day and all day long," Paris sang.

"We don't have to do anything complex, right?" Isha asked.

Paris turned to Alfred. "Are there reports that correspond to my department's cases?"

"Yes, Agent Beaufont. There will be a backlog of them."

"Great," Paris chirped. "Pull those reports and give them to the squirrel. He'll analyze them, and we can decide where and how our efforts to intervene and orchestrate casual romance can be best served."

"This sounds like work," Holly repeated.

"The squirrel analyzes things?" Isha pointed at Faraday.

"When he's not crafting chemistry projects or devices that can blow something up," Paris answered.

Holly sighed, looking at her long pointy nails. "I don't think all this sounds necessary. We've been fine on our own, and it seems that you're kind of a joke and Agent Jasper doesn't want you here. So no offense, but maybe you should let us do our thing, and you can analyze reports, and everyone will be happy."

Paris nodded, having expected this. "Then there are hundreds of thousands of people who won't be happy because they didn't meet the guy who they started a relationship flirting with on the train or the girl who smiles at him while bagging her groceries. If we don't do our job, then there is so much love, however seemingly small and insignificant, that doesn't get to happen. Every butterfly flutter in a Cinderella's stomach or twitter of a heart from a look, well, it makes a difference in this world. Maybe those couples don't go on to be great love stories, but maybe that interaction gives them the confidence to find their Prince Charmings."

Paris glanced at Faraday, and he gave her an encouraging nod so she continued, "So yes, I'm considered a total joke, and almost everyone is betting on me failing. That's exactly what I'm not going to do. Along with your help, we're going to turn this ineffective department around, making it a huge success.

"Then Agent Punk Face and his buddy Agent Head-Up-His-Butt are going to look like the losers because we're making a real difference while they merely profit off FGA's endeavors. This place has lost its mission of creating love, but that's why I'm here. We're going to get things back to how they're supposed to be."

Although Paris would have liked an enthusiastic round of applause or cheering from her team, she had to settle for a few tail flicks from Faraday, who seemed to be the only one energized by her speech.

"I have a question," Holly ventured.

"Yes?" Paris groaned, trying not to feel deflated by their lack of energy.

"Why would we do all that?"

"You're fairy godmothers. Your mission is to create love."

"Originally," Isha corrected. "Since then, we've been informed that creating love only perpetuates heartbreaks, which adds to a deficit. So we're told to pretty much stay out of love's way. Some departments do a good job on their own, like Online Dating and Dating Apps. If we go around intervening, it could have a domino effect and ruin the whole balance."

Paris lowered her chin, at a loss for how this could be her current reality. "That's what the others all told you?"

"It's true," Alfred cut in. "The complex task of creating love has had some fairly costly ways of backfiring, so many of the departments are told not to do anything that upsets the balance."

"What balance?" Paris asked. "It sounds like we're complacent with low levels of love and playing it safe with online dating for our matches. There is so much more we can do."

Holly shrugged. "I don't see how. Casual Romance is kind of a joke department."

Paris shook her head, pointing at herself. "Leave that up to me. You two get to work cleaning up this place. Alfred, get Faraday those reports. We're going to start making big changes."

"But not today, right?" Isha asked. "I was planning on…"

The ultra-serious expression that jumped to Paris' face made her stop.

"You know what, my Pilates class can wait." Isha plastered a smile on her face. "Hols, why don't you help me start sorting through stuff? A little purging of old things will be a good detox ritual."

"Dress it up however you like, Ish, but that's still considered work."

The two women moved off toward the back of the department space. Paris turned to Faraday, bolstering her spirits.

"This is going to be a much bigger challenge than I originally envisioned," Paris remarked in a low voice so the others didn't hear.

The squirrel nodded, jumping up to the table beside her. "Yes, and the odds are stacked against you. Many want to stand in your way. Your very nature threatens so many things about this place, how it's run, and how it's currently operating. I've deduced that they've abandoned the operations of love for more profit-driven ones. However, I still think that despite all the obstacles you face, you're in the best position to turn this around as I know Saint Valentine desires."

"You do?" Paris needed the assurance. "Why me, though?"

"Because most would have let the mugger get away," he began. "Most would have walked out when they met the first jerk of the day. Most would have been defeated by finding an abandoned department with two loafers for employees and no real mission.

"However, Paris Beaufont isn't deterred. That's exactly why you're going to be the one to fix this place. I suspect many have tried. Many have investigated. I believe we'll face many challenges as we set out to succeed on our mission. With your tenacity paired with my genius, we're going to overcome the barriers that held all the rest back. We're going to make FGA what it once was again. No, we're going to make it better. A place that adapts with the evolving world, but always creates sustainable love."

Paris could've used a round of applause when she gave her earlier speech, but she didn't get it. That's the reason she enthusiastically put her hands together and clapped for the squirrel who was the reason she still had her chin up on what was proving to be the hardest day in a long time.

From the back of the large space, Isha and Holly looked over, curious about the clapping. Paris smiled and pointed at Faraday. "He made a good speech."

"Of course, he did." Isha shook her head. "And I thought Agent Crystal did a lot of drugs."

Paris glanced at her friend and smiled. "Thanks, Fare. I'm glad to have you by my side."

"I'm glad to be here."

"That's good because you might be here for a while," Alfred cut in. "I've run the backlog of reports, and there are over a thousand pages of old cases to review."

CHAPTER TWENTY-SIX

Roya Lane, London

Thankfully Faraday was happy to stay late at FGA Tower and start reviewing the reports that Alfred had run for them. That was good for Paris because she had a meeting that evening with her Aunt Sophia and Mae Ling. Something told her that it was important and she shouldn't miss it even to try to understand her department better.

Roya Lane, a hidden magical set of streets in a mysterious part of London, was where Paris had grown up, raised by her Uncle John. He wasn't her uncle or from a magical race of any sort. He was a mortal who ran an electronics repair shop in West Hollywood, California.

However, when Paris' parents had mysteriously disappeared, John rose to the challenge. Their old family friend took on the disguise as a fairy, got a job as a detective for FLEA—Fairy Law Enforcement Agency on Roya Lane—and raised Paris in a flat above the busy shops.

That was all to keep her safe and protected. You see, it was because Paris was so rare as the only half-fairy and half-magician with demon blood that her parents went missing. The Beaufont family and many close friends knew that protecting Paris until she was grown was paramount.

Even now, Paris knew that danger usually lurked around most corners waiting to get her. Where danger was absent, some jerk who didn't like Paris because of who she was, like Agent Punk Face, usually replaced it.

Now that Paris' identity was known and her parents recovered, Uncle John had returned to his old life as a mortal. Realizing that her life had been a big lie hadn't been hard to deal with for Paris. It was the fact that so many people had rearranged their lives for her. The weight of what she was supposed to represent to the world of love was overwhelming to say the very least. Prophecies existed about the halfling who would save the fairy godmothers.

Already Paris had helped eradicate evil agents and stop tooth fairies bent on destroying the fairy godmothers and Happily Ever After College. However, Paris knew that was only the beginning of her mission to protect the fairies meant to safeguard love. That was because love was the scariest thing in the world for most.

Nothing had more villains waiting to slay it—afraid of their hearts. Paris was learning that there were always those who wanted to destroy love because it threatened them at their very core. That was why there must be so many who were willing to fight to protect it.

That had been Saint Valentine's first mistake, Paris thought as she let the familiarity of Roya Lane wash over once stepping through the portal. For as wise and well-meaning as the fairy was in his leadership role, he'd also played it safe.

His focus had been on creating love but not understanding that love would inevitably and naturally grow in a fertile world. So one didn't have to plant seeds in the garden of love as much as get the weeds out so it could grow.

Paris wasn't cynical, but she believed that in this world, fighting for and protecting love was the most critical mission the fairy godmothers had—but fairies were the least likely race to fight for anything. Maybe it was because she was a magician or a Beaufont, someone charged with maintaining justice, that Paris took this unique stance on love.

The ancient cobbled streets of Roya Lane under Paris' boots felt different from the shiny marble floors at FGA Tower. The two-story buildings all nestled together with mismatched roofs and smoking chimneys were a welcome sight after spending the day in the ultra-modern skyscraper.

There was always a new shop on Roya Lane, some eager business owner who had a magical product or service to offer. Then there were the staples of the magical district that had always been there and always would be like the Rose Apothecary, Crying Cat Bakery, the Silk Armor, and Chimerick's Bar and Grill.

Paris' stomach rumbled as she passed a cart run by an elf selling talking tofu hotdogs. It wasn't that the hot dog insulted the person about to eat it that dissuaded Paris from trying the magical food. Even if she was a vegetarian, she didn't do tofu. There were way better ways of spending her calories. Also, she didn't want to be late for her meeting with Mae Ling and Aunt Sophia.

The pair were standing exactly where they'd promised in front of the Crying Cat Bakery, which was buzzing with customers. The bakery was run by maybe the strangest people on Roya Lane, which was saying a lot, but their magical pastries, breads, and cakes kept customers returning even if they risked being insulted and threatened.

"You haven't eaten." Mae Ling looked Paris over. The fairy godmother wore her usual loose-fitting black pants and blouse, which matched her short hair. Her expression was usually neutral, although compassion lurked in her eyes.

"It was a busy first day," Paris admitted, smiling at her aunt who hugged her immediately.

"Well, then we'll have to get you something delicious to fill your reserves," Sophia said. The dragonrider was in her typical blue and silver armor with her elfin-made sword on her hip. Like all the Beaufonts, Sophia had blonde hair currently tied back, the ponytail trailing down her back. She also had the trademark Beaufont blue eyes that held an unwavering glint.

"How about we get something at Crying Cat Bakery?" Mae Ling offered.

"Yeah, I'd like that, but they appear packed." Paris had noticed the line of customers trailing out the door.

"Are they?" Mae Ling waved her small hand at their backs. Paris turned. To her surprise, the bakery that was full just seconds prior appeared completely deserted.

Paris glanced sideways at the tricky fairy godmother, always surprised by her mystery and strange way of doing magic that was different from any fairy she'd met. Mae Ling was unlike those at Happily Ever After College or FGA. It was like she wasn't a fairy at all, or something new, or someone much more powerful than most yet also very unassuming.

CHAPTER TWENTY-SEVEN

Crying Cat Bakery, Roya Lane, London

"You made all our customers disappear," Lee, the owner and baker for Crying Cat Bakery barked when the three came through the shop's door. The bell *clanged* overhead to mark their entrance.

Paris tensed, looking back at Mae Ling, but she maintained a pleasant, unfussed expression.

"I'm not sure what you mean," the fairy said to the tall woman on the other side of the counter. Lee had short, light hair and was strong. Her two professions required it. Lifting big bags of flour and heavy trays all day baking created strong muscles. So did pulling back an arrow on a crossbow when she was assassinating bad guys at night.

"I'm sure you do." Lee crossed her arms. "I'd appreciate it if you stopped by regularly when we get busy like earlier and make all the demanding customers disappear."

Paris giggled, always entertained that the assassin baker was annoyed by her customers and wished they'd drop dead rather than pay her money for her magical pastries. They were lucky that she didn't murder them herself when they pestered her with special requests.

"What are you laughing at, mutt?" Lee looked straight at Paris. "Did you see your reflection in the glass display case?" She indicated the stocked case in between her and the three women, lined with colorful and delicious pastries and assorted bread and cakes.

Paris knew better than to take offense to anything that Lee said. Half the time, she was looking for a rise, so it was best to ignore her. "Nothing, I'm just delirious from hunger."

"Well, I can't help you," Lee sang. "We're all sold out of everything."

"Clearly, you're not." Sophia indicated the stocked displays. "The cases are all full."

"Clearly, you can't take a hint, pony rider," Lee spat. "I need a nap, and there's no way I'm getting one until you all leave."

"I ride a dragon." Sophia chuckled, like Paris more amused by the assassin baker than put off by her brazen threats. "We'll take three croissants. Then we'll be out of your hair."

"Fine." Lee sighed, pulled three croissants from the display case, and stuck them in a bag. "I don't feel like messing with the cash register, so don't try to give me money." She added a huge chocolate chip cookie before handing the bag to Sophia. "I added a cookie because the mutt looks like she has low blood sugar."

"Thanks," Paris remarked, realizing the assassin baker was talking about her. "That was nice of you."

"Don't insult me with such words," Lee muttered, narrowing her light-colored eyes.

"Why are you so tired?" Sophia asked Lee thoughtfully, looking her over.

She pointed behind her as a tiny woman with red hair and a mischievous expression strode in from the back. "Because of my wife. It was the middle of the night, and my phone ringing woke me up. I started, thinking that I'd missed a hit or something. I answered the phone without looking at it, and it was Cat calling me."

"Where was she?" Paris asked.

Lee scowled at the woman behind her. "She was lying right next to me and for some reason, thought it would be cute to call me in the middle of the night. She hung up, turned over, and went straight to sleep. I, of course, was wide awake the rest of the night."

"It's not my fault that your guilty conscience over all the bad things you've done keeps you up," Cat said in her thick French accent.

"No, what keeps me up is regret over the things I haven't done yet." Lee brandished a fist, waving it at her wife.

Paris and Sophia shared a small laugh, used to the couple's antics. They argued and threatened each other incessantly, but no two people were more devoted to each other.

"Lee, I do have a quick question for you before we leave," Mae Ling said in a low voice.

"You want to add just enough cyanide to the batter that it has an effect but not too much that the mark notices the bitter taste," Lee answered at once like she already knew the question. "Add nutmeg to neutralize the acidity from the other poisons."

"Thanks but this isn't a question related to recipes," Mae Ling said with a polite smile. "I know that FGA has the market cornered on wands right now."

Lee whistled with a nod. "They sure do. That trash they're importing from you-know-where can hardly light a candle using magic. And they've squashed all the competition thanks to their superior position in the fairy world."

"FGA produces wands?" Paris was surprised.

"Oh yeah, it's big business," Lee answered. "They've got deals with shady producers for the materials since they want to keep their profit margins high. So the result is fairies get substandard wands, and they continue to make a killing."

"All problems that we eventually hope to erase." Mae Ling glanced at Paris.

"Good, because I'm sick and tired of that corporation profiting and hiding behind their mission of love," Lee lectured. "They have about as much interest in love as the casinos do. Both make a lot more money on the lost and lonely, but they dress things up all romantically so they can break hearts and take everyone's money."

This notion from Lee suddenly made a lot of sense to Paris, especially after everything she'd seen that day in the various departments. Maybe there were agents and fairy godmothers at FGA who were still motivated to create love. However, numerous times she'd seen projects at the company that were about profiting from other things that were quite the opposite of love. It was entirely possible that in the interest of making money, the branch and department heads at FGA had moved away from the mission of creating love.

"If someone wanted a unique wand that was custom-made and not issued by FGA," Mae Ling continued, "where would you send them?"

To Paris, this was a curious question. Mae Ling didn't use a wand or any magical instrument. Maybe this was about to change, and the fairy godmother was looking to get one.

"Well, at the end of the day, a wand is a weapon," Lee mused. "Therefore, if it were me and I was a weak-ass fairy who needed such a thing and not the badass magician that I am, I'd go to see the Protector of Weapons."

Mae Ling nodded. "Yes, that's a good idea." She turned to face Paris and Sophia with a triumphant look. "It appears we will be paying Subner at the Fantastical Armory a visit next."

"Why?" Paris asked. "Are you getting a wand?"

Mae Ling shook her head. "Of course not, dear. I don't need one. We're going to have one made for you."

CHAPTER TWENTY-EIGHT

Roya Lane, London

"I don't need a wand," Paris remarked when they were out on the streets again. A drizzle had started, and light mist covered the cobbled road, making it darker.

"No, you don't *need* one," Sophia related. "Mae Ling and I think having one that's special will make you look like both a fairy godmother and an agent."

"The idea is to make you look like them," Mae Ling stated.

"And also not," Sophia added.

Paris took a big bite of her croissant, the butter-rich flavor satisfying her hungry taste buds. "Excuse me for not following this mind-bending line of reasoning."

"We recognize that you're going to face a lot of resistance at FGA," Mae Ling began. "You're different. Not just in being you, but as a woman in an agent role. So the idea is that you need to conform while also not conforming."

Sophia nodded in agreement. "So if all the fairies carry wands or instruments, you should too."

"Even though I don't need one?" Paris questioned.

"Well, that only reminds them that you're different," Mae Ling answered.

"Which makes them not trust you," Sophia added.

"If you carried something that was both a wand and a magical instrument, you'd appear like both—"

"An agent and a fairy godmother," Paris finished, interrupting Mae Ling. The idea was genius and struck Paris by surprise.

"Exactly," Sophia confirmed as they rounded the corner to the main thoroughfare of Roya Lane. "Although you don't need a wand to use your magic, having an instrument will provide an extra advantage for you."

"Like your sword." Paris pointed at Inexorabilis, Sophia's weapon sheathed on her hip.

"That's right. Similar to my sword, you'll want to bond with the weapon of sorts that we have made for you. Then it can aid you in times of need in surprising ways."

"Okay, I like this idea," Paris said as they headed toward the Fantastical Armory, a place that sold ancient and rare artifacts and weapons. It was also Father Time's home base.

However, as they neared the end of the lane, Paris noticed a huge crowd ahead. She would have paused no matter what to discern what was happening. A figure stepped out from the crowd, his hand raised and a serious look of warning on his very handsome face.

"For your protection, I shall have to prevent you from going any further," King Rudolf Sweetwater said in a stern voice. "Some idiot who was trying to replicate the running of the bull here has released a minotaur, and I fear he's about to charge."

CHAPTER TWENTY-NINE

Outside Fantastical Armory, Roya Lane, London

King Rudolf Sweetwater was like an uncle to Paris as one of her mother's closest friends. He was also the leader of the fae. Also, as a segment of the fairy race, the ancient fae was very young-looking and deadly attractive. However, what he was known for besides being loyal and brave was also being a complete and utter moron.

Sophia sighed, put her hands on her hips, lowered her chin, and regarded the man beside them with waning patience. "Who might this idiot be?"

"It was me," King Rudolf said at once, putting his hands on his waist. He was wearing a navy blue velvet suit and an endearing smile. "I thought I'd bring a little Spanish flair to this uncultured place."

"Roya Lane is the United Nations of magical races," Paris argued. "The Official Brownie Headquarters is here as well as the Elfin Office and Gnome Nations."

"Not to mention that there's a bar for just giants, the Fairy Law Enforcement Office, and Pegasus Corrections," Sophia added.

"I know, as well as a bunch of ugly magicians who are always begging for my help at Heals Pills," King Rudolf muttered.

"You don't call them that, do you?" Sophia narrowed her eyes at the fae.

She and King Rudolf co-owned Heals Pills, the place that sold a magical elixir made from dragon eggshells that healed various ailments and improved appearances.

"Don't worry." King Rudolf waved her off. "Magicians are all very ego-driven, so I pat them on the head and tell them they have big brains. They don't seem to remember being called ugly."

"I'm a magician, Ru." Sophia crossed her arms.

He smiled at her and went to pat her on the head. "You're the smartest little magician I've seen all day."

"Touch me, and I'll break your arm," Sophia threatened before Rudolf's hand made contact with her head.

"It is I who is trying to protect you, Soph." Rudolf looked hurt as he pulled back his hand. "How am I to do that if you break my arms?"

Paris peered around King Rudolf. "This minotaur…is it at the far end of the lane?"

"Yes, and Ramy is holding it in a trance," he answered.

"How is he doing that?" Skepticism lay heavy in Sophia's tone.

"It's a staring contest," Rudolf stated. "You see, a minotaur hates nothing more than to lose a staring contest, so all you have to do is lock eyes with one and not look away. He'll stay staring at you until he passes out from hunger to win."

"That's true." Mae Ling sounded impressed.

"It isn't," Sophia argued.

Mae Ling nodded. "It is. Minotaurs are very stubborn creatures, which is to their benefit and disadvantage."

"So Ramy is having a staring contest with the minotaur at the end of Roya Lane?" Paris pointed at the crowd behind them. "What happens when he blinks?"

"Well…he dies," Rudolf stated. "Better him than any of us."

All three of the women nodded in response. Ramy Vance, the clerk who ran Heals Pills, was a special case in many ways. He made strange decisions and ate more cheese than the entire state of Wisconsin. Most unique about the magician was that he couldn't be killed...well, not easily.

Ramy had accidentally fallen into the fountain of youth before Father Time had it demolished. The benefit was that he couldn't die easily, but the trade-off was that he was accident-prone.

So on a regular basis, Ramy found himself in a deadly situation where he usually met his demise. After about twenty minutes, he'd rise again, totally fine, all to trip and fall off a building or get hit by a bus and die once more.

That was pretty much how his days went, with him dying several times a day. Those around him had gotten used to it. The most taxing thing about the man's constant deaths was that they were usually avoidable and always created huge inconveniences for those around him.

"And after Ramy dies?" Paris asked. "What happens to the rest of Roya Lane when the minotaur is let loose? Who saves the people and stores from getting destroyed?"

"I do," Mae Ling stated with confidence like she was a professional bullfighter and not a tiny older woman with a spirit unlike most.

CHAPTER THIRTY

Beside Minotaur and Soon-to-be-Newest Site of Ramy's Death, Roya Lane, London

"You're going to stop the minotaur?" Paris asked Mae Ling, surprised, although she had seen the fairy godmother in action and knew she could be quite impressive. "How?"

"I need to lead the animal to a brick wall," Mae Ling explained, very confidently. "Then I'll move out of the way, and the creature will charge, sticking its horns into the bricks and be stuck. The Minotaur Sanctuary and Rehabilitation Society will retrieve him."

Paris shook her head, trying to dispel the many layers of shock. "Wait, that will work?"

"Yeah, about like a bull," Sophia said in sudden awe. "The minotaur can be led and goaded toward a target."

"They aren't all that bright so the dum-dum would charge at a wall." Rudolf clapped in triumph. "Great plan."

"Shouldn't this all be your problem?" Sophia asked. "You did bring the animal here."

"I brought a rage-filled bull-like creature to this place," King Rudolf stated. "Do you really think I'm equipped to fix the problems I've created? Or do you think I should go to the wine bar on the far side of Roya Lane and wait until you very competent women deal with things?

"I mean, this is like the time my wife let me do laundry, and I put a red sock in with all the whites. I'm not good at things. Don't let me do laundry. Don't make me fix problems. I'll mess them up." He held up his hands and strode in the opposite direction from the crowd. "I'm going to do you a favor and get out of here. You're welcome."

"Wow, that guy is the worst." Paris laughed, watching as the king of the fae retreated down Roya Lane.

Sophia nodded. "Sort of. I mean, he is, kind of, but he also in his usual fashion has done something right."

Paris' eyes perked up. "He has?"

"Well, I'm sure that King Rudolf probably found the minotaur using shady methods," Sophia explained. "The point is that he found one. I read a report recently issued by the Minotaur Sanctuary and Rehabilitation Society that they were worried about the creatures going extinct and needed ways of cataloging and tracking wild animals. They put out a request to know about any minotaur in nature. So it appears we'll be giving them something useful they could use to do a lot of good."

"Wow," Paris mused. "King Rudolf unknowingly does something right once again."

Sophia and Mae Ling nodded in agreement as the crowd ahead of them around the minotaur pulsed. Excited screams echoed from that area. The cobbled streets vibrated from a nearby assault.

Paris tensed. "Can't we call the Minotaur Sanctuary and Rehabilitation Society to take care of this problem directly? That way Mae Ling doesn't have to put herself at risk?"

The crowd dispersed suddenly, running past the three of them.

A voice vibrating with fear cut through the air. "I can't take it anymore! I'm going to blink!"

Mae Ling gave Paris a determined look. "It's up to me. You and Sophia go to the Fantastical Armory at once. I've got the minotaur and will handle things from here."

"But Ramy..." Paris urged.

"He's burned another match," Mae Ling said simply. "He'll be fine and so will I. There's no need to see what happens next or worry for me. We'll both survive to live another day."

Paris didn't want to leave the small, unassuming woman to deal with a bumbling idiot and a deadly creature on her own. However, she had to admit that from everything she knew about Mae Ling, she was more than capable of dealing with the situation, even if her means for doing so were mysterious and seemingly unorthodox.

CHAPTER THIRTY-ONE

Outside Fantastical Armory, Roya Lane, London

Still reluctant to retreat and leave this minotaur business to Mae Ling, Paris didn't move off toward the nearby steps of the Fantastical Armory with Sophia. However, her aunt was strong, and when she grabbed Paris by her arm, there was little she could do except be dragged up the stairs to the old shop's stoop.

From there, Paris viewed the scene transpiring at the end of Roya Lane. Backed into a dead end was a massive creature with horns like a demon, a face like a bull's, and a body like a wrestler. Unlike a bull, the minotaur stood on his back two hooved feet and was regarding the small man in front of him with red eyes.

Ramy stood a few yards from the minotaur in a sweater vest and tweed hat, appearing the opposite of menacing. Even from a distance, Paris read the tension on Ramy's face as he stared straight at the minotaur, trying not to blink. Tears were racing down his cheeks, and his eyes were growing redder by the moment. However, his efforts appeared to be working because despite the beast huffing and growling, it wasn't moving from its position.

Behind him, Mae Ling was a safe distance away and seemed

ready to bolt in the opposite direction. Her eyes were keen, and she didn't look worried about the monster that was about to charge in her direction.

However, there was still hope that maybe Mae Ling didn't have to deal with the minotaur. Paris held out hope that Ramy could keep the stare-off going until the Minotaur Sanctuary and Rehabilitation Society could get there in time to intervene.

No sooner had the hope crossed Paris' mind as Ramy swatted at something in the air. "Oh, darn flies. Now isn't the time."

Paris groaned, feeling like she could see the future.

Apparently more intent on smashing the fly buzzing around his head than going a day without dying, Ramy looked up and swung his hand through the air. Then realizing too late that he'd taken his eyes off the minotaur and lost the staring contest, very slowly and full of fear, Ramy pulled his gaze down.

The beast rocked forward, landing on all fours. Then the monster growled, making all of Roya Lane vibrate from the noise. All who were on the streets vanished indoors. All but Ramy directly in front of the beast, Mae Ling several yards behind him, and Sophia and Paris watching the events from the Fantastical Armory's stoop.

In a flash, the minotaur charged forward. Paris swung her head to the side, avoiding seeing the huge monster flatten Ramy. It wouldn't have been a pretty sight, but thankfully when Ramy rose in roughly twenty minutes, he'd look the same and be unscathed from the collision.

"Wow, that was a totally avoidable and senseless death," Sophia said when Paris looked up. She caught sight of Mae Ling moving faster than she thought the small woman could run. Faster than most. It was a good thing because the minotaur had spotted her and was racing and quickly catching up with her. However, Paris didn't see how this part of the story ended because Mae Ling disappeared around a corner. A moment later, the creature followed. A loud crashing sound that vibrated the ground underfoot followed. Then the cackle of a woman who sounded strangely like Mae Ling, although Paris had never heard her laugh.

"Is she okay?" Paris looked at Sophia, careful to keep her gaze from where Ramy's body lay dead in the lane.

"She's Mae Ling," her aunt replied. "Of course she's okay. Now that the show is over and another King Rudolf disaster averted, let's get you a cool weapon that will make you even more powerful."

CHAPTER THIRTY-TWO

Fantastical Armory, Roya Lane, London

The place where one could find the Protector of Weapons was always as Paris remembered. The shop with its many oddities was full of shiny glass cases that twinkled with bright and rare objects. Along the wood-paneled wall were large swords, claymores, knives, bows, and shields.

The forest green carpet and chandeliers were at least a century old, and Paris was sure there wouldn't be any remodels any time soon. Subner, the Protector of Weapons—who was also Father Time's assistant of sorts—simply didn't care about the shop's appearance enough to do any updates. Subner didn't care about much. Protecting weapons, yes. Father Time, called Papa Creola by those who knew him directly, yes. That was about it for the grumpy elf known as Subner.

When Paris and Sophia strode into the Fantastical Armory, Subner was in his usual place, sitting behind the counter next to an old cash register he hadn't used in—ever. What happened in this shop didn't involve exchanging money. Favors, usually. Knowledge was a frequent trade for weapons or artifacts. A future loyalty or a promise. Never money.

The sullen-faced man was looking down, reading a book. It was his usual activity. He was also wearing his usual black t-shirt that matched his long, greasy black hair. Being Father Time's assistant, Subner had always existed and would for as long as Papa Creola walked the Earth, managing all things related to time. In their current form, the pair were elves.

If something compromised Father Time's body, he'd regenerate into another form. Before this, they'd been gnomes, which suited Subner's grumpy attitude better than a free-loving hippie. However, he'd adapted to his elfin form, shedding all the hippie characteristics usually congruent with that race.

Papa Creola, on the other hand, had embraced his hippie attributes a bit more. The unassuming creator of time and everything related to it was doing a runner's stretch against a nearby case when they entered the shop. The tall, lanky man was barefoot and wearing running shorts and had a headband over his stringy brown hair. His hands pressed against the counter and one leg extended back, getting a deeper stretch in his calves.

He stood when the door chimed, marking Paris and Sophia's arrival, and offered them a small bow with his hands pressed in prayer in front of his chest. "Namaste."

Sophia copied the movement, murmuring, "Namaste."

Paris did the same, reading Papa Creola's t-shirt. It always had a phrase written on it that supported hippie-ism. Today's said, "And the day came when the risk to remain tight in a bud was more painful than the risk it took to bloom."—Anais Nin

"Oh, so you didn't try to be a hero and wrestle the minotaur," Subner said in a bored voice, not looking up from his book. "Too bad. I had already started to plan your funeral, Miss Beaufont."

Paris lowered her chin and regarded the Protector of Weapons with a scowl. "Although we're both Beaufonts, I'm going to guess it was my death you were pining for, Sub. Is that correct?"

"No, it's not." The man turned the page of his book,

pretending to read it. "My name is Subner. No abbreviation. Yes, it was you that I hoped the minotaur would flatten. Sophia is useful on this planet."

Paris rolled her eyes, used to the verbal abuse. Her mother, Liv Beaufont, was Father Time's warrior, going out on cases for him, saving time repeatedly. For her loyalty and bravery, Papa Creola showed a unique fondness to Liv. Therefore his assistant despised her and made a show of it.

By way of simply being related, Paris also received this abuse. She knew it was because much like her mother, Papa Creola valued her—not that he didn't appreciate Sophia. It was just that Father Time relied heavily on Liv. Mother Nature doted on Sophia, believing she was the best thing since pancakes.

"So you were hanging out in here, reading your book," Paris accused. "Knowing full well that a minotaur was loose on the streets of Roya Lane."

"Other people's problems aren't my concern," Subner muttered.

"How do you sleep at night with that kind of nihilistic perspective?" Paris challenged.

"With a fan on," Subner answered at once. "It has to be a crisp sixty-four degrees for me to get a good night's rest."

"Although Subner's uncaring attitude sounds cynical, it isn't wrong," Papa Creola offered thoughtfully, taking his foot in hand from behind for a quad stretch. "If we went around fixing the world's problems, no one would learn anything."

"I solve mortals' problems all the time," Sophia argued.

"That was the role you were born for," Papa Creola answered. "I created all of time and space and the intricate fabric that keeps things moving forward. I created the construct from which this reality unfolds. The passing of time and everything related to its science was my gift to you all. What you do with it, well, that's up to you. Neither my job nor Subner's is to fix the problems on these timelines but simply observe."

"You still manage things," Paris offered, still trying to understand what Father Time did since he often took this hands-off approach to things.

"I supervise," he corrected. "I've found that if I desert things that humans try to find cheats, creating time machines and whatnot. I might not be willing to fix mortals' problems, but I'm not letting them create a black hole in my universe."

"Our universe," Mother Nature chimed from the corner where she sat in a puffy armchair, sipping a cup of tea. "Aren't my humans so clever, always trying to find ways to mess with time?"

"Bloody brilliant," Papa Creola muttered unenthusiastically.

Undeterred, Mama Jamba, the affectionate name those who knew Mother Nature personally called her, smiled and winked at Paris. The woman who was as powerful as Father Time and had created everything on the planet wasn't what most would expect. She wasn't covered in vines and didn't have bark skin.

Instead, Mama Jamba appeared very much like a southern grandmother with her big *Dallas*-style grayish-blue hair and her mint green velour tracksuit. Pristine white New Balance sneakers perched on a small ottoman in front of her coffee table filled with colorful treats like macaroons and little sandwiches.

"Mama Jamba." Paris bowed to the older woman. "It's nice to see you."

"You as well," she chimed, her southern accent making her words sound melodic. "How was your first day as an agent at FGA?"

"You already know," Subner cut in. "She offended everyone she met. Confused most with her appearance and the fact she carts around a squirrel. And she has zero clue what she's doing or how she's going to figure out what's going on behind the scenes."

Paris turned and faced the Protector of Weapons. "If you know so much about my affairs, why don't you tell me what's going on behind the scenes at FGA?"

"Most are planning your demise." Subner casually turned the

page. "The fairy godmothers mostly think you're a showoff who got your position because you cheated the system. The agents don't like what you represent as far as change goes and want you gone. Making friends or even a real difference in a place pitted against you will be impossible. If I were you, I'd kill myself."

Paris growled under her breath, letting out a steadying breath. "Why don't you pretend you are me and do just that, Sub."

"Ner," he added, flipping the page in his book and pretending to be reading.

"Whatever." Paris turned back to face Mama Jamba. "It wasn't all that bad. Yes, there are some challenges at FGA, but I made friends with the shoeshine guy."

"Wow, talk about high-level networking," Subner interrupted.

Ignoring him, Paris forced a smile. "My team is a bit undisciplined and out of practice, but I think we have a lot of opportunities. I'm already noticing things of interest, so I think if I follow the clues, I'll be able to help Saint Valentine as he's requested."

"That's nice, darling," Mama Jamba sang, taking a bite of a pimento cheese sandwich and looking out the front display window like she was casually checking the weather.

"Mama, if you have any insights into FGA, what's going on, or how I could better do my job, I'd appreciate it." Paris spoke meekly. She glanced at Sophia, looking for a bit of encouragement. Her aunt offered her a sympathetic smile.

"You know," Mama Jamba said in a dreamy tone, not taking her gaze from the window and the happenings on Roya Lane outside the shop. "'Love never dies a natural death. It dies because we don't know how to replenish its source.'"

"Another Anais Nin quote," Sophia observed, mulling over the words.

Paris was too, but she didn't know what to make of that phrase, although it was inspiring. "So, are you saying that I need to replenish the source of love to help FGA?"

"I could be saying that," Mama Jamba agreed, still not looking directly at her.

"Or that you have to clean the source," Sophia guessed.

"No helping her with her homework," Subner warned. "She has to fail on her own. Then Mama will see how worthless she is, and we'll extinguish that drain on society."

"That's my life you're talking about," Paris muttered dryly.

"She's not going to fail." Mama Jamba picked up her teacup and saucer again and sipped. "Stumble, yes. Falter, well invariably. But we don't really fail in this world. Sometimes we take the longer path, but in the end, all roads will lead to Rome."

"So you think I can help FGA and therefore make love prosper worldwide?" Paris needed the confidence boost.

She wanted Mama Jamba to say, "Of course, you can, darling." Instead, the older woman smiled brightly with a twinkle in her eyes. "We'll see, my dear. We shall see."

CHAPTER THIRTY-THREE

Fantastical Armory, Roya Lane, London

"You'll be great and do what is needed," Sophia offered, giving Paris a reassuring look.

"There's no need to inflate her ego with false hope." Subner turned another page in his book.

"It's not false hope," Sophia argued. "Paris has already done so much in a short time for the fairy godmothers. She's in a unique position. I know how that feels, the weight and pressure of not knowing how to fix the world or fulfill your destiny."

"Therefore you can attest to the fact that you had to figure things out on your own." Mama Jamba sipped her tea.

"If we had handed you the problem and solution, it would have surely been counterintuitive," Papa Creola added, now stretching his neck to one side and other.

"It would've been a shortcut, but ironically led to further setbacks," Mama Jamba chimed.

Sophia turned and faced Paris. "Unfortunately, they're right."

"They're the creators of the universe," Subner grumbled. "Of course, they're right."

"As I was saying," Sophia continued, ignoring the grumpy elf.

"They're right, and the process of figuring things out on your own is part of your evolution. It will mold you into the person who can conquer the upcoming challenges. If they simply show you the problems and the solutions, you won't be the person who can solve them."

"We've taught her well," Mama Jamba said proudly to Papa Creola.

"That we did," he agreed, equally proud.

"Thanks." Sophia beamed at them before turning to face Subner directly. "We're here to see you for something that will help Paris rise to the challenge and become the person she needs to be to succeed."

Subner looked up, eyeing the two magicians. "I know."

"Great, then we can cut to chase," Paris chirped. "Can you help?"

"With what?" Subner asked dryly.

Paris sighed. "I thought you knew why I was here."

"I do," he countered.

"So then, can you help?" She sighed.

"With what?" he repeated, obviously enjoying this.

"As with discovering the problems you face and the solutions they'll need," Mama Jamba began, her attention directed out the window again. "There are no shortcuts. Even if someone knows what you need, it's always prudent to ask. The biggest problems in this world come from miscommunication or a lack thereof. You wouldn't want to assume that Subner knows what you want and he gives you a bag of nails because you didn't specify."

"Touché," Paris muttered, returning her focus to the wrinkly elf. "Subner, can you help me to find a wand?"

"That's also a magical instrument," Sophia added, sidling up next to her.

Paris nodded. "Yes, something that is both a wand and a magical instrument and uniquely its own thing."

"With a gem in it," Sophia tacked on. "Maybe a sapphire to match Paris' eyes."

"Good idea." She smiled at her aunt.

"I thought so," Sophia said proudly, blushing.

The two magicians turned to face Subner with expectant looks.

"Well, can you help me to find such a wand...or instrument... or weapon?" Paris asked.

Unhurried, Subner brought his gaze up and looked at Paris directly. "No, no I can't."

CHAPTER THIRTY-FOUR

Fantastical Armory, Roya Lane, London

"Wait, you can't help me find a wand?" Paris asked. "So you made me go through all that asking business, knowing ahead of time what I needed, and you couldn't save me the time and say no?"

"Yes," Subner said simply.

Paris growled, looking at Sophia, her expression begging for patience or help before she strangled Father Time's assistant. That would get her in trouble no matter how much Papa Creola liked her mother.

"So yes, you made me go through all that just to say no, or no, you can't help me?" Paris felt the heat rise to her face.

"Yes," Subner repeated, obviously enjoying this all more than she would have liked.

"You see how communications get muddied?" Mama Jamba asked casually, sipping her tea and taking a bite of a cookie, pure delight springing to her face. "The construction of questions is important. Don't even get me started on the written word and how texting has messed up a whole generation that disregards punctuation in favor of emojis."

Papa Creola nodded, rolling his eyes as he glanced at Paris and Sophia. "Definitely don't get her started on that. We'll be here for a century."

"Okay, well, you three might have time for that kind of conversation, but we don't." Sophia centered on Subner. "Let's break this down, Mr. P.O.W."

"I don't like that name," Subner muttered, glancing back at his book like he was going to jump back into wherever he left off.

"Okay, so no initials then? I was thinking P.O.W for Protector of Weapons, but you don't approve?" Sophia was apparently a master at getting under the elf's skin. Whereas Liv and Paris were outwardly rude, Sophia was much more diplomatic, which was why she was an arbitrator for mortals. "How about Mr. Pow then?"

"I don't like that either," Subner stated, turning a page after not reading anything.

"Yeah, I agree," Sophia related. "It makes me want Chinese food."

"Subner," Paris began, leaning forward and waiting for the man across the counter to look up. She thought they were about to have a reverse staring contest, the opposite of what Ramy and the minotaur did. However, Subner got tired of pretending to ignore her as she stared straight at the bridge of his crooked nose.

"What?" he barked, finally bringing his eyes up to meet hers.

"Can you help me find a special wand?" Paris worked hard to keep the annoyance off her face.

The grumpy old elf shook his head. "No."

Paris wanted to reach across the counter and satisfy her dreams and choke the man. Instead, she let out a breath. She decided to stop asking yes and no questions and put this all back on Subner. "Why is it, do you think, that Lee sent us to see you for a special wand?"

He studied her for a moment, something mysterious flickering behind his ancient eyes. Finally, as though curbing some of his irritation and his act of dismissing her, Subner closed his book and laid it on the countertop.

"What you're seeking is something that's a wand, but better than a wand, right?"

She glanced at Sophia, who nodded in reply.

Paris looked back at the Protector of Weapons and copied her aunt's gesture.

"Yes, because you're a magician. If you used a normal wand, your power would overwhelm it." Subner glanced down like he was figuring something out on his own.

Paris nodded again, not knowing much about wands, but that seemed about right. Magicians didn't use wands. Their magic was much more dynamic, whereas fairies usually needed assistance.

"This weapon also needs to have the properties of a magical instrument, right?" Subner questioned. Before she could answer, he added, "Again, it will have to be able to withstand funneling your magic and not be overwhelmed by it. The instrument needs to aid you and not make a show of being used by you."

Paris again looked at her aunt, who nodded, this time more enthusiastically than before. It was like they were finally getting somewhere.

Subner thought for a moment. "The gem, that's a tricky part because gems complicate magic. They add or take away from it. Fairies use them to track magic because it puts a signature on it in a way. Magicians have other, better ways of tracking magic. Of course, they did before Liv decided to have the House of Fourteen stop registering magic."

"You mean stopping the House from abusing the rights and privacy of innocent magicians," Sophia corrected.

"Whatever," Subner muttered.

Paris tapped the counter between her and the elf. "The wand, instrument thing. Can you please help me to find one?"

"No," he said coldly. "As I said before, I can't."

Paris lowered her chin, wondering how best to choke the man before her. Probably slowly, she joked to herself.

"The reason I can't," Subner continued, glaring up at her, "is that what you're asking for simply doesn't exist."

Paris deflated with a sigh. Beside her, Sophia did the same.

Her aunt smiled and patted her arm. "This is fine. We'll find other ways to make you appear like them while also different. Maybe we get you a suit, but one made for you."

"Maybe I jump off the roof of FGA Tower," Paris teased.

"The reason that this special wand slash magical instrument with a gem doesn't exist," Subner continued in a bored voice, "is that there simply hasn't ever been a need to create one."

Both magicians whipped around to look at him. He had their attention now.

Realizing that, Subner smirked wickedly. "A fairy has always needed a magical instrument. A magician never has. There has never been the need for a halfling who needed something her fairy magic could come through but wouldn't be overwhelmed by her magician power."

"So you can help me?" Paris asked in a rush, her heart suddenly pounding with excitement in her chest.

Subner tipped his head back and forth, thinking. "Again, the gem complicates things. If we add it to this wand, it could have assorted effects. There's no way of knowing until we test it, and the only one who can do that is you."

Paris gulped. This was much more complicated than she thought. Still, she felt like this was right. It was part of her next step. Slowly she nodded. "I want the gem. A sapphire. I'll take the risk."

"I think that's wise," Subner stated. "The benefits should outweigh them. In some magical clans, gems have stored magic the way gnomes can save up their power. Then they can use that vault to create a giant burst of magic."

"Oh, wow," Sophia said. "That could be useful."

"It could also kill the person using it." Subner looked straight at Paris.

"If gems can store magic, how does that work with a fairy's magical instrument?" Paris thought of the agents.

"Fairy magic is weaker," he explained. "Even if they stored up some, it would never equal what a magician could do. As you've witnessed, the gems on the agent's instruments usually sign their magic, track it, or link them to it somehow. Their gems are relatively small since something too big would be a waste and too bulky on their instruments."

Paris chewed on her lip, confused by all the misdirection on this subject and wondering what her options were.

"If I were making this instrument, a one-of-a-kind wand," Subner continued, "I'd make the gem as large as the carrier could handle. I think there could be a hidden benefit in that. This person is carrying a wand more powerful than any other in the world, so they might as well level it up as much as possible because who knows what they'll face with it."

Paris blinked at the elf. "And an extra hidden benefit is that it could kill me if it backfires, which wouldn't ruin your day."

"Although I prefer to make the finest quality weapons known to man or beasts, no, I wouldn't lose sleep if I created a wand that one day took you out."

Brightening, Paris glanced at Sophia, who shared her excited expression. She swung back to Subner, wanting to hug him after very recently wanting to choke him. "Are you saying that you're going to make me a custom wand with a gem that will also be a magical instrument?"

He nodded. "Yes, but you have to come up with a better name than that for it."

Paris thought for a moment. "How about Larry?"

Subner sighed and turned at once, making for the door at the back. "I'll get to work on the instrument. You should have a name when it's ready."

"When will that be?" Paris called after him as he opened a door. Darkness and cold spilled through into the warm shop.

"When it is," he answered and disappeared at once, slamming the door behind him.

CHAPTER THIRTY-FIVE

Fairy Grounds, FGA Tower, New York City, New York

"I don't care what everyone in my department says about you," Christine Welsh said from the other side of the coffee table. "I know who the real Paris Beaufont is."

Groaning, Paris went to sip her coffee and immediately regretted it. She'd ordered a shot of espresso, a cup of black drip coffee, and a sugary latte at Fairy Grounds. All three drinks were bad. It appeared that Alfred was correct. The pixies simply didn't know how to make coffee, but their shop still buzzed with customers. Apparently, most of them were there to get a scone.

"You and Faraday went to the same school of morale-boosting," Paris joked to her friend.

Although the friend she'd graduated Happily Ever After College with wore the fairy godmother blue gown, Paris knew that Christine's straight hair was orangish-red and not gray. She was surprised to see her wearing the outfit since Christine's assignment was the fashion department in the Basic Love branch.

Her job was to help Cinderellas look their best for a potential suitor. Or, as was more often the case, throw out all the baggy jeans from Prince Charmings' closets, making them not look like bums on their dates. The realm of the fairy godmother was assorted, and Paris was learning they dipped into many different areas of matchmaking, but not all of them seemed related to love.

Usually, Christine could be found sporting the newest fashions when not on duty and criticizing those who were making a wardrobe "disaster." The fairy godmother firmly believed that her job was to help the disadvantaged stop ruining their life with bad hairdos and fashion choices that the rest of the world had to look at.

"How do you like your department?" Paris asked her other friend and fellow graduate, Penny Pullman. Compared to Christine, who was loud and brazen with her hilarious quips, Penny was quiet and humble but smart as a whip. There weren't two better fairies that Paris would want by her side. From the beginning, these two women had proven their loyalty to her when the rest of FGA and the college had treated her like a freak for being a halfling with demon blood.

"Well, it's okay…" Penny stirred another packet of sugar into her coffee. It didn't matter how much she added. There was no disguising the burned flavor. "There have been a lot of changes already to get used to."

Paris nodded, reading between the lines and deciding to call out the truth. "Because you're in the Practical Love department, which used to share a floor with Casual Romance, and you all were quickly uprooted and forced onto another floor? Is that what you mean by changes?"

"Well, that…" Penny hedged sensitively. "And the new faces and bosses…"

"Oh, you mean Agent Punk Face, who moved your department and made it known that he didn't want you corrupted by my 'wrong' way of doing things?" Paris didn't want to put her friend in an awkward situation, but she also thought candor was the best approach.

To her relief, Penny laughed but covered the gesture. "He is mean. I went up to him to introduce myself, and he told me to put it in an email that he probably wouldn't read."

Paris slumped, not feeling any better that Agent Jasper had treated her friend equally rudely. She hoped he was only mean to her because she threatened his tiny manhood. "I'm sorry, it sounds like he treats everyone with the same level of dismissal."

Christine nodded. "Oh, yeah. I complimented his magical instrument because it's that pretty jasper phone case. He held it up and said, 'When I'm holding this, you hold your tongue because that means the big guy is busy and doesn't have time for your incessant babbling.'"

Paris shook her head. "He's the worst."

"Don't worry about all the haters here," Christine consoled, leaning forward so others couldn't hear. The coffee shop was full of people, but even if it weren't, all the mismatched furniture and weird abstract artwork on the walls would clutter it up. Paris was pretty sure that the pixies, who knew nothing at all about coffee, had gone and studied every coffee shop in the Pacific Northwest and reconstructed a conglomeration of it here in FGA Tower for their patrons.

Corduroy sofas with oversized pillows, huge armchairs, and tiny tables with chess boards printed on the surface might work in coffee shops in small college towns, but they were out of place in a skyscraper in Manhattan. Not only did the pixies not understand coffee, but they seemed lost when it came to décor too.

"Yeah, people are afraid of you because you're different," Penny echoed Christine's sentiment.

"I get it." Paris pushed away her espresso shot, her last attempt at finding a decent dose of caffeine on her second day at FGA. "I'm a woman in a role notorious for being filled by males. I have demon blood, which most think makes me dangerous. And I'm a magician, who fairies usually find overly cerebral and boring."

"Not to mention that you eat kittens for breakfast," Christine imparted casually.

Paris lowered her chin and regarded her friend with murderous eyes.

Christine held her hands up in surrender. "What? That's what everyone keeps saying. I told them I hadn't seen you do that, but also, I never saw you eat breakfast."

"We've spent every breakfast together for the past year at college," Paris argued.

"You drink coffee and never eat," Christine countered, indicating the row of mugs in front of her. "Case and point. So how was the kitten this morning?"

"Overcooked," Paris joked. "I should fire my chef."

"Can you do that when he's your uncle?" Christine mused.

Paris shrugged. "Probably not. That's why you don't go into business with your family."

Christine laughed. "Says the girl who is running a restaurant with all her closest friends and family, and the family business is pretty much running the magical world."

"Yeah, my dad says that the Beaufonts will soon be running this world, both magical and otherwise," Penny related in a low voice, taking a bite of her scone.

Paris shook her head. "The Beaufonts are a dying breed. Besides my mother, Uncle Clark, Aunt Sophia, and myself, there are no more. Get us together and bomb the place and the last founding family of magicians is gone."

Christine and Penny both exchanged morbid looks.

"Wow, that was dark even for you, Pare." Christine shook her head and stole a bite of Penny's scone. She widened her eyes as if in apology and held up her hands again. "What? I already finished my scone, and look at that line." She indicated a long line of impatient fairy godmothers and agents all waiting for their pastries.

"Wow, if the pixies could get coffee right, this place would be tops," Paris related.

"You said, tops," Christine teased. "You're the only one here who likes coffee, magician. The rest of us are fine with some juice or milk."

Paris shook her head. "You fairies are going to overdose from sugar one day."

Christine looked out with a dreamy expression. "What a glorious day that will be."

"Well, until then," Paris began, leaning forward. "I hope that your jobs get easier, that your association with me doesn't add stress to your lives, and that we all find a bit of happiness in our new roles."

Christine smiled at Penny. "Should we tell her?"

Penny blushed and nodded.

"Tell me what?" Paris looked between her friends.

"Pare, the only reason you threaten the uptight agents and their subservient fairy godmothers here is that you do things your way," Christine began. "Yesterday, during orientation, Alfred was taking us around, telling us about various departments and such, and we ran into Saint Valentine.

"He said, and I quote, 'You're the new generation. The new stock. The wave of the future. Before, we told you to do things the way we've always done them. However, I'm starting to appreciate that there's value in people doing things in new ways. Different ways. I'm starting to appreciate that when we celebrate people's unique abilities, we bring them to light and they bring merit to the world. So try doing that as you take on your new roles. Be you...and let's see where that gets us. Let's see what greatness that creates.'"

Paris was quiet for a long moment. Then she leaned closer to her friends. "Saint Valentine said that? Why?"

"Well, I think it's obvious," Penny whispered.

Christine shook her head at the mousey-haired girl. "You know, for being so polite, you can be rude sometimes. Things like that aren't obvious to Paris because she doesn't see stuff directly related to her."

SARAH NOFFKE & MICHAEL ANDERLE

"I think you're trying to be helpful." Paris shook her head. "It's hard to tell based on how you say things, Christina."

"My name is Christine and always has been. Thanks. What I mean is that you obviously inspired S.V.'s little speech. He's seeing how your graduation project set new standards. Before that, you didn't conform when you came to the college, and you didn't only learn. You became part of the positive change at the school. Now you're here, and you're already hitting the ground running. He's spouting your gospel and encouraging us to follow you…not his department heads. You."

"That has to be more than intimidating for Agent You-Know-Who and the other one," Penny muttered.

Paris nodded. "I call the other one Agent Head-Up-His-Butt."

The other women laughed.

"That's accurate," Christine agreed.

"She's right." Penny pointed at the other fairy. "S.V. knows that things have to change. That's why I think you got recruited in the first place at Happily Ever After College. We need new blood. Different blood."

"Well, and it kept me out of jail." Paris remembered that going to fairy godmother college was like community service to erase her rap sheet.

"Now that he's taken that chance," Penny continued, "he sees that it's not the old ways that work. Conformity and uniforms aren't what has kept this place together. FGA has survived despite those things, not because of them. We have to push to express our creative freedom because that's an expression of love. By doing so, we'll help create it.

"For too long, we've followed some prescribed method that's stale and outdated and isn't working. I think the only love this place creates is artificial and short-lived. I think that S.V. is all too aware and knows we're dangerously close to losing what really matters in the world."

Paris nodded, conscious that if love, real love died in the

world, replaced by technology, simulated experiences, and the like, it would be next to impossible to recover. If mortals and magicals lost real love, it would be like a starship that had lost Earth for thousands of years and was trying to find its way home. It would be worth every effort, cost, and sacrifice, but getting back to Earth might be too difficult.

"Well, I think there are some genuine obstacles to love," Paris began. "Thankfully and sadly, they exist in the very place responsible for its protection and creation. So on a positive note, we know where to look to get rid of it. It's here. Sadly, we know where to look. It's right here, on our home turf."

"Sounds like we have a big mission ahead of us as fairy godmothers and agent." Penny proudly looked around the table at her friends.

"Yes, but we're not alone because we're going to help each other to get there," Christine stated with confidence. "We know that together we're stronger no matter what department we work in."

"So you'll help me to figure out what's going on here behind the scenes?" Paris had quickly filled her friends in on her suspicion before they entered the busy coffee shop that morning before work.

They both nodded with unwavering glints in their eyes.

Paris smiled triumphantly, absentmindedly took a sip from her closest coffee cup, and immediately regretted it. "Okay, but at our next meeting, we're going to Starbucks."

CHAPTER THIRTY-SIX

Third Floor, Casual Romance Department, FGA Tower, New York City, New York

"Why does it look like the home décor section of a Target shopping store in here?" Paris paused after entering her department, wondering if she'd gotten off on the wrong floor.

The walls of 1970s beads hung in various doorways or around cubicles were gone. Many of the booths had been disassembled or moved to the far back of the large open floor area. The shag carpet had disappeared, but under closer inspection, it simply was covered up. Hip armchairs sat in neat arrangements with lamps beside small makeshift coffee tables—magazines and knickknacks strewn on top.

A decorative throw draped over a couch that Paris didn't remember seeing. There were large puffy pillows in what appeared to be a reading nook of sorts. Beside it was an oversized basket filled with more blankets and books for those searching.

"We cleaned up like you told us to." Isha strode over to a sitting area, carrying a tray with a teapot and cups. She set it down next to a pillow resting on a tabletop. At least Paris had thought it was a pillow…of fur…until it moved and took the form of Faraday, the talking squirrel.

Straining to open his eyes, Faraday blinked several times as he tried to sit up.

"Hey, are you okay?" Paris asked the squirrel, rushing to him and looking him over.

He took a tiny cup of steaming tea from Isha and smiled at her tiredly. "Thank you." Then he looked at Paris and nodded. "I'm fine. Tired from staying up all night, but we can review what I found once I've had this."

"Okay, well, you could've gotten some rest," Paris offered, looking around. "There are more places to lounge here than in Fairy Grounds downstairs."

"There was no time to lounge," Faraday droned sleepily, yawning into his tiny, adorable teacup. "I promised that I'd review the Casual Romance departmental reports while you were hobnobbing with dragonriders."

Isha's eyes widened with shock as she poured another cup of tea and handed it to Paris.

Paris rolled her eyes at the squirrel and smiled at Isha. "Thanks. I wasn't hobnobbing. I was working on something important that I think will make me a more effective agent here at FGA, where the odds are currently against me."

"Was brushing your hair not on that list?" Holly strode over from the workout alcove. She was wearing pale blue yoga pants and an oversized hoodie.

Paris scoffed. "I don't own a brush."

"That's true," Faraday stated, blowing on his hot tea. "I can attest. But it does appear that after your important mission, you got to get some rest and dare I say…" He sniffed the air. "A shower."

"Are you jealous, squirrel?" Paris asked, putting her teacup down on a small ottoman so it could cool. "I'll give you a flea dip after your nap."

SARAH NOFFKE & MICHAEL ANDERLE

"Thanks." He let out a faint chuckle despite appearing ready to fall over.

"Faraday wouldn't have been able to sleep with all the noise we were making rearranging things here." Isha poured another cup of tea and offered it to Holly.

She held up her hands, shaking her head. "No, I'm only drinking things that start with the letter W today."

Isha pulled the tea back with a look of offense. "This is Jasmine Mint Green tea."

"Well, I can't have it. If it were white tea or water or—"

"Or if it were whiskey," Isha interrupted Holly.

She nodded. "Yeah, I could have whiskey today. Do we have any?"

Isha pointed behind her at the small kitchen area portioned off. "You know where we keep the good stuff."

Holly trudged off.

Paris whipped around, shaking her head. "It's morning. No day drinking. We have work to do."

"Maybe she's Russian," Faraday offered. "Maybe it's just drinking for her."

Turning back around, Paris sighed, looking at the squirrel. "You ready to tell me what you dug up in those reports?"

"Almost." He took another sip of his tea, starting to look more alert.

"Well, the department space looks…well, it looks like you two stole a bunch of stuff from Crate and Barrel," Paris began and looked at Isha suddenly, a worrying thought occurring to her. "Did you steal a bunch of stuff from a home décor store? Please tell me you didn't."

Isha laughed, plopping down on one of the large fuzzy pillows in the seating area and pulling a blanket around her shoulders. She was only wearing a workout top over her yoga pants, and the area was quite cold, as it had been the first time Paris had visited it. "No, we gathered up all the retro furniture that had been clogging this place up for ages and took it to the thrift shop down the road. Do you know how much they'll pay for a vintage lava lamp?"

"More than it's worth?" Paris guessed.

"Yep," Isha stated. "But everything in the shop isn't vintage. Since we're in Manhattan, the place where people live beyond their means, there's a ton of nice furniture there. So we doubled what they were going to give us for the hippie stuff by taking it in store credit." She indicated the modern décor all around them. "Therefore, for a lot less than anyone would've expected, we were able to make this place look pretty presentable in no time."

"Wow." Paris was impressed. "You two aren't worthless."

"Hey," Isha complained.

"No, I meant that in a good way," Paris amended. "I knew you two wouldn't be and you just had to be forced to work."

Holly returned with a tumbler that clinked with ice and a bit of liquid that swished back and forth.

Paris pointed at her glass. "You better tell me that's not whiskey."

"It's not." Holly tossed her long blonde hair off her shoulder, making the ice cubes in the glass clink.

"Why does it look like whiskey?" Paris inquired.

"Because that's what it is," Holly stated.

"I just said that better not be whiskey," Paris fired.

"No, you said, you better tell me it's not whiskey," Holly argued. "Which is what I did. You need to work on your communication skills. If you ask for something and I give it to you, then you need to be satisfied. None of these mixed signals."

Paris glanced at the modern clock on the wall that was new. "It's nine o'clock in the morning. Why are you drinking whiskey?"

"Well, my tennis elbow doesn't care what time it is." Holly held up her bony elbow for Paris to see. "So if you can make it

157

flare up at accepted times to drink, I'll follow these rules you have."

Isha laughed and sipped her tea. "Don't worry. She works better when she's had a whiskey. She complains less about her many ailments." She held the tea close to her chest as though for warmth. "Mmmm…isn't this tea the very best? It's soothing to one's soul."

"It's making me feel alive, so that's good." Faraday finished his cup.

"Yeah, it was lovely." Paris smiled at Isha and Faraday. "You ready to tell me what you found in the thousand-page report of cases from the Casual Romance department?"

"Sure," Faraday stated. "Let's first start with unraveling a mystery."

Paris' attention perked up. So did the other women's.

"What is that?" Isha asked.

"Well, I don't understand how you would think that Holly works better if she drinks whiskey," Faraday began. "Because from what I've deduced after reading over the case files for the department, no one has been productive. Over the last few years, there have been two hundred and thirteen potential cases, and you two have worked exactly zero of them."

CHAPTER THIRTY-SEVEN

Third Floor, Cozy Sitting Area, Casual Romance Department, FGA Tower, New York City, New York

"Say what?" Paris exclaimed, looking between Holly and Isha. "You two haven't worked a single case in how long?"

"I've done stuff." Holly lifted the tumbler to her mouth to take a drink.

Paris pointed, and a neat bit of magic shot from the end of her finger and exploded the glass into dust. It didn't harm the fairy, but it spooked her. The whiskey and ice was a chill when it fell into her lap.

Holly stood from her cozy spot at once, gawking at Paris. "That's not fair. You do magic and punish us."

"You do nothing when you're supposed to be working, and it punishes the world," Paris retorted.

"I cleaned this place up and decorated it," Holly argued.

"Great," Paris stated. "I appreciate that. But why haven't you done anything for years?"

"Well, we couldn't," Isha chimed in. "Agent Crystal would go to assign us cases, but then there were all the budgetary restrictions. So he'd tell us to lay low while he went to department meetings and he'd come back with solutions. Then nothing happened. He'd give up for a bit and leave us to our devices."

Holly brushed the drink off her clothes and nodded. "It kind of was lather, rinse, and repeat like that for as long as I can remember."

"I'm not buying this," Paris muttered, wishing someone would put some whiskey in her tea.

"It's true," Faraday stated, to her shock.

"What?" Paris whipped around to face the squirrel. "How would you know? You weren't here...were you?"

"No," he answered at once. "However, there are a lot of ways to tell what's happened historically at a place. One of the best is by looking at budget reports. For a very long time, the Casual Romance department has had a budget of zero, meaning..."

Paris nodded. "Even if Agent Crystal wanted to do something, he didn't have the means to do it."

"So he charged off to department meetings," Faraday continued. "Fought with the higher-ups—"

"Got knocked back down," Paris interrupted.

"And came back defeated," Isha added.

"Then lather, rinse, and repeat." Holly went to the kitchen again. "Who wants a drink?"

"I do," the two women and the squirrel sang in unison.

CHAPTER THIRTY-EIGHT

Third Floor, Around the "Whiskey" Table, Casual Romance Department, FGA Tower, New York City, New York

"So it comes down to money?" Paris held the shot of whiskey in her hand. "Who paid for this?"

"We stole this from the Practical Romance department," Holly admitted. "When they left, we told them they couldn't take anything because it was part of the space and would make us ache for them."

Isha nodded. "Then we sold all their drawer organizer things and pencil holders to the thrift shop for all this décor."

Paris lowered her chin. "We're going to need things for organizing, you know? Not only throw pillows."

Holly shrugged, sipping her whiskey. "When we get there, we'll go and steal from the Practical Romance department. They'll have restocked by then. They always had money for supplies and cases."

"Why is that?" Paris eyed her drink but didn't want to drink it.

"Well, probably because Practical Romance makes money," Isha explained. "Smart matches like Debutant Debbie with Mark from an oil tycoon family would be profitable to FGA."

"How?" Faraday didn't have any trouble drinking his whiskey.

"Well, because they'd have a big wedding and there's tons of money in that," Holly answered. "I mean, none have bigger weddings than those who aren't in love, as it happens in the Practical Love department. I mean, they're together out of practicality, as the name implies.

"So they have engagement announcements and parties, then bridal showers, and bachelorette and bachelor parties followed by huge weddings and honeymoons. The whole thing can easily be over a million dollars depending on the family. It's always families with lots of money who have practical romances."

"Why?" Paris didn't like what she was learning and felt like a fish out of water, educated in the wrong school...then hated herself for making the stupidest of puns. If Faraday heard it, he would probably bite her.

"Well, wealthy families have interests to protect," Isha stated. "They create smart, practical matches. The wife gets what she wants, and the husband gets a trophy. Everyone is happy, and the wedding and events around it are extravagant because that's how they make everyone believe it's real love, but it's never fooled us."

Holly lifted her glass of whiskey and held it up for her friend. "Cheers to that, Ish."

"Cheers," the fairy with short black hair repeated.

"So these matches bring in a lot of money," Paris stated. "I don't understand why FGA would care more about them. How are they profiting off weddings and the side parties?"

Both fairies regarded her like a monkey picking her nose at the table.

"You do know who runs the wedding industry, right?" Holly asked.

Paris glanced around the table. Then it dawned on her. "FGA..."

"Wow, were you born under a rock?" Holly asked.

"To magicians, who are in love and hid me away to save me

from a life of torment until I was old enough to fight for myself, with a secret identity and a fake parent," Paris said in a rush.

Holly yawned. "Yeah, me too."

Isha laughed. "You were born in Malibu with a silver spoon in your mouth that you broke, and that's why you're here."

"Well, at least I'm not you, the one with a degree in environmental economics who can't make coffee without having a moral dilemma," Holly spat at her friend.

"Well, we don't compost here," Isha stated. "Who knows where those coffee beans came from…"

"Can we focus for a second here?" Paris snapped, recapturing their attention. "So FGA has interests connected to financial gains, I'm learning. Departments like Practical Romance get money for cases and whatnot because their matches lead to big profits."

Faraday nodded. "Casual Romance is usually short-lived and only leads to short dinners, coffee dates, or a few flirty interactions."

"It doesn't have to," Paris argued. "I think that romance on all levels is important because it all has the potential to lead somewhere. What's the value in matching the Humphreys with the Rockefellers so we can make bank on a wedding if the couple sleeps in separate bedrooms? What if it's Cindy and Derek who meet in the elevator and have a casual romance that leads to the big one that creates huge fireworks on the love meter?"

Isha patted Holly's arm, looking at Paris dreamily. "Isn't she cute?"

Holly nodded, pouring more whiskey for everyone but Paris, who hadn't touched her glass. "Yeah, she's like we both were when we started. All ready to change the FGA world."

"I am going to," Paris asserted.

"She hasn't lost her angst yet." Isha smiled at her boss.

"It's not angst," Paris argued.

"She has so much hope that hasn't been wasted," Holly said.

She grabbed her shot of whiskey and threw it back, taking it in one swallow. She slammed the glass down and wiped her mouth with the back of her hand before pointing at the two fairies. "First off, what did I say about talking about me like I'm not here?"

They both tensed.

"Not to," Isha guessed.

"Or we'll turn to fire," Holly added.

"Second," Paris continued, "we're changing things. I don't care if Casual Romance doesn't make money. It's important and can lead to big things. We're going to increase its instances. Then we're going to keep doing more until this department gets noticed."

"I don't see how without any money." Faraday turned the pages of the report he'd been reading all day and night.

"We're going to get creative to start with." Paris smiled at her friends...well, employees, but she wanted them to be her friends. "You all showed a lot of genius today, redecorating this place with no funds. I need you all to do the same thing but in creating Casual Romance."

"So you want us to go and take other people's things and sell them for money?" Holly asked, quite seriously.

Paris shook her head. "No, and although you don't have money, you have magic."

"Yeah, but that's costly too," Isha stated. "We have wands, but still, fairies aren't like you, magician. We don't have an infinite supply. We can't eat a bagel and recharge. Each department is only allotted so much magic in our budgets."

Isha pointed at the large corked bottle sitting on the pedestal that Paris had noticed originally. Her mouth dropped open as she realized the implications.

"Oh, that's your magical reserves, isn't it?" Paris questioned.

"Yep," Holly stated. "Unlike you magicians, we're limited on how much magic we have each day or month or year. We can't eat carbs and be powered up. Our wands help channel magic and conserve it, but we only have so much. So some departments like Potions and Practical Love get more in their reserves."

Isha nodded. "That way fairy godmothers don't have to use their own 'at home' magic on the job."

Paris nodded. "Because why would you burn through your own if you didn't have to?"

"I'm not lifting a finger to cook dinner if I don't have to." Holly lifted her elbow. "I told you about my injury, right?"

"Yeah, you got it lifting the whiskey bottle." Paris chewed on the inside of her cheek. "So the higher-ups keep us ineffective by taking our budgets and also our magic."

"Yeah, so we've sat around for a few years and worked out," Isha said proudly. "I have rock-hard abs."

"You can bounce a quarter off my butt," Holly bragged.

"But you're ineffective as a department and a complete joke," Faraday interjected.

"Hey now," Holly protested.

"He's right," Paris stated. "They're trying to break me with no budget, two dimwits, and isolation…"

"Hey now!" Isha exclaimed.

"But you two aren't dimwits," Paris added. "And I don't need money because I do have magic, which means you two do too."

Paris pointed at the corked bottle on the pedestal, and it filled with thick pink liquid from the bottom to the top. As it did, Holly and Isha tensed and rose suddenly, their mouths falling open. Their eyes flew wide.

"W-W-We have magic!" Isha exclaimed.

"Lots and lots of magic!" Holly rejoiced. "Disposable magic."

Paris pulled her finger to the side, pausing them both. "It's not disposable. It's crucial that you use this in place of our lack of funds. I want you to use my magic that I've supplied you with, but only to help Casual Romance."

"She always ruins everything." Holly groaned.

SARAH NOFFKE & MICHAEL ANDERLE

"You've known me for two days so don't use absolutes," Paris admonished.

Holly nodded. "So far, as long as I've known her, she ruins things."

Paris rolled her eyes. "Don't talk about me like I'm not here."

Faraday looked excited. He jumped up and flicked his tail. "Pare, you have a plan?"

She nodded. "Yes, I want these two to go out and find people that need to 'bump' into each other. Go to coffee shops and find two people who should talk. Use magic to mix up their orders.

"Or find people and set them up on blind dates. Wait until two suitable people are in an elevator and use magic to break it. Let them fall for each other and exchange numbers. Who cares if any of it amounts to more than a few heated looks. The point is to spend your day making casual romance."

Isha smiled, gazing off in excited thought. "You know, this could work."

"It sounds like just that…work," Holly muttered.

"If it works, we will have done something that matters," Isha countered.

"What if I lose muscle mass?" Holly argued.

Isha jumped to her feet. "Who cares. We can work out after work. Look at this. We have magic."

She pointed at the big jar full of Paris' magic.

"Yeah, it is pretty cool," Holly admitted. She pulled her small pencil-like wand from a pocket along the side of her yoga pants and tapped it on the bottle of magic. Pink sparks swirled around the wand and disappeared, and with it, the magic in the bottle went down a little. "That's totally rad."

Isha nodded in agreement and did the same, refilling her wand with magic.

The two turned to Paris, smiling with true and rare excitement.

"You know what to do?" Paris asked.

"Yeah, we'll figure it out," Isha stated. "We'll make you proud."

"We definitely won't waste it on pranks," Holly remarked. Her friend beside her gave her a punishing look, and she quickly shrugged. "Okay, seriously, no pranks. We'll...I mean, I'll be good. We'll go and make people flirt and all."

"Good," Paris stated. "That's a start. We'll do small stuff, and we'll work up to big stuff. We're going to put this department on the map."

The fairies smiled. They didn't say it, but they seemed to believe Paris. The hope in their eyes was rare and something they'd longed for without knowing it.

When Isha and Holly had left, Faraday gave Paris a serious look. "You depleted your magic with that stunt."

"You mean when I filled up the bottle of magic so my employees could work?" she corrected.

"It was impressive. The fairies wouldn't have expected it since it's not something they can do, bottling magic for others to use," he stated.

"Hey, what would you think if I could store up a bunch of magic for me to use in one burst?" Paris thought of the gem that would be attached to her wand.

"Well..." Faraday thought for a moment. "With that magic reservoir you created, you could use it the same way you use your internal stores. But one stored for a burst of large magic, well, that could be great or very dangerous. It could backfire."

Paris nodded. "Yeah, that's what I thought too."

"We'll have to talk about it," Faraday stated. "For now, I need a nap, and you need a donut."

Paris pointed at the kitchen. A moment later, a pink donut with sprinkles appeared in front of her. However, that last bit of magic was almost too much. She thought it would make her pass out before she could stick the donut in her mouth and replenish her calories.

Thankfully she mustered enough energy to pick up the pastry

that felt like it weighed a million pounds. Slowly she took a bite and chewed and swallowed like it was cardboard rather than a sweet doughy treat.

When she'd had the single bite, Faraday seemed relieved. "Very good. Well, I'm going to take a nap. We'll catch up in a few if that's okay."

"Great." Paris felt on the verge of passing out. "I'll eat this and do some planning for the department."

Faraday yawned and stretched out on one of the fluffy pillows in the seating area. He pulled a soft blanket over his body and smiled up at Paris. "You're doing a great job so far. We're going to squash those purse-string holders."

"Thanks." Paris tried not to slur her words from the exhaustion tunneling in her head. "I couldn't do it without you. Rest up for the next adventure."

"Okay." He was snoring within a minute.

That was a good thing because Paris hated to admit that remaining upright after expending all her magic reserves was too much. Her eyes went to the donut. She reached out, knowing that the sugar was the fastest way to replenish her magic.

However, she knew before her fingers connected with the pastry that the only way she was refilling her magic was through good old sleep. She fell over sideways, landing on the pillow next to her squirrel and falling asleep just as fast—exhausted.

CHAPTER THIRTY-NINE

Third Floor, Makeshift Sleeping Area, Casual Romance Department, FGA Tower, New York City, New York

Scratching sounds made Paris stir from the heaviest slumber she remembered having in ages. As though trying to swim up through quicksand, Paris pushed up through the layers of sleep but kept feeling tugged back into dreamland. She was aware that she was asleep but shouldn't be.

Something soft tickled Paris' nose, making her slap herself in the face to bat whatever it was away. That did the trick. Paris bolted upright, her hair matted to the side of her face with a nice drool glue.

"Ouch," Paris groaned, feeling the side of her face where she'd hit her cheek. "Nothing like smacking yourself awake to start the day."

Blinking around, Paris tried to clear the bright spots partially obstructing her vision. The light streaming through the row of windows around the department space was bright—brighter than Paris had remembered earlier.

It must be mid-day, she thought, remembering falling asleep after expending all her magic reserves for Holly and Isha.

Soft snoring pulled Paris' attention back down. She found Faraday lying on the pillow next to where she'd fallen asleep. However, that's not what had awoken Paris. It had been a feeling —something tickling her face.

Paris didn't have to wonder for too much longer because that something jumped onto a nearby table. Sitting up, Paris held up her hand, ready to defend herself. However, she slumped at once, although she was still perplexed by the sight of the creature before her and how he got there.

Standing with his puffy orange tail high in the air was the large cat who belonged to Happily Ever After College.

"Casanova, how did you get here?"

CHAPTER FORTY

Third Floor, Sitting Area, Casual Romance Department, FGA Tower, New York City, New York

"Huh...what...I didn't use your hairbrush," Faraday said, mostly asleep.

"Wake up, you weirdo who won't stop using my hair stuff," Paris demanded.

The squirrel sat up. His eyes widened as he shook his head, his current reality catching up with him. He blinked at her, and as if he'd been part of a waking conversation the entire time, he sort of grinned. "Well, why shouldn't I use your hair stuff since you don't?"

Paris scoffed at him, running her hands through her messy blonde hair. "Your concern shouldn't be my hair or yours. Instead, why don't you tell me what he's doing here?" She pointed at the bright orange cat still standing on the table, peering at them with his usual annoyed expression.

"Casanova." Faraday narrowed his eyes at him. "What are you doing here, nemesis?"

As if in answer, the tabby cat jumped off the table and hurried for the exit to the department.

"You had to call him a name." Paris groaned while hurrying after the cat. "Now we might not know why or how he got here."

"He earned that title with all his spying," Faraday spat while scurrying after Paris, who was speeding after the cat.

"Of course, he's a spy," Paris said mostly to herself. "He's watching us...but why?"

Casanova, the house cat at Happily Ever After College, was a tattle cat. He usually meandered around the old mansion where the students lived and learned, looking for troublemakers and reporting them to Headmistress Willow Starr.

How did he get into FGA Tower? And again, why?

By the time Paris reached the elevator, the door had already shut, and the compartment was descending. She spun and darted for the stairs with Faraday following her.

"What is that feline up to?" Paris hurdled three and four steps at a time, making quick progress down the three flights of stairs. She didn't know which floor Casanova would get off on, but it made sense to her to go to the lobby.

Apparently, Faraday agreed with her because the nimble squirrel had leapt onto the railing and made quick progress down, passing Paris and reaching the door to the lobby first.

In one swift movement, Paris whipped it open, and she and the squirrel spilled out of the stairwell, running straight over to the bank of elevators.

Casanova had gone to the lobby, but he was already heading toward the entrance to FGA Tower. Quickly changing directions, Paris darted for the revolving doors, watching as fairy godmothers gave the feline curious looks. Some of them recognized the cat and waved. Casanova didn't return the gestures. Instead, he glanced over his shoulder to ensure that Paris and Faraday were still following him before slipping through the door and out into FGA Plaza.

Paris darted around the crowd of gabbing fairy godmothers and into the bright sunlit plaza. Across the mostly open space, she spotted Casanova already on the far side next to the street where the barrier was.

"Damn, that cat is fast." Paris ran again.

"It could be a trick," Faraday offered, keeping pace with her as he bounded forward.

"It could be, but I'm not turning back now," Paris said between breaths.

"Me either," Faraday agreed as Casanova slipped through the barrier and crossed the busy street. The nimble cat swerved around cars, slipped under tires, and safely made it to the other side of the road. He then snuck into the crowd on the sidewalk. Paris worried that they'd lose sight of him. That's why she made the impromptu decision to use magic, holding out her hand as they came to the busy intersection.

All the cars barreling forward stopped at once without any braking noises or screeching tires. They magically halted in place. The drivers' faces registered their confusion as they pressed on their gas pedals, but the vehicles didn't move.

With the intersection momentarily clear, Paris and Faraday hurried across, waving for the crowd on the other side to disperse. Having witnessed an impressive use of magic, the mortals did what Paris wanted and scurried in opposite directions, out of her way.

As soon as the crowd divided, Paris saw Casanova. The cat was casually standing halfway down the block. He watched as Paris and Faraday progressed in his direction and unhurriedly slipped into an alley next to his spot.

Paris shook her head, realizing that this could be a trick. An enemy could be luring her to her death. Someone could be trying to take her hostage. There were so many nefarious things this could be leading to. Paris didn't care. She had to find out what Casanova was doing at FGA.

Turning down the alleyway without checking it for dangers, Paris found herself in a narrow passage darkened by the brick

SARAH NOFFKE & MICHAEL ANDERLE

buildings being close together. Ahead was a dead end. If this was a trick, an attacker would have Paris trapped.

She paused, looking around the dark alley for the orange cat.

"There." Faraday pointed at a metal fire escape on the second floor.

Casanova was glaring down at them, his green eyes full of annoyance as if they were keeping him waiting.

Paris huffed, taking a running start before leaping high to catch the ladder connected to the fire escape. Faraday simply jumped from one side of the brick wall to the next until he grabbed one of the rungs above Paris' head and climbed the rest of the way up.

By the time Paris arrived on the fire escape's second-floor landing, Casanova had disappeared through an open window. Lacy white curtains partially obscured it.

Peering sideways at Faraday, she gave him a look that said, "Well, now what?"

He nodded and mouthed, "Let's do this."

Paris nodded. More carefully than before, she edged forward and peered through the window into some stranger's private dwelling. However, the person she found sitting in a cozy living room and knitting wasn't a stranger at all. It was someone Paris trusted very much.

"Headmistress Starr," Paris said in shock as the drapes blew in her direction. "What are you doing here?"

CHAPTER FORTY-ONE

Private Hideout, New York City, New York

"Come on in, Paris," Headmistress Willow Starr said as casually as if she was inviting her in for afternoon tea through her home's front door and not the fire escape off a random alley in New York.

Looking over her shoulder to see if anyone was watching her, Paris glanced briefly down at Faraday who simply shrugged as if to say, "Just go with it."

"What are you doing here?" Paris repeated after she'd climbed through the small window, careful not to pull the curtains down with her. She looked around the small apartment that instantly reminded her of the mansion on the Enchanted Grounds of Happily Ever After College.

The cozy living room, much like the headmistress' office at the school, looked like "grandmother's" home with its paisley couch and rocking chair and shelves with knickknacks.

Headmistress Willow Starr didn't appear like a grandmother though, although her thick hair was grayish-blue since she wore the fairy godmother gown. She'd arranged it into a smooth bun on top of her head. Her brown eyes sparkled with an innocence

175

that made her appear young, although also wise with years of experience.

Willow Starr was someone who Paris intrinsically trusted. It was the great Ernest Hemingway who said, "The best way to know if you can trust someone is to trust them." That's what Paris had done when she met Willow, and the other woman had never done anything since to lose that trust. However, luring Paris to her location was definitely outside the sweet fairy godmother's character.

"I needed to see you," the headmistress explained, laying down her knitting into a basket beside the rocking chair where she sat. Curled up next to her, already snoozing and purring like the trek through the streets had worn him out, was the fat orange cat. "I'm sorry I had to send Casanova like that to lead you here. That's not my usual style."

Paris thought for a moment that the headmistress was reading her mind, hearing her thoughts about the move being out of character. She shook her head, forcing a smile. "Why did you send Casanova to get me? Why not call my phone if you want to see me?"

Headmistress Starr pursed her lips. A look of regret surfaced in her warm eyes. "I never like to be cynical or paranoid. However, I have reason to believe that sending you messages directly wouldn't be wise."

"Why is that?" Paris continued to study the small apartment. So many questions popped into her head.

"Do you have your phone?" Willow rocked in the chair.

Paris nodded, pulled her device from her pants pocket, and held it up.

"Very good." Willow directed her gaze to Faraday. "Well, hello. I'm glad you joined us as well. Please pardon my manners, both of you. I should have started this conversation properly. It's nice to see you, both Paris and Faraday. I look forward to hearing all about how you've been. Would you like some tea?"

Paris had just awoken from a magic-induced coma after depleting her reserves. Now she realized that she was quite thirsty and hungry. Calories were the best way to replenish her stores now that she'd slept.

"Yes, please," Paris answered. "That would be great."

"Of course." The headmistress picked up a quill pen on the side table next to her and twirled it. Blue sparks radiated from the feather that was also Willow's magical instrument. A moment later, a tray with tea, cookies, and sandwiches appeared on the coffee table beside the fluffy couch. "Please make yourself comfortable and eat up. You are safe here."

Paris didn't need any more encouragement and plopped down on the sofa, grabbing a cream cheese and cucumber sandwich at once. Through her first bite, she looked around. "I still don't understand. Why would you say we're safe here? Are we not at FGA Tower? What is this place?"

"I'll explain everything as best I can based on what I know and also what I don't know but suspect," Willow answered with a polite smile. She turned her soft gaze on Faraday, who had dug into the sandwiches as well. His long all-nighter had depleted his reserves too. "Do you think if there is spyware on Paris' phone that you can find it?"

Headmistress Starr had gotten to know Faraday during a series of missions at Happily Ever After College, where the scientific squirrel helped save the school. His knowledge of technology had stopped a spell that made cell phones addictive and much more. The headmistress had become so indebted to the squirrel for his expertise that she had a science lab created for him on the mansion's third story.

Paris swallowed her bite without fully chewing. "Spyware on my phone? How? When? Why?"

"It's only an assumption," Willow said in a calm voice much different than the panic that had quickly arisen in Paris'.

"I can take a look." Faraday brushed his paws together to shake off crumbs.

Paris slid the phone in front of the squirrel on the couch and poured some tea for the group.

"This apartment is a little place I keep that's close to FGA Tower so I can keep an eye on things when needed," Head-mistress Willow began, turning her full attention to Paris while Faraday went to work investigating her phone. "Proximity is helpful in certain situations."

Paris tilted her head, confusion heavy in her gaze. "I'm already under the impression that there might be things going on below the surface at FGA," she began, not wanting to disclose that Saint Valentine had told her to keep an eye out for anything worth noting. It felt best to keep things to herself until she knew more information. "However, is there something specific you can tell me about why you think I have spyware on my phone or seem to be secretly monitoring things at FGA Tower?"

Willow folded her hands and calmly laid them in her lap. "You know from recent events that there have been problems within the ranks of agents at FGA. Saint Valentine is entirely aware that he has opposition inside his organization.

"The FGA board is full of respectable fairies but also ones who know how to play the game and probably do things for selfish gains. We know this, yet we don't know who fits into which category."

Willow sighed, suddenly looking overwhelmed. "Since FGA is an old and established organization, it's hard to know who is corrupt and who is simply entrenched in old ways of thinking. You see, Saint Valentine believes there are people with good intentions working for him with wrong ways of doing things. Then some have bad intentions but know how to make themselves look good. Does that make sense?"

"Yes." Paris watched as Faraday tapped on her phone, scrolling through multiple screens. "People aren't black and white. The world is full of gray."

"That's right. Although for a long time there have been things that have made Saint Valentine believe those in his ranks are working against him rather than for him, never before has that notion been more prevalent."

"Why is that?"

"Well, Saint Valentine recognizes that FGA needs to adapt, so he's been pushing back on the board, creating tensions. He's been making unpopular decisions—"

"Like promoting me to agent," Paris guessed.

Willow nodded. "Because of FGA's long-established organizational structure, many of the branches and departments work independently from Matters of the Heart, Saint Valentine's ruling office over the company."

"That means there's a lot he can't see." Paris chewed her lip and thought about the conversation she'd had with the leader of FGA on her first day. He'd said, "Most think that a leader is in the perfect position to see. However, from on top of the mountain, usually one is stuck in the clouds. It is those on the ground who see the army approaching. They see the whites of the enemy's eyes, whereas the general only sees the troops after they stormed his army."

"Yes, and this problem is big and complex, and we want to keep things as quiet as possible when it comes to our suspicions…"

"I get that." It wouldn't be diplomatic for Saint Valentine to start accusing. Nor could he very well start snooping when he was already under such scrutiny. It was probably why he put people he trusted into places to keep an eye out for him. People like her, and Willow, and who knew who else.

"Yeah, you're being spied on, all right." Faraday tapped on Paris' phone, gaining both her and Willow's attention.

"I am?" Paris was shocked. "By whom? Since when? How?"

179

SARAH NOFFKE & MICHAEL ANDERLE

"I don't know, and the same answer applies to the other two questions."

Both the squirrel and the halfling looked directly at Willow.

"How did you know?" Paris asked the fairy godmother.

"I didn't. I simply thought it was a possibility. You are being watched by many. We know that much. We can only work with what we know, and I'll tell you that." She held up her hand and ticked off one finger. "We know that there are those at FGA who can't be trusted."

"Because they want to bring it down?" Paris asked.

Willow shrugged. "That would be too obvious an answer. I think more often, people want what they want, and it's not always in the best interests of the organization or more importantly, love."

"What else do you know?" Paris questioned.

"We know that love is constantly under attack," Willow continued, ticking off another finger.

Paris nodded, remembering her thoughts on how love was the single biggest fear for some—challenging them at their core.

"We believe that there are those at FGA who aren't doing their job." Willow held up a third finger. "We don't know anything else and making accusations is dangerous in this world, so we are going to move stealthily."

"But my phone, why was it bugged?" Paris questioned.

"Probably to keep an eye on you," Faraday answered. "It seems to be a simple remote bugging software. You're the new kid on campus. People at FGA, any of them, might have wanted to see what you were doing or if they could trust you. Just the same way you're looking around and suspicious of others, they can be thinking you're the corrupt one and trying to harm love."

Willow nodded in agreement. "He's right. We simply don't know."

"You knew," Paris argued.

"I suspected," Willow corrected. "So I sent Casanova to retrieve you so no one would know about our meeting."

"Well, I have a few questions about that," Paris stated. "Why did you send the cat to lure me here? Why not visit me at FGA?"

"She didn't want anyone to suspect her," Faraday guessed.

Willow smiled and nodded. "It's best if I don't look like I'm snooping into things. I need to remain objective as the headmistress of Happily Ever After College. I can't simply waltz onto FGA Plaza. I have to request permission. Then others become aware and would start asking questions. If I visited you, that might look like favoritism if I'm not visiting all our graduates. Although I want the best for them, I only wanted to see you."

"Why?" That was her most burning question.

"Paris, I need your help with something that I've discovered. Saint Valentine is aware of it. It has far-reaching, devastating effects on love."

"Really?" Paris' voice went an octave higher. "Then is anyone at FGA working on helping too?"

"That's the thing. It appears to be going unnoticed, which is suspicious in itself. This is why I've recruited you to look into the matter for me. I need access to information that's only available inside FGA. Saint Valentine would look into it, but it's a bit outside his scope, and he can't draw attention to himself if someone catches him. We need someone on the inside to look into this for us, and we're hoping that's you.

"It could be nothing related to FGA and simply going unnoticed by agents. Or it could be an inside job. We simply don't know enough. That's where you come in. I need you to do some investigating, but I'll warn you that it will involve sneaking into places inside FGA. Are you interested in hearing more about this?"

Paris smiled, glanced to the side, and met Faraday's gaze before she looked straight at Headmistress Willow Starr. "Absolutely, I am."

CHAPTER FORTY-TWO

Headmistress Willow Starr's Private Hideout, New York City, New York

The fairy godmother grinned with relief and nodded. "Okay, well then I'm going to need to play you something that will demonstrate what I just became aware of."

"Oh?" Paris watched as Faraday continued to type on her phone, hopefully getting rid of the spyware.

"Yes," Willow answered. "I observed the love meter going down at an alarming rate, something that hinted at a very specific cause."

"Like when phones were addictive," Paris guessed.

"Yes," Willow affirmed. "So I did some research. Mae Ling and I found something that we think could be the cause." She twirled her feather quill again, and on the table's surface appeared a little bluebird and two tiny rosebuds with no stems.

Paris had used this music listening device at Happily Ever After College when studying music and how it related to love.

Tentatively, Paris went to place the rosebuds into her ear, but Willow held up her hand, pausing her for a moment.

"Remember that the music's spelled and what you feel won't

be your true emotions," Willow warned. She twirled the quill again, and a small bottle of thick, bright red potion appeared beside the bluebird and rosebuds. Even if it wasn't for the intense color, Paris could tell it was a powerful magic potion.

Reading the question in Paris' eyes, Willow said, "That's to combat the spell afterward."

"Okay." Paris wasn't sure what she was about to get herself into. Spelled music? Something that affected love and needed what appeared to be a strong potion? Paris was curious, but she was also intensely nervous. She eyed Faraday, reassured by his nod of encouragement.

Paris picked up the rosebuds and placed them in her ears. The bluebird began singing, but only for her to hear. The beat that began was immediately enticing, but Paris didn't think that was part of the spell. The notes played by the guitar and keyboard were also very alluring and catchy, but that was only the power of good music.

It was when the singer started his vocal that Paris knew what was so magical about the song. It was the lyrics, and without her permission, they were breaking her heart.

CHAPTER FORTY-THREE

Headmistress Willow Starr's Private Hideout, New York City, New York

Although Paris' instinct was to yank the rosebuds out of her ears and not feel the anguish the song was causing, she knew that she needed to experience this. Paris had to understand what was going on here. That was the way to fix it, and that's what had to happen because without a doubt, this music was tearing lovers apart. It was magically breaking people's hearts.

She brought her eyes up to meet Headmistress Starr's gaze. The look of sympathy in the fairy godmother's eyes told Paris she understood how the younger woman felt.

The lyrics on their own would've been enough to bring a tender ache to Paris' heart.

She listened, appreciating their poetry.

"Every year a thousand places. Every night a thousand faces," the guy sang, his voice raw and full of persuading emotions. "That front row space I saved for you. Its emptiness haunts me, that heartbreak view."

Unprovoked by any situation or thoughts, Paris suddenly was painfully angry at Hemingway. She had the sudden urge to call him up and break things off. That wasn't right because Paris loved him madly. Deeply. Forever. Yet at her core, she desperately wanted to end her relationship with the love of her life.

Finally unable to take any more pain, Paris pulled the rosebuds from her ears. Willow twirled her quill, and a handkerchief appeared in her free hand. Paris was confused when the fairy godmother handed it to her, but then she felt the tears on her face. They'd appeared without her knowing it.

Paris took the handkerchief and dried her tears, but that didn't take away the pain burning in her heart. This was powerful music. There was no doubt that someone had spelled it. No matter what, she had to stop it.

CHAPTER FORTY-FOUR

Headmistress Willow Starr's Private Hideout, New York City, New York

With a shaking hand and tears still streaming from her eyes, Paris pulled the cork from the potion and took it in one gulp. The sludge tasted rancid, and Paris worried she wouldn't be able to choke it down. She had to, though. She must do whatever it took to erase the pain and heartbreak the music had caused her.

Pressing her eyes tightly shut, Paris held her breath and swallowed, willing herself to keep the thick potion down as the last of it drained from the bottle. Her gag reflex was begging to send the concoction back out of her mouth.

However, Paris persevered and forced the gunk down her throat where it settled in her stomach uncomfortably, making it rumble. She let out a deep breath and willed herself to remain calm, knowing that would help the potion work faster.

Thankfully, the ache in her heart receded, covered up now by nausea. Paris didn't care and would take being sick over the pain. However, she didn't have to endure either for too long.

Magically, the unease in her stomach went away as fast as it came on, along with the torment in her heart.

Her eyes sprang open to find Willow and Faraday staring at her intently, concern radiating from their gazes.

"How are you?" Willow looked Paris over like she'd been in a physical fight and not had her heart figuratively stabbed by lyrics.

Paris nodded, not sure she trusted her voice to speak yet.

"I'm so sorry I had to put you through that," Willow said with genuine remorse. "The only way to show the song's effects is to experience it."

"What happened?" Faraday looked between Paris and the headmistress.

"The song Paris heard breaks people's hearts," Willow explained. "There's no way to avoid it, and it leads to heartbreak and therefore the loss of love."

"The song is spelled to break couples up," Faraday stated, his brain already racing with thoughts.

"Yes and the only cure that we know of is that potion," Willow elaborated. "That's obviously not a viable solution."

Paris shook her head, never wanting to drink that revolting stuff again. "We have to stop that song from being played."

Willow nodded. "That's the problem. The band that sings that song is famous, and it's now number one on the charts."

Paris sighed, feeling the weight of this heavy situation. "People worldwide are experiencing this heartache."

"Which is why we saw the most dramatic dip in love that I've ever witnessed," the headmistress stated.

"What are they doing at FGA?" Paris looked out the window toward fairy godmother headquarters.

"That's the thing." Willow shook her head. "It appears to be going unnoticed. This supports my already growing suspicions about there being problems inside the corporation. However, I don't have anything concrete, and it could simply be that no one has pinpointed that the song is to blame."

"Music often inspires people either with happiness or

despair," Faraday stated, going back to typing on Paris' phone. "What's the name of this band?"

"Punch Line. Don't listen to the song because that's all the recovery potion I had with me."

"I won't, but I want to check something out. Spelled music would involve powerful magic. If we figure out what it is, maybe we can create a counterspell."

"That's a good idea." Willow looked at Paris. "I hoped you could do some research for us at FGA. Maybe there's something there that can fix this that no one is considering."

"I can do that," Paris said at once, motivated to stamp this problem out as fast as she could.

"I'm afraid that there's only one way to fix this problem," Faraday interjected, his eyes transfixed on the phone screen.

Both women dropped their gaze and gave him their full attention.

The squirrel looked up with a heavy look in his eyes. "We have to stop Punch Line from singing this song. That's the only solution."

CHAPTER FORTY-FIVE

Headmistress Willow Starr's Private Hideout, New York City, New York

"What did you find?" Willow asked.

Faraday turned the phone around to show a recording of a band performing. The bottom said, "Punch Line playing their newest hit—*Heartbreak View*."

Instinctively Paris flinched like she'd hear the heartbreak song again. Thankfully Faraday had turned the volume down on the device, and all they saw was the performance, which didn't have the same effects as hearing the music.

"Look at the lead singer's arm," Faraday encouraged, pointing at a man with a black ponytail holding a microphone. His bicep flexed as he belted out his song, tears and sweat streaming down his face as he evoked emotions through the lyrics. Even without hearing them, the sight moved Paris. The man was heartbroken.

"Are those words tattooed on his arm?" Paris squinted at the phone for a clearer view.

"Yes," Faraday confirmed, zooming in on the tattoo. "I didn't hear the lyrics to the song, but I think it's them. Look, each word is glowing as he sings."

Paris saw what he meant. They *were* the lyrics to the song. Although Paris didn't consider herself a lip reader, she thought the glowing words corresponded to what the man was singing.

"So the lyrics are spelled through a tattoo," Paris mused, shaking her head. "Why would someone do that?"

"To break hearts," Faraday offered.

"Yes, but it has to be deeper than that," Willow mumbled, thinking. "This lead singer—"

"Archer Finch," Faraday supplied.

Willow nodded. "Thank you. Yes, this Archer Finch. We need to know more about him if we're going to stop Punch Line from singing this song."

"Yes." Paris' mind raced with ideas. "Because this isn't just someone trying to break hearts. Archer tattooed these lyrics on his arm using magic. There's something deeper going on here."

"The fifth floor of FGA Tower is where they keep records. It's quite a spectacular system and documented using very complex magic. Every romantic relationship is stored there. As things happen in a relationship, more is added to the lovers' files."

"How is that possible?" Faraday was impressed.

"It's similar to the magic that runs the Great Library," Willow explained.

The Great Library, located in Timbuktu and magically hidden from most of the world, was the place that stored every book in all of time. As soon as someone wrote a book, whether published or not, it showed up on the library shelves. When edits happened in the book, it updated itself in the Great Library.

Few had access to the Great Library since knowledge in the wrong hands could be extremely dangerous. However, as fairy godmothers, they had access to the secret location. It therefore made sense that the Records department of FGA would have similar magic for recording romantic liaisons.

"Wow," Faraday gasped, obviously impressed by this new insight.

"We need to find out as much about Archer Finch as possible," Willow continued. "Maybe he's only singing a spelled song for fame and riches, but my instinct tells me there's more to this."

Paris agreed with a nod. "This is personal. The emotions on his face when singing, they say so much."

"I think so. Good idea to look up the performance." Willow smiled at Faraday, who blushed at the compliment.

"So you think I should sneak into the Records department of FGA Tower?" Paris guessed, asking the headmistress.

She nodded. "Yes, and you'll have to sneak because you don't have clearance to that area. I'd request access, but I think we need to be discreet and not let anyone know what we're researching."

Paris nodded. "Yes, if there's someone behind this besides the band, we don't need them knowing that we're figuring things out."

"This feels like a very dangerous situation." Willow's tone suddenly turned haunted.

"Well, it is," Faraday related. "Punch Line wants to hurt hundreds of thousands of people. They don't appear to be magicians from what I've seen, so that means they got the magic from somewhere."

"I fear this goes deep and we're going to have our work cut out for us uncovering the truth," Willow warned.

Paris forced a look of confidence on her face. "Don't worry. I'll get into the Records department and find out why Archer Finch is heartbroken. From there we'll figure how to stop him from singing that song."

CHAPTER FORTY-SIX

Plaza, FGA Tower, New York City, New York

"So, have you figured how you're sneaking into the Records department?" Faraday asked as they looked up at the skyscraper from beside the fountain at the front of the building.

Paris grinned at her friend. "Yeah, but I'm not sneaking in there."

"You're not?" Faraday was shocked. "But the song. The heartbreak. You've got to stop it."

She nodded. "Yes, silly. Read between the lines. I can't sneak into the Records department because…well, look around." Paris waved around FGA Plaza, where fairy godmothers and agents were crossing to the building or sitting on benches and chatting. However, no matter what they were doing, they weren't hiding their curiosity.

"Everyone is looking at you," Faraday guessed.

"Exactly," Paris affirmed. "There's no way I can breeze onto the fifth floor unnoticed. Sooooo…"

"That means you plan for me to do it," Faraday guessed.

She nodded victoriously. "Yeah, you're the perfect choice."

He smirked. "True, but still, I can't simply get off the elevator and trot into the department."

"No, but I bet if we get you to the fourth floor, from there, you could take the air vents up to the fifth," Paris offered, working out the idea as she spoke.

"That could work," Faraday whispered. "I'm excellent at finding information quickly. So I'll locate the information on Archer Finch's past relationships and see if there's anything that can help us."

"Okay, well, we have a plan." Paris started for the entrance to FGA Tower. "We have to be fast. The longer this goes on, the more heartbreak that happens."

CHAPTER FORTY-SEVEN

Fourth Floor, Gnome-Mance Department, FGA Tower, New York City, New York

Paris remembered from her tour with Alfred that the fourth floor was devoted to Interspecies Love. She hadn't noticed then that they didn't visit the fifth floor on that tour, but there had been some levels they didn't see, and she hadn't thought anything of it. Now Paris realized it was because the fifth floor was devoted to the Records department and would have been off-limits. They'd skipped quite a few areas, so she guessed those were all restricted.

Thankfully, there wasn't much staff on the fourth floor since most didn't regard Interspecies Love as an important department. Probably because it didn't bring in profits, Paris assumed.

"Keep an eye out for me," Paris murmured when she and Faraday found an air vent in a less-traveled hallway outside some meeting rooms.

She pointed at the vent and used a spell to unscrew the metal panel on the wall. As quietly as she could manage, Paris grabbed the vent cover and lowered it enough so Faraday could climb into the long, dusty shaft. The squirrel's claws made a scratching noise inside the metal tunnel.

"Do you think you can find the way up to the fifth floor?" Paris asked in a whisper.

Faraday scowled at her. "I have multiple advanced degrees in various areas of science."

She nodded as though she understood. "So that means you know string theory but can't tie your shoe. I get it. I'll draw you a map."

"I don't wear shoes," Faraday muttered.

"Because you can't tie them," she teased. "Seriously, we won't have any way to communicate so you need to know where you're going and what you're looking for."

"You can rely on me, Pare. I've got this."

"Fine." Paris sighed. "Well, I'll be here waiting for you."

"How about you don't," Faraday stated. "You're not supposed to be on this floor, and the last thing we need is you drawing more unwanted attention to yourself."

"Fine." Paris shuffled Faraday forward as she lifted the front panel back onto the vent and screwed it back into place. "Be careful."

"You too," Faraday whispered. His gaze darted to something over her shoulder as he held up his paw in front of his face, shushing her.

"What are you doing there?" a stern voice said at Paris' back.

CHAPTER FORTY-EIGHT

Fourth Floor, Hallway, FGA Tower, New York City, New York

Paris tensed, gulped, and let out a deep breath. Faraday silently retreated several feet down the vent shaft so he wasn't visible.

Paris turned to find an agent standing at the far end of the hallway—a man with a pock-marked face in all black. His suit was nicer than most of the other agents, but like many of them, he wore a black bowler hat. Also like many of them, he had a serious expression and a scrutinizing look in his cold dark eyes. On the man's right shoulder was a silver pendant of a sword that glinted in the light.

With a light-hearted giggle, Paris flipped her hair over her shoulder and threw up her hand. "I'm totally lost. It's only my second day so I guess that's not unexpected."

"What are you looking for?" The man strode toward her.

"My department." She worked to keep the light expression on her face although her heart suddenly beat fast and she sensed something intensely evil around her. It was like when she and her father tracked demons to FGA Tower, and she felt their presence. However, the man before her wasn't a demon. She knew that.

Paris figured her adrenaline had spiked from nearly getting caught putting Faraday in the air vent.

"Your department is on the third floor." The man paused a few feet from her.

"Yep. The third floor."

"You're on the fourth," the man stated.

Paris slapped her forehead. "Of course. No wonder I can't find my way. I'm such an airhead."

"You graduated at the top of your class at Happily Ever After College."

"That was luck," Paris stated at once.

"Your aptitude test when we assessed you for placement at FGA put you scoring in the top ninety-ninth percentile of fairy godmothers."

Paris shrugged. "I picked C on all the multiple-choice questions. The answer is always C."

"You're a Beaufont, meaning that you have more power on a bad day than most other magical races when at full steam," the man countered.

"Yeah, but I'm inexperienced with my magic."

"Miss Beaufont, I know exactly who you are. I dare say I know more about you than you might know about yourself. So don't think of me as a fool you can lie to and deceive. I won't fall for it like everyone else in this place."

"Who might you be?" Paris narrowed her eyes at the man. "Since you know so much about me and I don't know your name." Her eyes flickered to the silver sword on his shoulder. It was no doubt his magical instrument. She noted that it was the sheath pinned to his jacket. The sword was removable for easy access. "Are you Agent Silver?"

"I'm Jackson Zelle. I don't go by an agent title or have my magic tracked using gems."

"Much like Saint Valentine." She thought of the leader's silver cane.

SARAH NOFFKE & MICHAEL ANDERLE

"Yes, very much like him."

"And you are?" She scrutinized him, undeterred by his intimidating glare.

"I'm the man who runs this place."

"Oh, I was under the impression that was Saint Valentine."

"Well, you have a lot to learn, it seems."

Paris smirked rebelliously at the man. "And here I thought, according to you, that I was so very smart."

"There's smart, and there's being wise. You can have all the intelligence in the world, but if you don't know how and when to use it, well, it will do you no good."

"So, Mr. Zelle, what department is yours that apparently runs this place?"

He returned the smirk, his expression much more sinister than hers. "Finance," Jackson Zelle answered simply and then turned and strode back the way he'd come, not giving her another moment of his attention.

A cold chill shot down Paris' back. She realized that the man striding away from her probably did run FGA. If he controlled the money, he controlled everything in that place.

CHAPTER FORTY-NINE

Fourth Floor, Air Vent Shaft, FGA Tower, New York City, New York

Distance muffled the conversation between Jackson Zelle and Paris, but Faraday had heard enough of it to know that the finance director seemed to have sat on a pinecone. The antagonistic quality in the man's voice was clear to Faraday. There appeared to be a lot of uptight jerks with boundary issues in FGA.

Careful not to make noise, Faraday lightly ran along the cold metal tunnels of the air vent. The dust covering the inside of the ducts tickled his nose, threatening to make him sneeze.

As he neared another vent covering, he heard more muffled voices from someone else talking on the fourth floor. Faraday held his breath, knowing that a sneeze from inside the walls wouldn't go unnoticed.

Paris trusted him to sneak up to the fifth floor and into the Records department. Not only did he not want to let her down, but Faraday also wanted to see this place that magically held the records on every romantic relationship. The power that maintained the Great Library was still confounding. Seeing something with similar magic would be a real treat for the scientific squirrel.

Ahead, Faraday spotted a vent shaft in the ceiling that went up. That should be his way to the fifth floor. Although climbing wouldn't be as easy as running horizontally, Faraday was a squirrel so the challenge wouldn't be taxing.

Faraday was about to launch himself at the opening so he could use that momentum to climb up the slick surface. However, a voice he'd just heard echoed from a nearby vent.

As quietly as he could, Faraday edged farther down the shaft, closer to the opening. He passed the way up but figured he could double back. Something told him that he should take this opportunity to hear the conversation happening on the other side of the wall.

Holding his breath so he didn't sneeze, Faraday pressed his ear close to the vent opening and listened as Jackson Zelle talked on the phone.

CHAPTER FIFTY

Fourth Floor, Hallway, FGA Tower, New York City, New York

"I want you to keep an eye on her," Jackson Zelle muttered into his phone, then paused as if someone was speaking on the other end of the line.

"Because she has a reputation for sticking her nose into places where it doesn't belong," he continued after a moment.

Faraday strained to make out every word the finance director said, but his pacing up and down the empty hallway made it difficult. The loud *slap* of his leather loafers on the tile floor told Faraday that the man was agitated. However, the squirrel had already deduced that from Zelle's conversation with Paris. He pictured that Jackson Zelle spent most of his time annoyed about something or another. He seemed like the type. The good news was that the man's noisy footsteps gave Faraday a chance to breathe.

"I think you're underestimating her," Jackson Zelle spat, annoyance heavy in his tone.

He was talking about Paris, Faraday believed. However, he couldn't assume that simply based on her being the last person he interacted with before this phone conversation. Those were congruent pieces of information, and mistakes happened when scientists made correlational assumptions instead of tested hypotheses based on facts. Faraday needed more information.

"Did you bug her phone like I told you?" Jackson Zelle continued to pace.

Faraday's tiny heart beat even faster. He was talking about Paris. He had to be.

"What do you mean, she's undone it?"

A loud sigh echoed down the hallway. "See, this is what I'm talking about. She's not like the silly fairy godmothers we're used to dealing with. She's trouble."

Faraday leaned closer to the vent as Jackson Zelle's voice grew fainter. He must have been walking farther away.

The dust from the slats tickled Faraday's nose. He held his breath, afraid he was about to have a violent sneezing attack. That would give him away. Then he'd give Paris away.

Deciding that it was best to save their cover over eavesdropping, Faraday backed up, hurrying the opposite direction from Jackson Zelle's position and toward the next tunnel that would lead to the fifth floor.

CHAPTER FIFTY-ONE

Elevator, FGA Tower, New York City, New York

Paris was grateful that the elevator was empty when she boarded. The last thing she wanted to do was make small talk with a ditzy fairy when her mind was racing with thoughts. Jackson Zelle seemed not to like her from the start. However, that was pretty much status quo for management at FGA except for Saint Valentine. Agents Emerald and Jasper hadn't given her a warm welcome.

However, there seemed to be an extra bit of disdain in how Jackson Zelle treated her. It was like he had a personal reason for not liking her. He'd seemed to know a lot about her, which was odd. Maybe that was part of his job as the director of finance, the department over the three main branches: IT-slash-Operations, Basic Love, and Advanced Love.

Pressing the button for the third floor, Paris hoped that Faraday was okay as he snuck into the Records department. She'd planned to hang out on the fourth floor and wait for signs of his return to retrieve him. However, with Jackson Zelle thundering around the floor and seemingly paranoid about her, she decided it was best to return to her department and wait for the squirrel. He would no doubt find his way back.

"Hey, what are you doing?" Paris asked the elevator as it went past the third floor and continued down.

Several times she tapped the button with the three, but the elevator didn't heed her requests. Then she remembered what Alfred had said about the magitech elevator. It apparently would take lone riders to the floor that it "thought" they needed, rather than where they wanted to go.

That was more perplexing to Paris when the crazy elevator paused on the first basement level. The doors opened to total blackness. Paris narrowed her eyes, squinting into the dark, trying to see what was up ahead. A blast of cold air shot through a narrow passageway and hit her in the chest as if she'd entered an arctic storm. A howl followed, and a violent chill ran down her spine.

Deciding that the elevator was wrong about where she *needed* to go, Paris slammed her hand on the button to close the elevator doors, then the one for the third floor. She held her breath, not understanding what she'd witnessed in the basement. It was like it was haunted.

What was wrong with the Advanced Love department that it was in such darkness? Faraday had thought there was more to that place and it was worth investigating. It appeared that he was right, and they would—when time allowed.

Paris let out a breath of relief when the elevator decided to take her to her floor, and thankfully, away from whatever resided in the basement of FGA Tower.

CHAPTER FIFTY-TWO

Fifth Floor, Air Vent, FGA Tower, New York City, New York

Faraday's heart was in overdrive when he arrived at the grate for the fifth floor. He knew that this mission was critical, but he desperately wanted to get back to Paris and warn her.

All he could do was be quick and return to Paris with what he'd learned. When he thought about it, Jackson Zelle didn't appear inherently bad. Grumpy, yes. Threatening, sure. Still, all he'd told the person on the phone was that they needed to keep an eye on Paris and that they shouldn't underestimate her. That wasn't false. No one should ever underestimate the halfling with demon blood.

Faraday could understand why agents and fairy godmothers who were used to things running a certain way at FGA would be intimidated by the change with Paris taking on a department.

However, the fact that Jackson Zelle had been the one to bug Paris' phone was disconcerting. Again though, Faraday couldn't entirely blame the finance director. It was wrong, and he'd over-stepped boundaries, but he might be protecting FGA from what he saw as a threat. Or Jackson Zelle might simply be trying to keep tabs on Paris until management deemed that she was trustworthy.

She was a magician, a big point of contention when she first came to Happily Ever After College. Then when everyone learned that she had demon blood, many were downright afraid of the halfling, not understanding that this part of her made her more charged against evil rather than prone to it.

Trying to focus on the mission at hand...or rather, at paw, Faraday pushed all this speculation from his mind. Jumping to conclusions would be no good. He should try to maintain objectivity, especially when relaying the new information to Paris. There was no reason to be overly paranoid about Jackson Zelle until they perceived a real threat.

The squirrel reminded himself that coinciding information wasn't proof of anything. Drawing unfounded conclusions was dangerous. That's why Faraday had come to the Records department, to find facts.

It was simply astounding how many facts he could find in this place. The realization hit him as he peered through the metal grate into the Records area. It was vast, filled with hundreds of thousands of documents, and controlled entirely by magic.

CHAPTER FIFTY-THREE

Fifth Floor, Records Department, FGA Tower, New York City, New York

Standing on the other side of the metal grate on top of a filing cabinet, Faraday looked around the vast space, mesmerized by the sight before him. From his perch, he had quite a view of the Records department. The scientific squirrel had never seen anything like it—which was saying a lot because the squirrel who was once a man had seen a lot. However, before him was the thing of fairy tales. Right out of storybooks. It was magic incarnate.

Thousands of filing cabinets formed rows that went on for as far as Faraday could see, disappearing into the darkness. Randomly a drawer would open magically, and a thick roll of parchment would rise into the air. From across the space, a quill would fly over and scribble on it as if held by an invisible giant. Then the parchment would roll up and drop into the open filing cabinet drawer before it shut once more.

That scene happened hundreds and hundreds of times over the next few minutes. Faraday watched in awe, his gaze jumping

207

from parchment to parchment as records were magically recorded on the scroll before it filed itself away.

How the romantic history of lovers got documented, Faraday couldn't even fathom. It was the same strange magic that worked in the Great Library. There was some very strong spell that made it so books and events related to love became the domain of this place and the Great Library.

Faraday had so many questions as he watched events of other people's relationships recorded and filed. However, his time for observing was over when he heard voices a few rows over in the room. Thankfully the filing cabinets were so high that whoever it was couldn't see Faraday on his perch.

Before he could be spotted, the squirrel jumped down to the floor and scampered in the opposite direction.

It didn't take Faraday long to figure out the filing system's setup. Then he only had to find the row for "F" where he believed Archer Finch's file would be. Thankfully he was quick on his feet because the Records department was massive. He realized that it had to be to store the romantic history of every single couple. The idea of what the archives looked like was simply astounding.

Faraday shook his head, wondering if that's what they kept on the twenty-sixth floor of FGA Tower. One thing was certain, and that was there were so many secrets to unlock in this place.

CHAPTER FIFTY-FOUR

Third Floor, Casual Romance Department, FGA Tower, New York City, New York

Paris paced back and forth in her large department space, suddenly wishing it wasn't so big with so many places where monsters could be hiding. She knew that seemed silly and childish, but ever since being taken to the basement, she couldn't shake a strange foreboding feeling.

Although she hadn't seen anything in the darkened corridor on the first level of the basement, she felt like she had. It seemed as though she'd met something sinister down there without seeing it directly. There had been no words exchanged or introductions made, yet she had the distinct impression that she'd been in the presence of someone or something down there.

Shaking off the cold, mysterious fear, Paris continued to pace, wishing that Holly or Isha were there to make her feel not so lonely. For a girl who grew up mostly alone, isolated on Roya Lane for her protection, Paris didn't know the pain of loneliness. However, since returning from the basement, she felt like she'd never know anything but permanent isolation for the rest of her life.

Whatever seemed to curse the basement was very dark and powerful magic, Paris reasoned as the elevator *chimed*, signaling that someone had arrived on the third floor. Halting in place, Paris held her breath, hoping that whoever was coming around the corner was a friend and not a poltergeist she'd let loose from the basement.

Relief flooded Paris' chest when Faraday hurried into sight, his eyes bright and his tail bushy.

"You're back!" Paris ran over, looking him over like he could've gotten hurt during his mission. He seemed fine, although no doubt a bit frazzled.

"Are you okay?" He studied her like she might have an injury as well. "Jackson Zelle rattled you, didn't he?"

"Not as much as whatever I encountered in the basement here."

He tilted his head, giving her a curious look. "What was that? Why did you go down there?"

"I didn't mean to," she explained. "The possessed elevator took me down there without my permission. Honestly, I don't know what I saw down there...or met... I can't explain the experience. It filled me with a really dark emotion."

Faraday nodded as though he understood. "I knew something strange was going on in the Advanced Love branch. There's something odd about locking it underground with no real information about it. We'll have to do more research on it."

"Yes," Paris agreed. "However, our priority right now is that song and stopping it from breaking hearts. Did you find out anything about Archer Finch? Is it possible that he wrote the song or is he a pawn?"

"I think both," Faraday stated. "His girlfriend, a Miss Ella Sparrow, broke up with him recently. He fought her on it, but she's been adamant that they don't belong together. Before that, she was always at many of his shows in the front row, in a seat he always had saved for her."

Paris nodded, remembering the lyrics from *Heartbreak View*. She mumbled them, almost afraid to sing them as if doing so might cause her pain again. However, she didn't have the tattoo on her arm that spelled the lyrics Archer Finch sang so she said them more clearly for her and Faraday to interpret.

"Every year a thousand places," Paris began, trying to remember the lyrics exactly. "Every night a thousand faces. That front row space I saved for you. Its emptiness haunts me, that heartbreak view."

"Yeah, that seems much too personal for Archer Finch not to have written about the woman who broke his heart," Faraday mused.

"You think that someone is behind it?" Paris asked.

"Well, as we thought, all of the members of Punch Line are mortals," Faraday stated. "So how they got hold of magical ink or a spell that powerful is perplexing. I think the only way to determine what's going on and stop this song is to visit Archer Finch."

Paris nodded. "Okay, I'm game for that. Do you know where to find him?"

Faraday's gaze skirted to the side. "I do. Before we go anywhere, I need to tell you something. Then we're going to have to create a diversion before we can leave this building."

CHAPTER FIFTY-FIVE

First Floor Stairwell, FGA Tower, New York City, New York

"Are you sure this is going to work?" Paris looked around to ensure that people were watching. As soon as Faraday told Paris that others were spying on her, she became understandably paranoid. However, it wasn't a hard reality to accept since someone had bugged her phone. Bitterly she thought of the jerk she'd met that day on the fourth floor. How dare Jackass Zelle trespass on her privacy like that.

"As with all things magical, there are no guarantees." Faraday scribbled notes on a pad, deep in focus.

Paris glanced up at the floors above. "How do we know that they haven't followed us here and whoever is supposed to be spying on us is about to witness this?"

"They could have, but I'm guessing that they have eyes on the lobby," Faraday explained. "No one can portal out of FGA Tower. All personnel must go to the plaza no matter what, so that means individuals are always traceable from the building. Whoever is watching you is probably alerted when you enter the lobby to leave for a new location. So now, we're going to help them out, making their jobs easier."

Paris laughed, delighted by Faraday's plan for a diversion, although it was a new level of complicated. "So I create this diversion, and you think it will give me the distraction I need to get out of here without being followed?"

"Again, I don't know. It's our best bet. If someone is looking for a Paris Beaufont to watch, we give them one who is over the top that no one can take their eyes off."

She sighed. "I'm not sure if I like that part of the plan."

He blinked. "Well, the thing is that you might not like it, but you can't ignore that it will get people's attention, which is what you want, right?"

"Yes," she said in a monotone.

"So we do it," he stated with determination.

"Yeah, I guess." She pointed, then paused. "So I only have to follow your spellwork on this to create it, and you tell it what to say, right?"

He nodded. "I think so. It's a robot in a way, so it only can say prescribed messages." Faraday turned his pad of paper he'd been working on. "I have some phrases I've been working on and need your quick endorsement. What do you think?"

Paris squinted at the squirrel's writing and winced, reading, "'The squirrel is master.' 'I'm dumb, dumb. Just listen to the squirrel.' 'I eat cheese curds, but the squirrel knows everything.'"

Paris planted her fists on her hips and pursed her lips. "Seriously, you're going to have full access to make me sound like whatever you want, and these are the liberties you're taking?"

Faraday innocently turned his pad around and pretended to glance at it. "You don't like?"

"Fare…"

"Okay, I might make you sound like a dumb human…"

"I was thinking that if you were making my doppelgänger do things that it would make me as an actual person sound insulting."

He waved her off. "Of course. A misunderstanding. I got it. You want to sound not dumb while I sound smart."

"Fare..." she repeated.

"Okay," he groaned, tearing off the sheet of paper and getting rid of it. "You want to sound like you, and I sound like me... which means a quiet rodent who does nothing."

"Faraday, this distraction is supposed to take the notice off me so I can get out of the building. That's all. It's not a glory moment for you. It's not anything but a diversion."

He nodded. "You're right. I won't make you look like my slave at any point, even if I can control your speech."

Paris leaned down and regarded the squirrel with a severe expression. "Seriously, you'll make my doppelgänger do and say whatever you want. If you make me regret this, I will turn your front half into a purse and your back half into a hat."

"I don't think there's that much of me for either," he squeaked.

"Then don't mess this up or I'll stretch you to make both."

He nodded as Paris finished the doppelgänger spell. She nodded at him when it was complete.

CHAPTER FIFTY-SIX

First Floor Stairwell, FGA Tower, New York City, New York

It was impressive magic, Paris had to admit. Faraday's spell was pure genius. After his little trick of trying to make her sound dumb, she wasn't admitting that to him. Instead, she simply pursed her lips in quiet appreciation.

He folded his arms like a gangster rodent and nodded proudly too.

"She looks pretty convincing." Paris checked out the holographic projection of herself that stood straight in front of them in the stairwell. She wore what Paris was wearing and had the same proud expression.

"Yeah, she does," Faraday said proudly.

A moment later, the doppelgänger Paris said, "Yeah, she does." She'd impersonated Faraday's tone and all, sounding exactly like him.

The real Paris propped her hands on her hips. "Okay, you can't mess this up. Whatever you say, this fake Paris will say. So speak quietly and diligently. Mostly stay out of sight. But also be in view in case anyone wonders where my squirrel is. They might think I'm a fake if they don't see you."

215

"So be seen, but not in the way. Speak, but not loudly. Be and don't be. Not at all confusing."

"Shut it," Paris admonished.

"You see why our relationship is complicated, right?"

"Do you have this, Faraday? I'm leaving you in charge of a real-life form of me. Whatever you say will come out of her mouth. I need to know I can trust you with this. It's big."

"I've got this, Pare. All I have to do is march her out into the lobby and make a scene so you have the chance to make a getaway. I'll be the best diversion ever."

Paris sighed. "That's what I'm scared of."

"Don't worry," Faraday stated. "I know how to control her also. When you created the spell, she linked to me. So I make a slight movement, and it's a big one for her. No biggie. I walk, and she walks."

Faraday started forward, and the fake Paris walked straight into a wall.

The real Paris rubbed her face like she was the one who hit it. "Can you try not to make me look like a dum-dum?"

"Are you talking about the real you or the fake you?" he asked, quite seriously. "Because I don't know how to make the real you do anything."

"Oh, never mind." She sighed. "Okay, are you ready to make your entrance into the lobby?"

He nodded. "Get ready to sneak out. Everyone is going to be staring at Paris Beaufont making a complete scene. It's going to be epic."

She groaned. "Oh, the things I do to save love…"

He grinned. "Yeah, you're pretty awesome… And about to be the talk of the FGA town."

CHAPTER FIFTY-SEVEN

Lobby, FGA Tower, New York City, New York

The fake Paris paraded through the stairwell door and past the bank of elevators. The real Paris watched from a crack in the door as Faraday scurried behind her doppelgänger into the lobby's center. Real Paris knew what would happen and why, but she still cringed inside.

The plan was sound though, and even she had to admit it. To get the attention off her, the person watching Paris had to think they were watching Paris. How could anyone look away from a person making such a scene?

Still, that knowledge didn't make it any easier when the fake Paris took off her leather jacket, whirled it over her head in front of Fairy Grounds, and yelled, "What do I have to do to get some real coffee? I'm dying here!"

Everyone in the lobby turned and politely paid attention to Paris like they thought the display might die down after that one explosion. Faraday and Paris had planned for it. That's why from the corners in the shadows, no one saw the squirrel scream, "Seriously, I need some brew that gets my demon blood boiling. I need some caffeine that makes my magician brain think. You fairies wouldn't know anything about that...would you?"

The fake Paris repeated those words seconds after Faraday. Real Paris was about to die from embarrassment. She'd never draw such unwanted attention to herself, pointing out the things she liked to downplay. However, she had to admit that the situation warranted it.

When security stalked out to apprehend the fake version of her, she had to admit that this whole thing had worked. The lobby was now full of onlookers. The person who was supposed to watch Paris for Jackson Zelle had to be in the crowd. If they knew that security had apprehended Paris, they wouldn't follow the real one when she left the building and portaled to Hollywood, California.

"Okay, little lady." A security guard ushered the hologram of Paris to a back area. "I think you've had a bit too much excitement and need to cool off. Your supervisor will come to see you once you've settled down."

When all eyes were watching the fake Paris Beaufont get escorted away, the genuine one quickly snuck out to do the real work.

CHAPTER FIFTY-EIGHT

Rooster Records, Hollywood, California

Although Paris wanted to tell herself that the most humiliating part of her job was over for this mission, she seriously doubted it. She knew what lay before her and it felt like a lot more embarrassment was in store. These were the things she did to save love.

Paris shook her head, shrugging off her ego as she started for the music recording company with nothing but her leather jacket and her magic to arm her. That was all she needed, though. Her trusty jacket was her confidence, her magic was her insurance, and she needed both, not one more than the other.

As she expected, there was a nice receptionist with a perky ponytail and a lip gloss smile when Paris entered the recording studio. Also as she expected, hiding out of immediate sight but still visible was a thug with broad shoulders, a nose he'd broken a few times, and a bad attitude.

"Hi, what are you here for?" the receptionist asked.

Paris smiled at the young mortal and decided not to use magic. She'd save that for when she needed it. Instead, she said, "I'm here to see that guy." She pointed a very discreet finger at the bouncer standing next to the big black door that might as well have had a big stop sign on it. However, Paris was getting through it.

The girl glanced at the bouncer. That's when Paris shot a tiny bit of persuasive magic at him. He looked confused. His beady, close-knit eyes glazed over before he nodded like he'd remembered something. Then he waved Paris over.

"Come on through, darling." He opened the door to the recording studio and allowed her through.

Paris breezed past, wondering if it would all be this easy. If so, she was going to stop by and get nachos with her mom, who lived down the street in West Hollywood, and maybe she'd get a nap.

However, as Paris waltzed down the bright hallway to the recording area, thinking about the toppings she'd get on her nachos, something sticky and reeking of magic caught her in an invisible net and pulled her up to the ceiling. The trap pinned her in place...ready for whoever had laid the ruse to find her.

CHAPTER FIFTY-NINE

Hallway Ceiling, Rooster Records, Hollywood, California

Paris was having a bad day…*Nah,* she thought. She was having the worst day. She tried to fight the invisible restraints that pinned her to the ceiling, looking down on things like a sitting duck, ready to be caught by whoever had set the magical trap.

What she figured out from her precarious position lying horizontally against the ceiling was that the trap would catch anyone with magic. It was also magical, created with a spell. That meant a fairy, a magician, or the like had set it.

Unlucky for Paris was that her trusty squirrel was watching over her doppelgänger. Also, the crafty spell had pinned her hands—she'd love to learn how. That meant the only tool Paris had at her disposal was her mouth, and usually, she only used that for persuading and insulting. That didn't leave her with any options, making the darkness set in.

Paris realized that she had no way of defending herself until whoever had trapped her cut her down. Then her mind raced with all the possibilities. She'd suspected that there was someone from the magical community behind Punch Line's spelled song since they were mortal. However, this cemented the whole thing.

Someone owned and operated Rooster Recording Studios, and they were behind this horrible song, *Heartbreak View*. They had her trapped. That didn't matter because once they cut her down, she would go after them with a vengeance. She wasn't going to give up until she stopped this person or organization who'd created so much misery through heartbreak.

However, to find out who was behind this, Paris would have to wait. Thankfully it didn't seem that would take long. A door at the back of the hallway opened, and a figure strode out. A man was whistling. A very attractive man...one she recognized. One who Paris had thought she could trust.

He didn't look up as he passed under her like he didn't know she was trapped there. He could have forgotten that he set the trap just as easily as he could've forgotten what his name was. He'd done that on multiple occasions.

Paris let out a hot breath, deciding it was fine to draw attention to herself. "King Rudolf Sweetwater, tell me why you've trapped me up here now!"

CHAPTER SIXTY

Hallway, Rooster Records, Hollywood, California

The king of the fae, who was also like Paris' godfather, glanced up and grimaced at her in confusion. Then he frowned like he didn't recognize her in that precarious position pinned to the ceiling. Then he did and grinned.

"Hey, Pare. Are you the new receptionist I ordered from the temp agency?" he asked, quite seriously. "If so, I'd prefer for you to sit at the front desk if that's okay…"

Paris sighed, used to dealing with King Rudolf's idiot ways. "No, I've been trapped here by some mysterious magic. Please tell me that it belongs to you and that you'll get me down."

He shook his head. "I didn't create any booby traps here in the hallway of Rooster Records." Then he laughed, covering his mouth. "I said booby."

"Can you please focus?" she asked. "Are you telling me you're in charge of this place? Rooster Records?"

He nodded. "Yeah, it's one of my many pet projects."

"But you didn't create this trap?"

He shook his head. "No, I would never."

"Then who did?"

"Well, I don't know. It would have to be someone who wanted to trap someone not supposed to be here so I'm guessing that's a discrimination spell." The fae rubbed his chin, musing on the problem. "There are mortals, fae, and fairies through here regularly, so if someone didn't want, say, magicians or halflings or what are you, hellish—"

"Demon," she corrected.

"Right," he chirped. "Your father is Satan."

"A demon bit my father." She lost patience as she tried to break her invisible restraints. "He's not hellish, and neither am I."

"I'm just saying that if you got tied up upon entering here, it would have to be something that sets you apart from the others," King Rudolf reasoned. "You see, mortals and fairies like me come through here but no one else."

"So if a magician came through here..." Paris wondered why they were still talking this out while she lay like a bat on the ceiling.

"I'm guessing they'd get tied up."

"This is your recording studio," Paris prodded. "So who did this?"

He shrugged. "Beats me. I can't know everything that goes on here, all the time. Or anything that goes on anywhere, most of the time. Or some of what goes on wherever when I'm not around. But also, nowhere—"

"Focus, King Rudolf!"

"Right. We should probably get you down. Then we can figure it out who set this trap."

"You think?"

King Rudolf reconsidered. "I don't know. Maybe you like it up there. Do you want to stay?"

"I will kill you in your sleep," she threatened.

He gave her a fond look. "You're so much like your mother

that it's scary. Now hold on tight. By that, I mean get ready to fall to the floor fast."

The king of the fae twirled his finger. Paris' invisible bindings immediately released her. She fell to the carpet and landed in a crouch. Frustration and adrenaline rushed through her.

CHAPTER SIXTY-ONE

Hallway, Rooster Records, Hollywood, California

Paris was pretty sure that she was close to clocking the king of the fae, but to her shock, he turned surprisingly fast upon her touching the floor, not giving her a chance to hit him. He strode back to the office he'd come from. His urgency showed in his steps.

"Where are you going?" Paris rushed after him.

He didn't look back. "To my office. You better follow. It sounds like we have a detective case to crack. Get out your telescope, Watson."

"Don't you mean magnifying glass, Holmes?" Paris followed the fae into a very posh office with lots of gold embossed records, leather furniture, and even a hot tub.

He shrugged once more, closing the door behind them. "Honestly, I don't watch *CSI*, so you tell me the lingo they use."

"Never mind." Paris was confused. She looked around the strange office. "I need to understand things, and I don't get what's going on here. You, King Rudolf, own Rooster Records?"

"Correct." He nodded and grinned good-naturedly.

"But you didn't set the trap that put me on the ceiling?" she continued questioning.

"Correct. Impressive magic, but not my style. I prefer to tie people up with rope, and usually just my wife."

"That's weird." Paris shook off the admission. "So are you aware that the band Punch Line is recording a song that breaks hearts using magic?"

"Punch Who?" King Rudolf looked confused.

"So that's a no?" she questioned.

When he scratched his head, Paris decided to dig deeper. "Is this recording studio something you're involved in?"

"I only wanted to learn how to play the piano," King Rudolf confessed. "I bought it, and all the equipment and all the labels that went with it, and I've had zero time to learn anything because all day long, I have to sign contracts and there's all this legal mumbo-jumbo and whatnot. It's very annoying."

Paris let out a long, slow breath, wondering if anyone would care if she killed the man before her. She realized that his three children might…or his kingdom. "You realize you could have simply taken piano lessons, right? You didn't have to buy a recording studio."

He threw up his arms and sighed. "Well, now you tell me! Where were you several million dollars ago?"

Paris put a hand figuratively down on the part of her that was prone to murder. "This recording studio has been releasing a song that's breaking people's hearts. So to confirm, you know nothing about that or can offer any insights at all?"

He shook his head.

Paris knew that King Rudolf was a lot of things. He was dumb. He was annoying. He was the bane of the Beaufonts' existence. However, he wasn't nefarious on any level. So she believed him when he said he didn't know.

"Okay, then when I get to the bottom of this, will you help me shut down the song that's causing pain?" she asked.

"Of course. All you have to do is tell me what to do. Like, step by step. Tell me like I'm a toddler. One who doesn't follow directions very well."

"Okay, first thing, I need to know who is behind all this. Someone set a trap in the studio, maybe suspecting that the House of Fourteen or FGA or someone would come to shut down the song at some point. Whoever is behind this had to think that a magician or Saint Valentine would figure it out," Paris mused, chewing on her lip.

"So you don't know who the producer is for Punch Line? Or can you figure it out? I'm guessing it has to be a magical person who put that booby trap on the ceiling to catch any magician or whatever who entered this place without permission? Someone who was coming to shut down the song. Me, of course…" Paris sighed.

However, Rudolf snickered. "You said booby."

"I need you to focus," she warned.

King Rudolf shook off the laughter. "Of course. I don't know who the producer is. There are so many different bands and their personnel who come through here. I mostly sit back here, sign things, and beg people to teach me to play the piano."

"Again, you realize that you're rich and can hire an expert, right?" she asked.

"Now you're telling me this," he huffed.

"So someone is working with Punch Line who we need to stop," Paris said mostly to herself. "Can you at least look into the contracts for the band while I talk to the lead singer? I hope they're here, or maybe at least you can tell me where to find them."

"Of course, I'll look into it for you." Rudolf glanced at his desk where a logbook was sitting. "You're in luck. This Punch Line band is on the schedule for right now. They're recording their new hit or a remix. You'll want to wait until the red light is off or you'll interrupt recording."

Although much of what had happened wasn't what Paris had planned for, she'd come prepared for this next part. She pulled noise-canceling earbuds from her jacket and smiled. "I think I'd very much like to interrupt this recording before it gets too far and does too much damage."

CHAPTER SIXTY-TWO

Rooster Records, Hollywood, California

Leaving King Rudolf to dig into who was behind Punch Line, she cautiously snuck back out into the hallway. Thankfully it was empty, and hopefully, there weren't any other traps ready to pin her to the ceiling again. King Rudolf promised to come looking for her if she didn't return soon.

It wasn't hard for Paris to figure out where the recording studio was—the room marked by the "On Air" sign outside the door. Currently, the light was off, which meant that Paris wouldn't be interrupting the recording. Still, she kept her noise-canceling earbuds in just in case.

When Paris opened the door to the recording studio, she was ready to face the villain behind this whole mess. She'd prepared to disarm any bouncers that attempted to hold her back. What Paris hadn't expected to find was a sobbing musician, all alone.

The man she recognized as Archer Finch from the video of *Heartbreak View* was sitting on an amp and looking at his phone with tears streaming down his cheeks. Around him were abandoned instruments like a guitar, bass, drums, and piano. Behind the performance area was a clear glass window where technical things like recording and sound engineering happened. Thankfully it was empty too, leaving it only Archer Finch and Paris.

Maybe her luck was turning around, Paris thought as she closed the door to the studio and softly cleared her throat.

Archer Finch quickly wiped the tears from his face, turning around and putting his back to Paris. "Oh, is the break over already? I thought y'all were leaving to get dinner…"

Paris smiled inwardly, grateful that the rest of the band and production team seemed to be gone, giving her a chance to talk to the lead singer.

"Hey, Archer Finch. I'm Paris Beaufont, and I'm here to see you about an extremely important matter."

The guy with a black ponytail and puffy face spun, his eyes suddenly burning with anger. "How did you get in here? Will you all never stop? I don't want you."

Paris nodded, conscious not to do anything that seemed threatening. She held up her hands as if in surrender. "I get it. I'm not here to harass you. I'm close friends with King Rudolf Sweetwater, the owner of Rooster Records. He let me in here. I need to talk to you about this song, *Heartbreak View*. You have to stop singing it."

He rolled his eyes and slid his phone into his black skinny jeans. "That's not going to happen. That song is making us a killing."

"That's the thing. It's killing love all over the world. I've heard it, and it's the reason you're miserable. It's making lovers all over the world miserable."

He shook his head. "No, I wrote the song because I was already miserable. The rest of the world is sentenced to the same fate as me now. If I can't have love, why should anyone else?"

Paris got it now. That made perfect sense…well, in a corrupt, very sad way. Of course, the heartbroken lover wouldn't want anyone to have the romance denied to him. Of course, he'd want others to feel as desolate as him. Misery loved company.

To get to the bottom of this, Paris would have to be a proper fairy godmother. She would have to repair the rift between Archer Finch and Ella Sparrow. Only then could she get him to quit singing the song because someone who was madly in love wouldn't be able to sing a song about heartbreak. She grinned victoriously inside, thinking that if she could reverse things, she could undo all this damage created by *Heartbreak View*.

If Paris could get Archer and Ella back together, maybe he'd sing a romantic ballad, and that would make people fall in love. All she had to do was fix whatever had gone wrong between the couple. How hard could that be...

CHAPTER SIXTY-THREE

Recording Studio, Rooster Records, Hollywood, California

"Archer, will you tell me what happened between you and Ella?" Paris kept her tone sensitive as she calmly approached him.

The rockstar backed up as his eyes narrowed. "Who are you?"

"I told you. I'm Paris Beaufont, but more importantly, I work for the Fairy Godmother Agency, and I'm here to help you."

He threw up his arms, and Paris spotted the tattoo of the lyrics on his arm. They weren't glowing as they did on the music video, probably because he wasn't singing them. *Such strange magic*, Paris thought.

"You can't help me. Why do you think I'm doing this? And fairy godmother…" He laughed coldly, shaking his head. "That can't be real."

"We are," Paris said with conviction. "Our job is exactly that. To help people with love."

Another hollow laugh fell from his mouth. "Love for me is over. There's nothing you or anyone can do."

Paris pointed at the tattoo on his arm. "That's magic. You know that, right?"

Archer glanced down at his arm and shrugged. "Yeah, so? The song would be a hit even if we didn't use magic."

"It would," Paris reasoned. "Every song Punch Line releases is a hit. However, the magic is making it break people's hearts."

"So?" he argued, anger simmering in his eyes.

This guy was tortured. He was hurt to the core. However, Paris didn't think he was a lost cause. He wasn't evil. Archer was lashing out at the world that he thought had hurt him. It instantly reminded her of a quote from Stephen Crane's *Open Boat* when the crew of a ship got stranded at sea.

"When it occurs to a man that nature does not regard him as important, and that she feels she would not maim the universe by disposing of him, he at first wishes to throw bricks at the temple, and he hates deeply the fact that there are no bricks and no temple."

Archer Finch believed that he would feel better by maiming the world he thought broke him, but he only felt worse, Paris realized. He'd sunk his ship by allowing the negativity inside him. *Not only can water float a boat; it can also sink it,* Paris thought, remembering the Chinese proverb.

She felt very philosophical and thought it had to do with the importance and inspiration of the mission.

Love was sinking Archer's ship, but it could as easily be what made him float. She had to help him fix the leak.

"As an agent for Fairy Godmother Agency, I have magic similar to what someone else used to spell your song, *Heartbreak View,*" Paris explained. "That magic can fix things for you. It so happens that you've used it to break things even more. If you allow me to help you, I think I can mend things for you. Then if you sing from a place of happiness and love, think of how much more success you'll have. More importantly, you'll feel better. Not worse, like you do now."

Archer's eyes softened slightly, and his expression seemed to say, "Yeah? Keep talking."

Paris had hit on something. Archer had the magical tattoo put on to get revenge on love, thinking that would make him feel better. As always was the case with revenge, it made the person feel worse.

Vengeance was a vicious cycle that only led to more destructive emotions. The only way to stop it was through love. Forgiveness was the cure for the feelings related to betrayal. One truly only had to love their way out of something, but telling the scarred and heartbroken that was about like asking them to pick up the very weapon that had wounded them and carry it for the rest of their days.

"Please tell me, why did you and Ella Sparrow break up?" Paris kept her voice low.

The mention of Ella's name made Archer flinch like it burned his soul to hear it. To think of her. To know that she was out in the same world as him, living life but without him.

He threw up his arms, the crazed anger suddenly returning to his eyes. "I wish I knew. She wouldn't tell me. Just said that we were better off apart. Nothing I could do or say would make her talk. E-E-Ella…" He stumbled on her name. Emotions almost broke loose on his face.

"She won't return my calls. I went to see her a few times at her work, but she disappeared. It's not like I'm someone who can sneak into her place of business. I can't even get to the front door without a mob crowding around me."

Paris nodded, realizing that this would be a bit more complicated. However, that didn't deter her. "So what if I go to Ella and find out her side of the story for you? I don't know that I can fix things, but I can try. I have resources and people and we all really, really want to help you."

"Why?" Despairing soberness filled his voice.

"Because I heard the lyrics you wrote for Ella," Paris explained. "Even without the magic that song is incredibly powerful. You don't write those kinds of songs except when it's true love. I want to help you two be together. If you have the power to break up the world, I want to believe that you, the lead singer of Punch Line, have the power to bring it back together."

"What do you want out of it?" Archer asked. "You want a cut of the profits? The rights to the song I sing about it?"

Something occurred to Paris, but she didn't rush into that line of questioning yet. First, she still needed to calm Archer down. Disarm him. Get him to trust her. Then she could get the important information she needed for the next part of this mission.

"I don't want anything of yours," Paris stated honestly. "I definitely don't want money. I want you to be happy. I want you to stop singing the song that's harming your soul and the rest of the world as well. At the end of the day, my job at FGA is to bring love to the world. If I want anything, it's that."

He looked at her like she wasn't real. Like before his very eyes, she'd turned into a Pegasus or a unicorn. "Who are you? Where did you come from?"

Paris blinked at him, wondering if he'd done too many rock-star drugs and had forgotten her introductions earlier. Before she could ask, he shook his head and continued.

"In my life, in this business, everyone wants something if it benefits them," Archer stated. "It's rare to meet someone like you who wants the world to have love simply for the reason that it's good and the right thing."

Paris smiled. "Well, that's what we do at FGA. At least, that's what we're supposed to be doing. Also, I'm a Beaufont, and we can't rest unless we help the world to be better."

"Well, Paris Beaufont, I don't know where you came from, but I hope you can help me because what I've been doing isn't... You're right. Singing that song only makes the pain worse. I don't sing it anymore, but I'm not sure if I can get out of it."

"How?" Paris was grateful that she could finally uncover the next part of this mystery. "How did you get that tattoo? Who is behind this?"

Archer drew in a heavy breath, looking at the tattooed words on his arm. "This man came to me. He said that there was a way to make our next song even bigger than any other. The last few songs I'd written and released with Punch Line were about my breakup with Ella. The man asked if I could write the most gut-wrenching one yet. I could, and I wrote *Heartbreak View*. He then supplied a special ink and said that when I sang the tattooed words, it would create a spell that would break the hearts of people around the world."

"You did it." Paris kept any judgment out of her voice, only a statement to confirm.

He nodded in shame. "The guy said that heartbreak sells. He said, 'Those who are broken always want a song that drives the dagger deeper into their wounds.'"

Paris narrowed her eyes. "Who was this man? A magician? A fairy? An elf? He had magic, right?"

"I think so," Archer answered. "I mean, he told us the ink was full of magic, and at that point, I didn't care. I don't know his name. He signed the contract Mr. J."

"Hmmm…" Paris mused, thinking that wasn't enough to draw any reasonable conclusions. Faraday would say that it was simply correlational evidence that would get one into trouble if they relied solely upon it. Mr. J could refer to Jackson Zelle, Agent Josh Emerald, or Agent Barney Jasper. It wouldn't be smart to assume based on this limited information.

"I never got a good look at the man's face," Archer went on. "He had a black hat on."

"Oh?" Paris' voice rose an octave.

"Yeah. He wore a black suit."

That could've been any of the agents at FGA, Paris reasoned. Or it could be anyone, anywhere… It simply wasn't enough to go on.

"This contract you signed. Rooster Records will have it, right?"

"Yeah, they should. That's the other thing, even if I don't play the song anymore, *Heartbreak View*, it's still playing on streaming services and the radio."

Paris nodded. "Leave that part up to me. Don't record the remix today. Don't sing the song anymore. I'll talk to Ella. As soon as I can, I'll get back to you."

Paris made for the door, ready to have King Rudolf pull the tracks of *Heartbreak View* from all the channels. The recording studio would have access to that. By the time Mr. J found out about it, it would hopefully be too late. This person, whoever he was, wasn't going to push a contract that would cause his identity to become known. He was going to skulk off into the dark, knowing someone had foiled him.

The question would then be, who was this Mr. J and why did he want to create heartbreak so badly? He'd told Archer that it sold. That, "Those who are broken always want a song that drives the dagger deeper into their wounds." Paris had to believe there was something deeper for this criminal breaking hearts. It couldn't only be money. It sounded like it was similar to Archer's motivation. That if he couldn't have love, no one got to.

Mr. J would have to wait, though. First, Paris would find Ella Sparrow and complete the next part of the plan. She had to get the two star-crossed lovers back together. Only once Archer Finch sang love songs would he repair all the heartbreak worldwide. Paris believed that not only could Punch Line do that, but they could create more love than before this whole mess started. If they did things the right way, love would benefit from this instead of taking a massive hit.

CHAPTER SIXTY-FOUR

Great Electronics Superstore, Hollywood, California

The last place Paris expected to find the ex-girlfriend of the hottest rockstar in the world was at an electronics store. However, according to the information she'd received, that's where Ella Sparrow worked as a floor manager for the retail chain. However, this only endeared this girl more to Paris since her mother had spent her formative years working in an electronics repair shop in West Hollywood.

That store had belonged to Uncle John, who was the one who raised Paris most of her life. It was the small, unassuming shop that repaired toasters and vacuums where Liv Beaufont had found herself during a very confusing time in her life. That's where she'd made a fresh start, finding solace in electronics instead of magic. Later that would lead to discoveries in magitech and so forth.

Anyway, Paris realized that judging where anyone worked was ill-advised. That was where people started. Who knew where they would end up—like Liv Beaufont, pretty much running the magical world as a Warrior for the House of Fourteen.

Although Paris was making an assumption, she thought she

spotted Ella Sparrow once entering the television section of the store. Large screens all broadcast the same football game. Many guys were standing around, watching the televisions like this was a sports bar and not a retail place.

Besides the distracted customers, a few employees wore blue polo shirts. All of them were men who were either skinny, overweight, had bad skin, too much hair, or not enough. Then there was Ella Sparrow—or at least who Paris thought was her.

The only female employee was in her mid-twenties and had dark brown dreadlocks, a nose ring, and a sleeve of tattoos on her right arm. The striking part about the woman, which drew Paris' gaze, was her contagious smile as she helped a customer. She seemed like the type who laughed easily and often and made others do the same.

Taking the spot behind the customer, Paris waited until she'd pointed them in the right direction. When they strode off, Paris smiled at the woman, reading her name badge. She was the right person—Archer Finch's ex-girlfriend.

"Hi, I need help with something," Paris began.

"I'm the right person to ask." Ella's eyes twinkled as she continued to smile. She appeared as though she wanted to help.

"I need to know why you broke up with Archer Finch."

Yes, Paris could've been a bit more diplomatic in her approach. She could have tiptoed around the question. She could've used a spell to soften Ella. However, she didn't have time for all that.

Archer couldn't hold off on recording the remix of *Heartbreak View* for long. The band would be skeptical. As soon as Mr. J found out that Rooster Records was pulling the song from channels, there might be trouble. Paris needed to work out a solution as fast as possible.

However, the look of fury that replaced Ella's cheerful expression told Paris that she hadn't made a fast friend with her instant prying.

"How dare you?" Ella seethed, shaking her head, her long dreads knocking her in the shoulder. "Who put you up to this? Was it Archer? Or are you one of his stalkers who want to know about our past? When will you tramps stop?"

Paris offered a sympathetic look. "I work for Fairy Godmother Agency, and I want to help. We create love at the agency, and it's come to my attention that the upset with you and Archer Finch has led to a lot of heartbreak. It's my job to fix it."

To Paris' surprise, this softened Ella, although she was confused. "You work for fairy godmothers?"

"Technically, they work for me," Paris corrected. "But yes. We promote love. In this case, we're trying to avoid things that detract from love, like Punch Line's newest hit single."

"Yeah, I heard about that stupid song Archie wrote." Ella started for a display, pretending to be checking the inventory.

"Have you heard it?" Paris questioned.

Ella shook her head. "I quit listening to that band's music when I quit him."

"Look, I know this is none of my business," Paris began. "But I do work for FGA, and we have a big problem. That song is creating all sorts of heartbreak all over the world. If I could understand why you broke up with Archer, maybe I can fix it. That's my job after—"

"Fix it?" Ella interrupted, whipping around to face Paris. "You can't fix someone who's irreparably broken."

"You mean Archer? I get that he's sad about you two, but if—"

"Oh no, he's broken because he is at his core."

Paris drew in a breath, studying the girl before her. "Archer said that you wouldn't tell him why you were breaking up with him. You simply said you were better off apart. Is that because you didn't think he could be 'fixed?'" She put air quotes on the last word.

"You get it a lot better than I think he would have. Yeah, what was the point in telling him that his rockstar lifestyle was never going to work for me? Sure, I'd show up at a gig on my night off, but that was hardly ever because most of the time he was in Amsterdam or Berlin or Madrid or New York."

She threw her arms wide, indicating the electronics super-store. "I work here. This is my life. It's not glamorous, but it suits me. It allows me to be home in time to take care of my grand-mother and her Yorkies and see my nieces and go to college. That's what matters to me. I can't live the rockstar lifestyle he wanted for me."

"That's what he asked you to do?" Paris was piecing it together.

"Yeah, Archie wanted me to give up my life and be some roadie. I told him I couldn't. For the longest time, we made it work. I'd see him when he came to town, but that was usually from the front row of his show. Then I'd have to wait in line to spend any time with my boyfriend afterward. Standing there watching girls throw themselves at him night after night got to be too much."

The girl went quiet, and Paris felt her frustration. She'd opened up easily because, in truth, this was something Ella had wanted to confess for a long time, but she hadn't and for a very specific reason.

"You never told Archer because if you did—"

"It would make me look insecure. There's no future for Archie and me. My life is here. He's a rockstar. The fact that we made it as long as we did, well, that's something to behold. At the end of the day, I can't stand knowing that he's flirting with girls every night and doing who knows what with them. It was better if I let him go and we ended things without him thinking of me as the possessive girlfriend who was jealous of all the tramps throwing themselves at him."

Paris wanted to dive into excuse after excuse for Archer. However, she couldn't find one. It was reasonable for Ella to feel how she did, given the situation. However, it wasn't fair to Archer.

Not only was this problem more complex than Paris had envisioned, but it reminded her how complicated love was. It was never as easy as throwing two compatible people together. People had two different lives that weren't always compatible, even if they were. Plus, there were egos, insecurities, and a bunch of other factors that made love difficult.

Paris wanted to believe at her core that true love, real love, could overcome even the biggest of obstacles.

She hoped this was true for Archer Finch and Ella Sparrow.

CHAPTER SIXTY-FIVE

First Floor, Security Center, FGA Tower, New York City, New York

There was a lot to do to fix things for Archer and Ella and all the heartbreak their breakup had created. None of that could happen until Paris did one important thing. That was to get her doppelgänger out of security's custody, and more importantly, free Faraday from his supervising job.

For the first time, Paris put on the blue fairy godmother gown before stepping through the barrier to FGA Plaza. With the hood up, covering her face, she hurried to the Tower entrance.

Thankfully it was a chilly evening in New York City, and many of the fairy godmothers had been making use of their hoods to keep their ears and cheeks warm after entering the drafty lobby.

That gave Paris the coverage she needed to sneak across the space into the security area where the guards would be holding her doppelgänger. She still couldn't believe what she'd said in public, bringing so much attention to herself in front of everyone.

She reasoned that they were all gossiping about her anyway, so at least she'd fed straight into their rumors with her outburst.

The cause was worth it. Paris had to get out and investigate Rooster Records, Punch Line, and Archer Finch without whoever Jackson Zelle stuck on her tail to spy.

She'd been able to do that and needed to move on to the next phase of the plan—which she had no idea what it would be. Before that, Paris had to figure out how to continue sneaking around without being watched. Whoever was spying on her could be Mr. J or working for Mr. J. If they didn't want her to succeed in stopping heartbreak, they might try to sabotage her efforts.

The last thing Paris wanted to believe was that someone at FGA was responsible for bringing love down. However, it wasn't completely far-fetched.

What had Lee said at Crying Cat Bakery when they'd been discussing the wands that FGA had the monopoly on? She'd likened FGA to gaming clubs, saying, "They have about as much interest in love as the casinos do. Both make a lot more money on the lost and lonely, but they dress things up all romantically so they can break hearts and take everyone's money."

For some reason, it suddenly seemed even more relevant. Especially after learning that Mr. J believed heartbreak sold and kept people coming back for more—making it lucrative.

It was sick that someone would want to profit off others' pain and loss, but there were all types in the world. The most villainous were the ones who tried to bring love down, afraid of it at their very core.

Paris shook this off, remembering that she didn't have any evidence. She simply had to keep her eyes open and pay attention. Mr. J would reveal himself in time, she hoped. In the meantime, she had to undo what he'd done to sabotage love.

Right outside the security station's custody holding area, Paris threw off the fairy godmother's blue gown where no one could see. Then she snapped her fingers, making her doppelgänger disappear from the other side of the door as she walked through it.

The lone security guard reading a thriller paperback looked up when she entered. He did a double-take, looking between the real Paris and an empty chair in the corner of the warm room.

"Where... How... What are you doing there?" The man pointed at the chair where Paris spied Faraday hiding in the shadows underneath. "You were sitting in that seat."

Paris shook her head, striding over and taking the seat. "You should ask your supervisor for a day off. They're working you too hard. I asked you if I could go to the bathroom and you said that was fine."

"I did?"

"Well, you sort of muttered," Paris amended. "You weren't able to pull your eyes off your book. What are you reading?"

"Oh, it's this really good space thriller about a guy who... Wait, I wouldn't have let you out of my sight. Not when your boss was just here and told me not to."

"Well, you're not supposed to go in the women's restroom, so I think you made the right call letting me wee-wee on my own," Paris joked. "I'm not a prisoner, even if Agent Jasper said I wasn't allowed out on my own. I simply had an outburst. You would too if you were addicted to caffeine and couldn't get a good cup of joe. Not to mention that it's only my second day and this place is stressful."

The security guard nodded in understanding. "Yeah, it's a lot at first. Don't tell anyone, but many fairies crack the first week. Usually, that means they cry a lot, but you're half-magician so I get you having a different reaction."

A confused look crossed his face. "No, I get that it's a lot to keep up with, but your boss, the guy here earlier, was Agent Emerald. Maybe you'll talk to him when he returns so you can get out of here and I can finish my book."

"Agent Emerald isn't my boss," Paris argued.

The guy shrugged, returning his attention to his book. "Whatever. Like I care."

"I hear you made quite the scene," a voice said from the doorway. Paris glanced up to find Agent Barney Jasper regarding her with mild disinterest before he returned his attention to the device in his hand.

"It's been a long couple of days," Paris said in reply.

Agent Jasper nodded. "Yeah, most fairies cry during their first week."

The security guard pointed in his direction, smirking at Paris. "I told you."

"Well, I'm not a fairy," Paris stated and added, "Well, not entirely."

"Yes, thanks for reminding us of that fact, once again." Agent Jasper pivoted and waved for Paris to follow. "Walk with me."

Paris sprang to her feet, glancing back at Faraday briefly, waving for him to follow too.

Paris easily caught up with the tall man. They walked briskly in silence for a moment, Agent Jasper scrolling through his phone and making people in the lobby move to avoid running into him rather than him swerving not to hit them.

"So what are we saying to the higher-ups about why you had such an outburst?" he asked in a bored voice like he was simultaneously reading an email.

"How about that I acted out because it's come to my attention that my department has no budget and no magical reserves? I wonder if that's a direct result of *you* not wanting me to be successful and quit or because you want to sabotage my efforts so I fail and the department gets cut."

Agent Barney Jasper smiled at this, although it appeared that he wasn't listening, his attention mostly on his phone as he strode for the bank of elevators. "Your department doesn't have any money because budgets get cut like this place is a barbershop at a boot camp for entry-level soldiers. Magic isn't something that we have in great supply."

"Yeah, but what about the Practical Love department?" Paris asked as the three of them boarded the elevator.

"What about it?" Agent Jasper asked.

"They have budgets and magic," she argued.

"They make money," he stated.

"With bogus matches!"

He yawned, putting his phone into his pocket, although he appeared to miss it instantly. "You run the Casual Romance department. Don't delude yourself into thinking that you're making any matches of great significance.

"Over time, it's been decided that this department isn't that important. Each year we lose a line item on the budget. I have to devote funds to the places I think they have to go. That's all there is to it. You want to be an agent here, then fine. Stay out of my way. Stay out of my hair. Don't keep making outbursts that make me look like I'm not managing my agents."

Paris got off on the third floor and figured that would be it, but Agent Jasper disembarked with her.

"For the love of the angels, if you can stop reminding everyone that you have demon blood, that would make me have a lot fewer headaches."

"I do have demon blood," Paris argued, striding into her department, surprised that Agent Jasper was still walking with her. She reasoned he had more threats to make. "And I have a lot of ideas for how I can turn Casual Romance around."

"I don't think…" Agent Jasper's voice trailed away as he took in the newly renovated department space. "What happened here?"

"I gave Isha and Holly the job of cleaning up the space and making it more conducive to our work," Paris stated. "They sold off the old furniture and used the funds to buy this."

"Conducive to your work?" His eyes were wide with surprise

as he took in the area that was organized and fashionable and appealing to the eye.

"Yeah, I figured that even if you don't give us any money, we can use magic to coordinate matches."

"You don't have any magic." Agent Jasper stopped as he took in the sight of the large bottle full of dazzling pink magic.

"As a magician and probably as a demon, I have huge, I mean simply gigantic stores of magic," Paris boasted. "I don't need a wand to direct or conserve my magic. I just eat a burrito and bam! I have enough to fill a bottle to supply my department."

"Then why were you complaining about not having any magic in your reserves?" he seethed.

"Because as my manager, I thought your job was to supply me with what I need to be successful with this department."

He drew in a breath, looking like he was trying to count himself down from murdering Paris. She knew the feeling. "I have a lot of jobs, but currently, it's not ensuring you have decorating money or magical reserves so your fairy godmothers can make two people bump into each other and have a superficial interaction. My job is to focus on the departments that can make a difference. From my experience, that's not Casual Romance. Lay low, keep the attention off yourself, and don't make trouble for me. Do you think you can manage that?"

The only thing that Paris could manage at that point was to say, "Sure."

Under her breath, as Agent Punk Face retreated to the elevators, she mumbled, "No, I've just started making trouble for you. So watch out."

CHAPTER SIXTY-SIX

Third Floor, Casual Romance Department, FGA Tower, New York City, New York

"Man, that guy is a real pill." Holly strode out from the kitchen, eating yogurt from a plastic container.

"Yeah, it wouldn't have killed him to say something nice about our décor." Isha was drinking a green protein shake.

Paris tilted her head, eyeing her employees. "So you two were hanging out there eavesdropping and not going to come to my defense or shower me with praise?"

Holly plopped down on the oversized pillows. "Oh, right. I tell him that I matched six different couples today, and he'll reset his expectations. He'll probably reassign me to a different department, thinking my skills can be better put toward something useful."

"You matched six couples today?" Paris was impressed.

"Well, one set were some squirrels," Holly stated. "But yeah."

"Squirrels count." Faraday scurried over and looked between the two women, Isha having taken a seat on the opposite set of pillows. "Are there any snacks in the kitchen?"

"Yeah, there are peanut butter protein bars," Isha stated. "They are simply the best thing in the world, all creamy and nutty and chock-full of protein."

"He's allergic to nuts," Paris pointed out.

"There are double-stuffed Oreos," Holly offered. "They're stale and so sweet that they'll make your teeth hurt. And they'll go straight to your butt."

Faraday flicked his tail. "I don't have so much of a problem in the rear-end department. Usually, I have to figure out how to keep my winter weight on."

Holly stuck her spoon in her yogurt container and grimaced at the squirrel. "I hate that for you."

"Order yourself a sandwich," Paris offered, handing the squirrel her phone. "And check to ensure it's not bugged again, would you?"

"You were bugged?" Isha finished her protein shake but didn't appear to have enjoyed it a single bit.

Paris nodded. "Yeah, and it was probably Agent Punk Face. That guy seems to have it out for me, and I think he's in cahoots with Jackson Zelle."

Holly shook her head. "Oh, you met that guy. All he cares about is money."

"In his defense, he is the director of finance," Faraday muttered, tapping on Paris' phone. "Your phone looks clear for now."

"I'm glad you two are here." Paris sat next to the others. "I have an important mission, and I need all hands on deck. There's a band called Punch Line and—"

The scream that shot out of Holly's mouth cut Paris off. "Yeah, talk about the best band ever!"

"So you've heard of them," Paris said in a rush. "You haven't listened to their newest single, right?"

Holly leaned forward. "They have a new single?" She jerked and glared at Isha. "*They have a new single.* We must hear it!"

Paris held up her hand, halting the raving women. "Stop.

Don't listen to it. Hopefully, you can't even find it. It's spelled to break people's hearts and has been breaking up couples."

Holly threw herself back. "Oh, man. I don't care. I must hear it."

"You won't, and no," Paris stated. "Our job is to figure out how to get Archer Finch back with his girlfriend, Ella Sparrow. Then they—"

"Are you insane?" Holly's blue eyes widened. "Archer is single? We're not hooking him up with that hussy. If I book an appointment right now, I can get my hair extension fixed. Then we arrange for Archer to run into me, maybe at his concert or the food bank where I volunteer."

Isha laughed, doubling over. "Volunteer. You're funny."

"I volunteer," Holly argued.

"You volunteer complaints about everything in your life," Isha fired back.

Paris snapped her fingers, regaining their attention. "Hearts broken worldwide. Nefarious magic. Love emergency. Can we focus?"

Holly sighed with defeat. Isha nodded, smiling.

"Someone spelled Punch Line's newest song," Paris stated. "I talked to Archer, and he's—"

"You spoke with Archer!" Holly interrupted. "Seriously, where was I, and will you hook your best friend up with him?"

Paris turned to Faraday. "Do you want to meet Archer Finch? I'll arrange the meeting."

He shook his head, picking his toppings on his sandwich to be delivered. "I'm good. But thanks."

"Okay, well, as I was saying," Paris muttered. "Archer has agreed not to play the song in question, *Heartbreak View*. But I promised to get him back with Ella. Also, I've had my uncle, King Rudolf Sweetwater—"

"Your uncle is the king of the fae!" Isha yelled. "I've had a crush on that man since I could talk. Not only is he the dreamiest man on this planet but he's so smart—"

"Okay, you've obviously never met King Rudolf," Paris interrupted. "No one who has would ever call him smart. He's sweet and funny, but not because he's trying. He's special, like a blind chimpanzee on a bike, but he's not smart.

"Anyway, yes, he's my pseudo uncle, a godfather of sorts. The man has more power than he probably should, and with that, he's able to pull down the song from all streaming services and channels, although it will take a bit to erase all instances of the song. For that, we'll need some techie squirrel…"

Paris looked around like she was lost and searching for something.

Faraday lowered her phone and nodded. "Yeah, fine. I can create a reverse system that goes and finds downloads of the song and deletes them from systems. It's going to take forty… maybe fifty minutes."

Paris shook her head and rolled her eyes. "I swear, it's so hard to find good help these days."

"Ha-ha." Faraday lifted the phone. "I need bread and cheese first."

"By all means," Paris encouraged. "In the meantime, the three of us have to figure out how to get Archer Finch and Ella Sparrow back together. I know there's a way. There has to be because I talked to both of them, and they're still madly in love with each other. They both want to be together, but as with many relationships, there are insecurities.

"I feel like if we put our heads together, we can figure this out, but that's where you two come in. I need your savvy. The brain cells that you usually use for doing crunches and calf raises or to calculate your caloric intake? I need you to devote them to this mission right now."

Isha and Holly leaned forward, both appearing to give Paris their full attention.

"If this helps Archer to be happy, even it's not with me, I'll do it," Holly said.

"If you promise to introduce me to King Rudolf, I'll do everything to help," Isha stated.

Paris beamed, thinking that they had a chance of reconciling the lovers. "Okay, start taking notes, and let's do research. This is Archer's and Ella's story as I know it..."

CHAPTER SIXTY-SEVEN

Great Electronics Superstore, Hollywood, California

"Okay, where is that witch and how should I take her down?" Holly asked as they entered Ella Sparrow's workplace.

Paris pointed toward the back where the television department was. "She's back there, and you're not taking anything down except for probably a carton of Ben & Jerry's later."

"If I'm not here to claw out that ungrateful woman's eyes, I'm not sure what my purpose is," Holly muttered and crossed her arms. She wore a workout top, although she hadn't worked out that day. For a first, she and Isha had done FGA work instead.

Paris swung around to face her and Isha. "Remember that I have someone following me on Jackson Zelle's orders. Also, we're reversing the effects that someone very powerful has created to get rid of love and spread heartbreak. We're going to be creating enemies on many different levels. So I need you two to have my back."

Isha looked around, suddenly nervous. "I don't know if anyone told you this, but as fairies, we don't do danger. We're in the business of love for a reason. I'm afraid of the dark, so if you think I can handle some unknown threat, you're wrong."

Paris sighed. "Leave the danger to me. Tell the squirrel if you see anything strange. He'll alert me."

She glanced down at Faraday, who nodded and saluted. "Go and mend some hearts, Pare."

She turned at once and marched for the back where Ella Sparrow was helping a customer. When they'd had their questions answered, Paris cleared her throat, getting the girl's attention.

Ella turned with a smile that quickly faded. "Oh, dear. You're back. I thought that you would take a hint. I told you what you wanted to know. More importantly, I told you what I wanted. I want to forget that Archer Finch was ever a part of my life. It's easier that way."

"I understand that," Paris began, her phone in her hand. "It's just there's something I wanted you to watch."

Ella considered this and shook her head. "I get that you're a fairy godmother or something. Your job is to create love or whatever. But Archie and I aren't meant to be. I hope you get that song taken down. I don't want people hurt, and he should never have agreed to it. Again, I just want to move on with my life."

"I realize that Archer being on the road and the distance created so much stress for you," Paris stated with conviction. "You thought that he had all these girls all over him and even if he did, you didn't see—"

Ella held up her hand. Her eyes narrowed with hostility. "I've had enough. I'm working here."

"If you let me show you something," Paris cut in.

"No!" Ella said loud enough that many looked over. "I don't think you understand how long I had to fight to live my life again. It's taken me what feels like forever to get over Archie. I'm not letting him back in. I'm not going to let you convince me that he deserves a second chance." She pointed at a group of waiting customers. "Look, I have people who need my help. They aren't you. And they definitely aren't Archie."

Paris let Ella walk away. This wasn't over. They merely had to resort to Plan B. She glanced at Faraday and nodded as she chose an option on her phone. He confirmed, clicking a remote in his paws.

The pair turned their attention to the bank of televisions visible all over the store along the back wall. All the screens flickered and turned to snow. Then they simultaneously broadcast the same video.

The first scene was Ella Sparrow and Archer Finch backstage at a concert. In the distance, the crowd of thousands chanted, screamed, and called Archer's name.

He cupped her chin and pulled her close. "The only person I need calling for me is you, my bird."

She smiled and kissed him as his guitarist pulled him away toward the stage where the audience was waiting for Punch Line to perform.

The video cut to several scenes in a row. Some would be footage Ella had seen, but most of it wasn't. What Paris and her employees had spliced together were videos from different social media platforms of Punch Line over the years. Most of the videos came from fans who had tried to get Archer's attention and failed.

The specific scene playing right then was of Archer singing the band's most loved ballad, holding the microphone, and peering into the audience at one girl like she was the only one on the planet. It was Ella Sparrow.

From what Paris could tell after combing through tons of footage that day, there was only one girl for Archer Finch. The proof was all there on social media. Paris and Isha and even Holly had put all the footage together, and it was currently playing for Archer's one true love right then.

"What are you doing?" Ella mouthed, her eyes welling with tears as everyone, including her, watched the montage play on the big screens all around the electronics store.

"I'm showing you the truth," Paris stated. "He loves you."

"But…"

"Watch," Paris encouraged, pointing at the screen as the video cut to an interview of Archer on the tour bus.

"Yeah, the hardest thing about being on the road is being away from my girl," Archer said to the camera. "She means more to me than any of this, the riches or the fame. I'd give it all up for her if she wanted."

"Do you think you two will make it?" the reporter asked.

"Absolutely," Archer stated with confidence. "Even if I stay touring, we have an unstoppable love. It might take an untraditional course. Maybe I see her on the weekends or every other week, but when I do, it's going to be the best part of my days…of my life. Ella is my one true love."

The video then cut to a fan's footage from her phone. It was a beautiful blonde built like a model, knocking on Archer's dressing room door.

"How did you get through security?" Archer asked after opening his door a crack and peering through.

"They like me," the woman said. "You will too. Just let me in, and I'll show you how much I'm in love with you. I'll show you anything and everything you want, Archer Finch."

He shook his head like he didn't even see her and shut the door. "Nah. I've got all that I want."

The video ended with Archer on stage at Punch Line's last concert, swaying back and forth, his eyes locked on one spot in the audience. The camera panned to that seat to show a place in the front row—the spot where Ella had always sat. But now Archer was heartbroken, and his gaze was unmistakably seeing her in the past and the love that they'd lost.

When the video cut out and the screens went back to broadcasting football once more, Ella Sparrow didn't look like she had moments prior. She didn't seem ready and intent on returning to work no matter what.

The woman was in a fit of tears, wiping them away over and over again, although they kept falling.

Paris cut through the crowd trying to form around Ella and paused, giving her a look of sympathy and respect. "If you want me to take you to him, I will. If you want me to leave you alone, I'll do that too. At this point, it's your call entirely."

CHAPTER SIXTY-EIGHT

Amoeba Music, Hollywood, California

The crowd outside the vintage vinyl record store in Hollywood was large. A line of crazed fans snaked around the corner and down the block.

Paris sighed, realizing that the timing had to be annoying like this. She turned to Ella, who had tearfully followed her to where Archer was supposed to be that afternoon. Thankfully it wasn't far from the Great Electronics Superstore, but sadly, with the number of people standing between them and the band, Archer could have been a million miles away.

"This is ridiculous." Ella assessed the size of the crowd as it came into view. She shook her head. "This is what I was talking about. This is why it never worked."

Paris spun, glancing at Holly and Isha behind the girl with dreads. Holly was nodding like Ella was right. Isha looked full of conviction.

She came forward and smiled at Ella, taking her arm. "No, it didn't work, but now you see why it's destined to. You and Archer are meant to be because you love each other. That's all it takes at the end of the day to overcome all odds."

Ella blinked at the woman with short black hair in confusion. "I'm sorry, but who are you?"

"I'm your fairy godmother," Isha said in a breathy tone. Then she giggled. "I mean, by that standard, I'm everyone's, but I'm a fairy godmother."

Ella looked her over in her yoga pants and hoodie. "Aren't you supposed to be wearing a blue gown or something or have a wand?"

"My wand is in my pocket, and my gown makes me look frumpy." Isha looked at Paris quite seriously like something had just occurred to her. "We don't have to wear that getup, do we?"

Paris laughed, waving at her appearance in a black leather jacket and boots, and grinned. "What do you think?"

"Cool." Isha returned her attention to Ella. "Now, we have to let Archer know you're here. Maybe call him on the phone."

"I deleted his number," Ella admitted.

"I just can't!" Holly exclaimed. She threw her hands up, shook her head at the girl with dreads, and looked at Paris. "I mean, she had Archer's phone number and deleted it."

Paris shook her head and pointed at the crowd. "Holly, go make yourself useful and go through and retrieve Archer. Tell him that I'm here, but more importantly tell him that I brought Ella for him."

"Ummm...how do you expect me to do that?" Holly asked. "Look at that crowd."

"Ummm...I don't know, try using magic, fairy godmother." Paris groaned. "Remember all that magic I gave you earlier? Butt your way in there with spells. Those are all mortals."

"Oh, right," Holly chirped. "I'm not used to having magic or someone encouraging me to use it."

"What did y'all do before I showed up?" Paris shook her head at Isha.

"Mostly we watched *Real Housewives of Wherever* and

pretended it was homework for nonexistent cases, did bicep curls, and took carb blockers while we ate pastries."

"Wow, that's sad." Paris watched as Holly thankfully did as instructed and disappeared into the crowd. She pointed her wand and made people back up like they suddenly realized they needed to do something else or be somewhere else. Or that the girl with fake blonde hair and eyelashes was a huge bully and would run them over. Holly might, to get to Archer, but it wouldn't work, and Paris knew that after seeing all the video footage they put together to get Ella there.

The love of Archer's life was there. Now all they needed was for him to come out and the real reunion could happen, followed by healing and love. Then Punch Line could spread it throughout the world through exponentiation.

But first, Archer had to come out, Paris thought as a fat rain droplet fell from the sky.

She glanced up at the graying clouds, and three more drops fell on her cheeks.

"Seriously, it rains like a handful of times in Los Angeles and this of all days," Paris muttered.

"I think it's another sign." Ella knotted her hands together, nervousness in her every movement.

"It's a sign that the angels are crying because they want you to be together," Isha offered.

Paris nodded at her friend, liking the encouragement she was offering.

"I don't know." Ella's tone was tense as the crowd grew antsy from the rain soaking them as they waited for the band.

It didn't often rain in Los Angeles, but when it did, it usually fell fast and furious, like the heavens wanted to get it all over with as quickly as possible so the sun could come back out to play.

Paris was trying to remain positive for Ella, but as they stood in front of Amoeba Music, her leather jacket quickly getting drenched, it was difficult. They could retreat and call Archer another time. However, Paris felt like she'd have lost momentum. She also reminded herself that they needed this win to combat the heartbreak from the song.

Archer had agreed to do a concert for Paris to mend hearts if she got him back with Ella. The funds for that would have to come from King Rudolf because strangely, Mr. J had taken all the profits from *Heartbreak View* and run, skipping town. Things had accelerated fast after they'd taken down the song, but Paris knew better than to think that the drama was over. She'd made an enemy, and he'd be back to seek his revenge.

She'd be ready.

First, she needed her reunion. As she looked at Ella's face splashed with raindrops and tears, she knew that she did too. Ella Sparrow needed her guy back. As Paris took in the annoyed and drenched fans, she thought that they deserved a reunion and a concert as well. Everyone deserved a win. She wanted to give it to them.

As Paris thought it, the crowd at the front of Amoeba Music parted. A bunch of security guards in black charged through. Paris thought they'd be hauling Holly in tow, about to chuck her into the streets for trespassing. However, Paris was grateful to see her employee proudly marching behind the security personnel. Behind her was none other than Archer Finch, his black ponytail soon drenched from the torrential downpour as he stalked out into the rain.

However, as soon as the rockstar spotted Ella Sparrow, he broke free of Holly's chaperoning and the security guards' protection and ran straight for the girl beside Paris.

In an instant, his hands pressed against her cheeks. His forehead rested alongside hers. He blinked at her like she wasn't real, but a dream—the one he'd wanted to come true since his nightmare started.

Thunder broke overhead. The crowd yelled, but not because

they were getting drenched. It was because they were getting a rare show. Everyone was.

"You're here," Archer Finch said in a whisper that only those close could hear.

"I saw the video," Ella replied, her lips only a breath from his.

"Video?" Archer asked.

Ella didn't take her eyes off him but pointed behind herself at Paris. "Your fairy godmother friend..."

"Oh, right." Archer laughed in relief.

"It showed the things I never saw, Archie... I never knew how much you loved me. I always thought when you were on the road, well, out of sight, out of mind..."

"Ella...you are the love of my life. Not for one moment are you out of my mind. How could you be?"

"I know that now. I've never been able to not think of you." Her tears mixed with the rain that soaked both lovers.

The crowd was soaked.

Paris was drenched. So were Isha, Holly, and the security guards. No one seemed to mind as they watched the two lovers embrace and kiss and begin to mend a heartbreak that would heal the world and create so much love. So much love that it would spread fast and wide and take Punch Line to bigger places than ever before.

More importantly, it would take Archer Finch and Ella Sparrow to a new level of happiness—where they would go on to do amazing things with their love.

CHAPTER SIXTY-NINE

Rose Apothecary, Roya Lane, London

When Paris had returned from Hollywood, she immediately got a message from Subner to tell her that her wand was ready. She was excited about the instrument she hadn't wanted and didn't need. It was more of a prop to make her look like fairy godmothers and agents. However, she knew hers would be special, and she was excited to have something unique and made specifically for her from the Protector of Weapons—even if he hated her guts.

However, when she messaged Subner to tell him she'd meet him the next morning before work, he stated that she'd be early.

Paris, always confused by the weird riddles and knowingness that Subner and Father Time displayed, replied that she'd come a little later.

He scolded her, saying that then she'd be late.

Sensing his annoyed tone even through text messages, Paris asked him when he wanted her to show up. To that, the elf said, "Come to see me when you plan but run an errand beforehand. Then I'll be ready for you."

That didn't make any sense to Paris, but she decided to go

with it. Knowing that she had some time to spare, Paris asked her mom if she wanted to grab some coffee on Roya Lane before Paris met with Subner. She thought it would be wise to caffeinate before work since Fairy Grounds wasn't going to welcome her into their coffee shop after her doppelgänger's public display.

Liv excitedly agreed to meet Paris and said she knew the perfect place to get coffee. For that reason, Paris was surprised when her mother led her into the Rose Apothecary after meeting her on Roya Lane.

Anyone who looked at Liv Beaufont would guess that she and Paris were related. However, they would probably think they were sisters rather than mother and daughter. That was because technically, Liv was only ten years older than her daughter. The Beaufonts were notorious for not aging the same as everyone else.

Sophia had sped up in age when she magnetized to her dragon. Liv and Stefan had been stuck in a parallel dimension for fifteen years where they didn't age and thought they'd only been gone from this world for a day. The Beaufonts' lives were very confused and assorted.

"I thought Bep mostly sold potions here," Paris muttered to her mother when they entered the small shop full of strange herbs, bubbling cauldrons, and an ornery potions expert.

Liv pulled her long blonde hair free from the long black cape she wore when on missions. "Who best to make a strong cup of coffee than someone who understands the chemistry of beans and things?"

"I guess so." Paris looked around the cluttered store, which was different every time she entered it. If her mother thought the Rose Apothecary had the best coffee on Roya Lane, she was probably right. Liv Beaufont tended to know the secrets that most didn't, thanks to many different factors, but mostly because she made friends with the most unexpected people. To Liv, people were the greatest resources in the world over riches, objects, and status.

"To get a cup of coffee, I think we're going to need some assistance," Paris muttered, looking around the Rose Apothecary for the potions expert.

"She's probably in the back sleeping and will show up when she feels like it." Liv picked up a jar of purple herbs and shook them, her gaze curious.

"Well, I don't want to be late." Paris pretended to look around, but her mind raced with a hundred thoughts. She had a super busy day, and although spending time with her mother was important, she couldn't help but feel that she should be preparing for the huge event that night. The concert that Punch Line agreed to do had to be that night because first, the sooner they could undo the effects caused by *Heartbreak View*, the better. Second, King Rudolf, who agreed to help fund the concert, said that the only night he could rent the Hollywood Bowl was that specific night.

"You'll show up exactly when Subner was planning based on his strange instructions," Liv explained, putting the container of herbs down.

"Yeah, it does seem that he's orchestrating the timeline."

Liv nodded. "That's his way."

Paris picked up a small pipe again, looking at it but not really seeing it.

"What has you so preoccupied?" Liv looked at her daughter with an empathetic gaze, her blue eyes dazzling.

"Besides the fact that I have a mystery man named Mr. J who tried to break lovers' hearts worldwide, and there's also someone at FGA keeping tabs on me who is also a mystery?"

Liv nodded with a grin. "Yes, besides all that. You know, you don't have to know who your enemies are to fight them."

"I'm sure those are great words of wisdom that you've learned firsthand in deadly battles, but they're also very confounding to me."

As a Warrior for the House of Fourteen, Liv Beaufont had fought many enemies. She'd unearthed a forgotten history of magic and released mortals from a prison of sorts where they couldn't see magic. To say that Paris came from the stuff of legends was an understatement.

"Pare, you know that you have someone out there trying to take you down. Probably a few somebodies. You have proof that someone is watching and someone wants to destroy love. Usually, we don't know what we're facing, but we should always act as if we know there's someone after us.

"It's when we walk through the street with our guard down that we are most at risk from our enemies. Treat most like they could be the culprit. Trust only those who are in your corner. And know that you don't have to name your villain to take them down."

"Okay." Paris loosened the tightness in her chest with a deep breath. "That makes sense…"

It did. Paris needed to be on high alert no matter what. Knowing who was after her might make it easier, but that could also make it so she only paid attention to that person and not to all who could potentially be of danger. She found it beautifully ironic that not knowing the information put her in a better position than if she knew all of what she was facing. Life was poetic like that.

"What else is making you frown?" Liv still looked at her daughter intently from over the display of herbs and essential oils.

Absentmindedly, Paris touched her forehead, mostly to cover up the constant tension she knew was written on her face. "Just that whole thing where I'm putting on a concert for fifteen thousand people tonight."

Liv nodded understandingly. "You've employed your resources, right?"

"Well, yeah. King Rudolf is taking care of many of the details for the venue. He's got press releases going out along with Punch Line, who is ready to perform. Headmistress Willow is helping with sending out invites, and the fairy godmothers are rounding up potentially compatible couples in hopes that we can make budding love blossom.

"The event is being recorded and will play on streaming music sites, so it will have an opportunity to create love. However, if we can make some actual love sparks in the audience, that would be a bonus."

"That's amazing." Liv sounded impressed.

"Yeah," Paris said but couldn't deny that even with all the things they'd covered with such short notice, she still felt unprepared. She let out another heavy breath. "I have security covered although I admit that it's sort of a group of misfits. Since there is an unknown threat, I wish that I had more safety measures...oh, and fireworks."

Liv laughed suddenly. "Fireworks?"

"Yeah, there are usually fireworks at the Hollywood Bowl after a big show. But for all his genius, Faraday says that pyrotechnics aren't something he should pull off with almost no prep time."

Liv beamed at her daughter, pride heavy in her gaze. "I still can't believe you're throwing a concert at the Hollywood Bowl. After fixing that near disaster with the heartbreak song. You're a maker of love. And so many other things. I wish I could be there tonight to see how successful you are and how much love you create."

Paris smiled fondly at her mother. "I know, but this is last minute, and you have important missions that demand your time."

Liv groaned. "I have politics to attend to in the form of peace treaties with rogue elves and gnomes who are threatening to fight with polar bears over land rights. I swear, you'd think that all the bickering idiots would take a day off, but they're the ones with a lot of free time and long agendas."

"Well, like I said, it will be broadcast so you can check it out afterward."

"Your father and I will relish the opportunity. I think I might be able to help with the extra security personnel, but I can't make any promises. Oh, and the fireworks too."

Paris arched a curious eyebrow at her mother. "Should I ask for details?"

Liv shook her head, hiding a grin. "No, but when all hope is lost, or the finale is about to rock on, look to the sky. Hopefully, you'll find some relief there."

"You're about as mysterious with your riddles as Subner and Papa Creola."

Liv laughed. "I learned from the very best. And Pare…"

She glanced up at her mother, pulling her attention off a set of candles that smelled horrid. "Yeah?"

"Even when you know who your villain is, there's usually someone behind them. Never think you know everyone who wants to bring you down. Unfortunately, we have a lot of enemies in this world, and it's because it's our job to protect things that are so crucial and sought-after like justice, love, and magic." Liv shrugged. "That's just my two cents. For what it's worth."

"It's priceless. Everything you tell me is." Paris was going to say that having her mother's support after so many years of being separated was a gift. However, before she had a chance, the pair were interrupted by the shop owner.

"I simply don't think it's possible to create a polish like that." Bep looked over her shoulder at whoever she was talking to as she carried supplies in from the back.

The potions expert had short curly hair and was tall and lean, and wearing her usual velvet cloak.

"I don't know. I think there has to be a way to create a shoeshine that makes shoes invisible." To Paris' surprise, it was Dwyer from the shoeshine station at FGA Tower.

"I simply don't know why you'd want to do such a thing," Bep stated. "It seems stupid."

"My mother said that stupid was a bad word." Dwyer sounded hurt as he crossed his arms.

"Your mother is right," Liv stated, drawing their attention to them waiting for service at the front of the shop.

"Oh, customers." It was unclear whether Bep was happy or annoyed about this realization. "Why didn't you tell me you were here, Beaufonts?"

"We're here," Liv said dryly.

"Ha-ha. What do you want?" Bep looked the two women over.

"Coffee," Liv answered. "And pronto…or take your time. We can't figure out if Paris is about to be late or early for her appointment with Subner."

"Hey there, Paris." Dwyer smiled at her. "It's good seeing you again. This is your sister?"

"My mom," Paris corrected. "Liv Beaufont."

Dwyer shook his head as if trying to dispel confusion. "Wow, whatever secret anti-aging potion you all are using, I want it."

"They're as likely to give you their secrets as you are to give yours away," Bep stated matter-of-factly, whirling her finger. A moment later, two steaming cups of coffee appeared on the countertop in front of her. "Come and get it. Drink it while it's hot. That way, you can't taste the secret ingredient."

Paris strode over, curiosity leading her way. "What's the secret ingredient?"

The woman gave her a sullen look. "It's a secret."

Dwyer laughed good-naturedly. "As we've just discussed, we all hold onto our secrets no matter what. The other day, Hester in the potions department was picking my brain, trying to find out if there was a recipe for a special kind of ink."

Paris nearly choked on her coffee and not because it was nearly simmering. "What did you say? Hester? A fairy godmother in the potions department? What did she want to know?"

Dwyer's gaze slid to the side like he was afraid he was suddenly in trouble. "Well, people in those departments are always stopping by and asking me questions about my polishes. The recipes are family secrets, and most of them are my special brew that only I know. Anyway, she wanted a special ink. Something that wasn't toxic and could hold a spell if tattooed on someone's skin."

He shrugged. "I don't know why someone would want to create a permanent spell like that, but I've never understood tattoos to begin with." Dwyer chuckled like he'd told a joke. "Anyway, I don't work in the area of inks. My job is polishes, and those are toxic if you tattooed them so I couldn't help her."

Paris glanced at her mother, who realized that she'd learned something of particular interest. However, Paris reminded herself of what Faraday would say in this situation. This was information. It was still only correlational.

Hester, a fairy godmother in the Potions department under the IT and Operations branch at FGA, might be behind the spell on *Heartbreak View*. Also, so could so many other people. There was still more to uncover, and as she did, Paris couldn't let down her guard.

CHAPTER SEVENTY

Fantastical Armory, Roya Lane, London

"You're late," Subner growled when Paris and Liv entered the shop, buzzing from the strong coffee they'd gulped down.

Liv shook her head at her daughter. "Isn't it cute how he does that?"

"Wait, I thought if I showed up when I was planning, I'd be early," Paris argued, glaring at the stringy-haired man behind the counter. "You told me to run an errand, then come to see you. That's what I did."

"An errand," Subner corrected. "Like stop by the Rose Apothecary for supplies. What did you do after that?"

"We stopped on our way here to pet a chimera," Liv remarked. "How can one not stop to? They're freaking adorable."

"There is why you're late," Subner barked. "An errand is one thing, but stopping to lollygag is quite another." He pointed an accusatory finger at Liv. "I blame you, although I have little hope that your daughter would be much different. The holly berry doesn't fall far from the bush."

"The phrase is the apple doesn't fall far from the tree," Liv corrected.

"Yes, but holly berries are poisonous," he added.

Liv nodded, smiling. "I see…"

"You said that my wand was ready," Paris cut in, hoping to steer things forward so she could get on with the day's demanding schedule.

"Yes, I did." Subner was slow to take his menacing gaze off Liv. Finally, he reached under the counter and retrieved something long and flat wrapped in burgundy cloth.

"Is Paris' wand composed of a phoenix feather and eleven inches long?" Liv leaned forward to get a better look.

Annoyed, Subner glanced up. "Is she Harry Potter?"

"I don't think so," Liv answered quite seriously.

"Then no," he answered plainly. "It is made from a rare sandalwood tree and was created to funnel the power of a magician, unlike an ordinary wand. At its end is a sapphire gem that once lay in a crown worn by Queen Anastasia Crystal of the fae. Etched along the outside are the symbols that represent the ancient language of the demons. It is one-of-a-kind, a rare instrument that will have powers I can't even begin to suppose and a future that only you, Paris, can guide."

After he finished, Subner pulled the cloth off the wand, revealing something that Paris hadn't expected to love at first sight. However, she did, and it felt familiar to her, although she didn't know how.

The wand was large, like a weapon. It wasn't straight but also wasn't like a gnarly branch. The cylindrical object had symmetry in its composition although it was an organic shape.

At its end was a large round sapphire, and as Subner stated, there were strange symbols engraved along its side.

"It's beautiful." Paris was suddenly breathless.

"Amantis," Subner corrected.

"Gesundheit," Liv said like he'd sneezed and she was wishing him good health.

He lowered his chin and regarded her with pure disdain. "Amantis is the name of the wand."

"What if Paris wanted to name it?" Liv questioned.

"Well, it's up to the maker to name their weapon, now isn't it," Subner fired back. "I've chosen Amantis because although this wand is still a weapon, I hope Paris will use it to bring love to the world. The name encapsulates that."

Paris reached out, hesitating, but wanting more than anything to feel the wand in her hand. "May I?"

He nodded. "From this point forward, this is yours, and everyone else must ask permission if they should ever touch it. However, I encourage you not to allow such things. The energy of others never belongs on someone's weapon. It is like a lover, and your hands are the only ones who should know it."

Paris nodded, feeling the weight of the momentous occasion as she picked up the wand. To her surprise, it was light in her fingers. The end with the sapphire made it tip that direction, but when she had her hand wrapped around it, that created a nice balance.

Although she wasn't sure exactly how to use the instrument, it also seemed like it would be as natural as walking or talking. It was like something she was always supposed to use and simply had to unite with it.

"Thank you." Paris looked up from the astonishingly beautiful wand and smiled with gratitude at Subner.

For once, he didn't look like he wanted her to die. He nodded thoughtfully. "I hope that Amantis protects you when your magic isn't enough. I hope that it brings goodness when it seems all is lost. And I hope that it elevates your powers when the time comes."

CHAPTER SEVENTY-ONE

Band Shell, Hollywood Bowl, Hollywood, California

The Hollywood Bowl was an iconic outdoor amphitheater nestled in the Hollywood Hills of Los Angeles, California. There wasn't a bad seat in the concave structure. It was an architectural masterpiece designed by Frank Lloyd Wright and was one of the largest outdoor venues of its type in the United States. It also was a no-fly zone, which gave its many concerts the peace they deserved as the performers graced the hungry audience with their art.

As Paris paced, trying to stay present, she couldn't shake Subner's strange words when she met Amantis—which felt more like a person rather than an instrument or a wand. *What did he mean by, he hoped that Amantis elevated her powers when the time came?* she thought, realizing that everyone on the stage was looking at her.

Paris halted and turned to her team. It hit her hard right then as she saw the empty rows of seats spreading out before them. They were about to put on a concert for tens of thousands of people. She shook off her speculations about the wand and slid it into a holster. Her mother had made it for her so Amantis could always be with her, much like how her mother and aunt kept their swords in their sheaths at their sides.

"Okay, so where were we?" Paris tried to collect her thoughts.

Lee, who was in charge of security for the event, pointed at Paris' waist. "We're wondering why you've got hip flasks on you. What is that, Midori? That stuff will get you sick, little one."

Paris glanced down, remembering what else was on her holster. There were also spots for potion bottles. Bep had mysteriously pushed a few different colored potions into her hands when she was at the Rose Apothecary, telling her that they might come in handy. It seemed that her friends were trying to help her, but Paris wished that they'd give her clues about what she was facing since they seemed to know more than her.

All Bep had told Paris was that the blue one was lucky, the green one unlucky, and the red one mixed. Paris hoped things went so smoothly that she didn't have to find out what the potions did. Then she could mix them when everything was done and have an interesting cocktail.

"They are insurance," Paris stated. "Really, if you all do your jobs, I shouldn't have to resort to hocus-pocus."

"The mutt said hocus-pocus." Lee looked sideways at Holly beside her. "That's not a real spell. I wonder if that means she isn't a real magician."

"I don't think that's her real eye color," Holly said loud enough for Paris to hear her. The acoustics on the stage made it so Paris could hear a lot from this place.

"This is my real eye color," Paris seethed. "You're one to talk, Barbie. Anyway, you five are the security detail."

Lee glanced down the line of fairies and shook her head. "Seriously, I think I'll do better if you lock up these ladies and let me run this place on my own."

Paris sighed, knowing this was their weakest place for the event. However, she'd already stretched her resources with getting the venue, publicity, the band, and staff. Of all the people she knew, these were the only ones who could do security on short notice. Paris' parents were busy saving the world or fighting demons. Sophia was running dragon missions. Hemingway and Uncle Clark were running the farmhouse restaurant.

It seemed absurd now, but Christine, Penny, Holly, and Isha, led by Lee, were all that Paris had for security. Hopefully, that's all they needed and things would be quiet.

"I get that you all aren't used to working security," Paris began. "However, I have faith that you all can step up to any challenges. I've taught Christine and Penny combat spells, and they've helped me out on other missions."

Christine nodded, looking at the other fairies. "We tied up a professor one time using a spell."

Penny nodded proudly.

"Oh wow, you should've told me that you've assigned me James Bond and Jason Bourne," Lee said dryly. "My job is surely much easier than I envisioned."

"We do a kickboxing class every other weekend." Holly motioned between herself and Isha.

"It gets better," Lee muttered. "Now I've got Bruce Lee and Jackie Chan at my side. What can go wrong?"

"Everything," Paris said heavily. "That's why I need you all to go and start doing patrols. The gates open in an hour. I want you to get familiar with all the ins and outs. Keep an eye out at all times. Always stay in communication. Faraday outfitted you with comms. Use them. Work together. Let's make this a safe and happy event."

Lee saluted and stumped off, waving at the four fairies. "Come on, you pansies. If we have time, I want to carb-load. That's how I prepare for all my battles."

"It's not Saturday," Holly stated. "I only eat carbs then."

"Strangely enough, I only choke blondes on Thursdays," Lee retorted with a mock-surprised expression.

Holly shrank back. "It's Thursday."

"So it is," Lee sang, ushering the group off the stage.

"Are we ready to do a soundcheck?" Paris looked at the side of the stage where she'd seen movement in her peripheral vision and expected to find Faraday working.

Instead, she was shocked to find Agent Barney Jasper scowling at her from the edge of the stage. Even more surprisingly, he wasn't holding his phone and pretending not to notice her. All of his attention seemed to hinge on Paris.

"What exactly is going on here?" he asked, his eyes narrowed as he stared around the large venue.

"Well, at sunset, we're going to do a tiny community concert," Paris said meekly, pulling up her clipboard and pretending to check off items. She didn't know how Agent Punk Face found out about her event, but she figured it had to do with snooping and spying and would probably be followed by sabotaging. She couldn't confirm it, but she heavily suspected he was the one Jackson Zelle told to keep an eye on her. That begged other questions that could indict him further. She'd get to that once she had more evidence.

"A tiny little concert?" he asked. "At the Hollywood Bowl? Rumor has it that Punch Line is headlining."

"You know how rumors go," she said dismissively.

"This rumor came from the top at FGA, and I for one, as your manager, am not happy about learning about this from my boss."

"Do you mean Saint Valentine?" Paris had to ask, wondering if he could've also been referring to Jackson Zelle.

"That's not important," he said dismissively. "Although Holly and Isha work for you, why do you think you can take my other agents and employ them for your pet projects?"

Paris let out a breath. "Christine and Penny are my friends. The last time I checked, it's officially after hours for FGA unless they're assigned to a special project, which they aren't. So if they want to volunteer to help me on this tiny pet project, I don't see what the big deal is."

"I'm not sure what you are up to here, but you need to remember that I'm in charge."

Paris blinked at him. "You want me to stay out of your hair, and I do. Then you want to know what I'm doing. If you must know, I'm working. I'm trying to promote love, but you don't seem to care much about that so why should it matter?"

"Agent Beaufont, we need to get one thing straight, or you're going to make a lot of mistakes—"

"Paris," Faraday called from the side of the stage, interrupting. "The band has arrived, and Willow Starr and Mae Ling are here to see you."

She nodded at once. "Okay, I'm coming." Returning her attention to Agent Punk Face, she offered an annoyed look. "I have a lot to do. Is it okay if I go, or do you want to lecture me about how I better not make you look bad?"

He held his arm out and nodded. "Go ahead. By all means, go do what it is you need to."

CHAPTER SEVENTY-TWO

Backstage, Hollywood Bowl, Hollywood, California

"You did it!" Headmistress Willow Starr exclaimed when Paris met her and Mae Ling backstage.

All the emotions from the last few days at her first week at FGA were catching up with her, Paris realized, feeling like she was about to burst into tears at the sight of her teachers from Happily Ever After College.

"I haven't really done anything yet," Paris said, her voice shaky.

"You got the song pulled from most channels," Mae Ling countered.

"That was King Rudolf Sweetwater," Paris argued.

"You got Punch Line to stop singing the song," Willow continued proudly. "And they've agreed to perform at this concert and sing ballads to promote love."

Paris nodded heavily. "Yes, but I haven't figured out who was behind the music." She glanced at the stage where Agent Punk Face had been with her and could be eavesdropping. She wanted to say something about Jackson Zelle spying on her but didn't think it was worth the risk. Instead, she simply said, "Even if I

SARAH NOFFKE & MICHAEL ANDERLE

don't know who we're up against, I think we're in a good position to defend ourselves from them."

"I know you're right." Willow's eyes were bright with excitement. "Tonight will be one for love. The fairy godmothers at Happily Ever After College have been promoting the event. If they had potential matches in the area, they invited them to the concert. Hopefully many fall in love here tonight or that at least it leads to positive feelings."

Mae Ling nodded. "As you requested, our students will be working the ticketing and concession booths. We have many of the areas covered. Is there anything else you need?"

Paris pointed at the wand on her hip and grinned, knowing that it was because of Mae Ling that she'd gotten the instrument. "A chance to practice with this. I hoped to do the fireworks show at the finale tonight."

Mae Ling shook her head with disapproval on her wise face. "I don't think this is the place to try such a spell. Unless the situation warrants it, I would only perform known spells with the wand until you've practiced it."

Paris deflated, realizing that her joke had fallen flat. In truth, there was no finale show. There weren't even t-shirts to sell. Honestly, she didn't know if there would be that many people in the audience. They'd started promoting the concert that day for an event that would happen in an hour. There were so many things that could go wrong.

Christine poked her head around the corner, her eyes snapping with adrenaline. "Sorry to interrupt, but…"

"Yes?" Paris wondered what it was now.

"The gates just opened. It looks like it's going to be a packed house."

CHAPTER SEVENTY-THREE

Hollywood Bowl, Hollywood, California

Paris knew that Punch Line was a huge band. The biggest. Why was she surprised that so many were filing through the gates, excited to find their seats at a free, invite-only concert? Because she'd organized it. Because it was last minute. Also because none of these would-be lovers knew that this was an effort to make them happier.

Although Paris had a lot of concerns right then, she could cross one off her list. She lifted her trusty clipboard and marked off the item that said, "Will anyone show up?"

It felt good to strike that concern. Paris wondered if she could simply cross off the rest on the long list and they'd magically disappear too.

"Pare…" Holly said behind her.

Not liking the tone of her voice, Paris lowered her chin and turned. "What is it?"

"You'll want to go and see the band backstage."

"Why?" Paris hoped that her employee would simply tell her.

However, Holly pointed at the upper deck. "I better go and

check out that area. There's a bottleneck, and Lee says those are security concerns."

Paris nodded, making her way backstage. She was relieved to see all of Punch Line's members were there, which had been her first concern when her mind briefly trailed through potential issues on her trek to that area. However, not only did their troubled expressions make her instantly worry, but something was missing. Something she couldn't quite put her finger on but seemed like it should be there.

"Archer, what's going on?" Paris strode over to the lead singer.

"Well, we had our instruments sent over this afternoon." Archer looked around the space.

"Yeah, I heard that they arrived and were getting set up." Paris remembered getting the information from Faraday, or maybe it was Holly. She couldn't remember at that point.

"Yeah, well, if they got set up, we don't know where." Frustration lay heavy in his voice. "Paris, we don't have any instruments. From everything we can tell, someone's taken them."

Doom and failure hit Paris' stomach like a bullet. She gulped, let out a breath, and decided that she wasn't out of options yet.

Holding up a finger, Paris forced a smile. "Give me one minute. I'll go and see about getting you new instruments."

"We need ours," he argued, the band members already protesting behind him.

"I get it," Paris stated. "If we can't find those, we'll get you the very best replacements. Let me go and find someone quickly."

"Who?" Archer asked.

"My uncle, the richest man alive," she stated. "If anyone can get you new instruments at a moment's notice, it will be King Rudolf Sweetwater."

CHAPTER SEVENTY-FOUR

Hollywood Bowl, Hollywood, California

Paris had been all over the venue and hadn't seen the blond fae anywhere. She decided to stop at Faraday's sound stage, where he was deep in concentration.

"Have you seen King Rudolf?"

"Not now, Pare." He chewed on a wire, deep in thought. "The sound system has some strange bug that keeps messing up the controls. If I can't fix it, the show is going to be a mess."

"Well, the show is going to be a huge mess if our band has no musical instruments," Paris spat, hating that she could trump the squirrel's real problems.

With wide eyes, Faraday glanced up, his mouth open and bits of wire hanging from it. "W-Wh-What?"

"Yeah, it appears that someone has stolen the band's instruments. Or maybe they've been misplaced. I mean, I have zero reason to think there is anyone in my midst who would try to ruin this concert."

"Are you sure?" He went back to work. "I mean, this is the same band asked to create and play a song that broke hearts worldwide with spelled lyrics by some mysterious Mr. J?"

"Yeah, that was sarcasm," she replied. "Anyway, I need to know where King Rudolf is. If I can get his wallet, maybe he'll let me portal to a music store where I can buy new instruments. Or maybe there are more at Rooster Records. Or maybe…"

The noise all over the amphitheater suddenly made Paris crazy. The sounds of someone tuning a guitar on stage made her cover her head. She could hardly think with the chattering crowd all around her and the pressure of the moment.

"I don't know where King Rudolf is." Faraday was back to work, chewing on wires and typing on a screen.

"Well, I need you to drop what you're doing and help me find him." Paris raised her voice so he'd hear her over all the noise.

"Why?" He didn't take his attention off his tasks.

"Because if you don't and we don't get instruments for the band, none of it will matter."

Without looking up, Faraday pointed a paw behind her. "What do you think is making that racket?"

Paris huffed, turning to see the stage crew tuning instruments. She gasped, choked on her sudden breath, then took off running toward the stage.

CHAPTER SEVENTY-FIVE

Backstage, Hollywood Bowl, Hollywood, California

"You found your instruments?" Paris nearly ran into the keyboardist for Punch Line when she rushed backstage.

Archer shook his head, downing a hot cup of tea and massaging his throat like he was preparing his voice for that night's performance. "No, it was this guy who helped us out."

He pointed, and Paris followed his direction until her eyes connected with the last person she would have expected to help out at the event.

Standing in the corner, holding his phone and smirking, looking smug, was none other than Agent Barney Jasper.

"That guy?" Paris asked. "Are you sure?"

"Yeah, when you left, he said that he could pull in some instruments they keep at FGA." Archer waved toward the stage where the sound of tuning instruments echoed. "I mean, they won't be what we're used to, but I can sing, and my band can play on paint cans with scrap metal if need be."

Paris narrowed her eyes at Agent Punk Face from across the room, trying to decide if she should shut down the whole operation. What if he'd rigged the musical instruments? What if someone had spelled them to play breakup songs instead of the ones they had on the setlist? She decided to deal with that in a minute.

Turning her attention back to Archer, she forced a look of confidence. "Are you and the band ready?"

"Not really." Archer looked around.

"What is it?" Paris' heart beat fast. Her head felt like it was going to explode from stress.

"I need something...someone." He was still searching the space. Then his expression transformed and a wide smile broke across his face when Ella Sparrow waltzed into the area wearing a short skirt, a white tank top, and thigh-high boots. With her dreadlocks, tattoos, and nose ring, Ella was the epitome of a rockstar's girlfriend. Paris knew she was more than that.

She'd proven to be Archer's rock. She was his muse. He was nothing without her. Most artists needed that support to do what they did, which was supply the world with inspiration. Still, they had to get it from somewhere, and Archer got it from Ella—the love of his life.

"There you are." Archer wrapped his arms around Ella and drew her close, their foreheads pressed together. Again, it was like they were the only people in the world as they gazed into each other's eyes. "You'll be in your usual spot?"

Ella nodded, smiling at him. "Of course."

"Good, because I wrote you a new song. No one but the band has heard it, and it's guaranteed to create so much love."

"I can't wait to hear it." Ella pressed her lips to his as the crowd went wild in front of the stage.

Paris tensed. It was almost time to start the concert.

From the side of the stage, Holly, who had taken a very professional demeanor although she had a huge crush on Archer, waved the band to their places. She then glanced at Paris and mouthed, "Get ready. It's almost showtime."

Paris drew a breath, looked down at her outfit, and realized that she hadn't had a chance to change and she was about to be in front of fifteen thousand people. She consoled herself that she was only announcing Punch Line and no one cared about her. Still, she probably should've combed her hair.

"It's almost showtime." Agent Jasper repeated what Holly said, having arrived soundlessly by her side.

Paris narrowed her eyes at the guy who still reminded her of some pompous high school football jock. "Why did you do it?"

"Get them instruments?" he asked.

"Yeah, especially after stealing their real ones," she decided to accuse.

He sucked in a breath, offense bouncing around in his eyes. "I didn't do any such thing. I got them instruments because I realized that we had some lying around in an old department at FGA. I figured I might as well help."

"That doesn't seem like your style," she fired back.

"Well, despite what you think, I don't want you to fail," he replied. "I'd like it if you weren't such a pain in my ass, but I'm starting to wonder if you might be of use."

"Like I can bring a lot of money to your department?" Paris questioned as the crowd started to chant, "Punch Line."

"You think that's what it's all about, don't you?"

"I think that in my short time at FGA, I've learned that most care more about budgets and money than about love," Paris answered. "And there seem to be a lot who care about money at the actual expense of love."

He nodded. "Astute observation. Remember that things aren't what they seem. What happens at FGA is a very political game. I'll warn you that if you're going to play, then get ready because the ones on the board don't fight fair."

Paris shook her head as she made her way for the stage. Looking over her shoulder, she said, "Yeah, I've been bugged, sabotaged, and trapped. All in my first few days on this job. All because I'm here to make a difference. That's fine. I'm ready to play this cutthroat game. Your move, boss."

CHAPTER SEVENTY-SIX

Terrace Boxes, Hollywood Bowl, Hollywood, California

As an assassin, Lee wasn't used to having the job of protecting people. Sure, she was about saving her butt. Or she was about saving the world from jerks by way of killing them. She wasn't a do-gooder like the Beaufonts. Lee, the assassin baker, thought of herself as more of a weed killer rather than a gardener who planted roses. She got rid of the pests.

However, when Paris Beaufont asked her if she'd serve as security detail at that night's concert, she had no choice but to say yes. The Beaufonts were good people. No, they were the best people. This world was spinning on its axis because of them. So although Lee would've preferred to be eating canned cheese in her oversized hoodie and watching bad French comedies that night, she'd volunteered.

Still, protecting and being a security guard wasn't natural for Lee. What she did find natural as she stood on her perch next to the amphitheater's terrace boxes, surveying the area, was picking out the criminals in the crowd. Thankfully, there weren't many since the fairy godmothers had handpicked the invitees based on their romantic inclination.

That meant most in the audience were single and receptive to the idea of falling in love. If the FGA was successful that night, there would be a lot of love created. *And a lot of babies,* Lee thought with a laugh.

She reasoned that her job would be easy. If anything, she'd have to stop a few catfights between women flirting with the same guy. Or maybe guys jockeying for the same girl. Well, the genders could be a toss-up, but the point was that any altercation would most likely be between Cinderellas and Prince Charmings fighting for their matches.

From her vantage point, Lee spotted a group of sorority girls who'd had too much to drink. She'd keep an eye on them in case they tried to climb on the stage. However, they had to get past Ella Sparrow, and that girl looked like she'd claw out a woman going for her man.

In the aisle were some meathead guys who were laughing loudly but not hurting anyone. Still, Lee didn't like it when people laughed loudly…or at all unless it was at her jokes.

The audience fell silent when Paris Beaufont strode out from the side of the bandshell. Lee continued to scan the crowd, looking for potential threats.

On the same side of the bandshell where she presided, but a few dozen rows higher was a photographer dressed all in black. He was perched on top of a small structure, giving him a good view for shots of the band.

"Thank you all for joining us here tonight," Paris began, making the crowd erupt with applause.

"I know you all are as shocked as I am about this concert," she continued, seeming like a natural, talking in front of the packed crowd. "We decided that it was time to spread some love, and Punch Line was happy to play this impromptu show for their favorite city."

The crowd went wild, but Lee kept her eyes focused on the photographer. The more she watched him, the more she realized that something wasn't right. His camera was strange. His demeanor too stiff. His clothes too black.

Lee pressed her finger to her ear, speaking into the comms to her security team. "We've got a suspicious figure on the structure to the left of the stage. Can I get someone from the front of the stage to give me a read?"

"I see who you mean," Holly replied over the comms.

"Does that look like a camera in his hands?"

"Camera?" Holly questioned. "I don't see anything in his hands. He's simply standing with his hands on his hips like he's about to break out into a River Dance number."

"Hands on his hips?" Lee stared straight at the guy with the instrument in his hands. It looked like a cylindrical object the more she focused. Not a camera. Maybe a screwdriver. "No, he's holding something. Maybe a wand."

"No, he's got his hands on his hips," Holly stated.

"On the left side of the stage. At nine o'clock?" Lee questioned.

"Yes, left," Holly answered. "If I'm facing the crowd, then it's... oh wait, that's my right..."

Lee's eyes darted to where Holly was referring. She instantly saw it. Standing on the small equipment buildings on the other side of the amphitheater was another figure. As Holly had stated, that figure was all in black too and had his hands on his hips like a stupid superhero about to dive into action.

Not on her watch. These guys didn't seem like invitees. They seemed like goons sent to ruin the festivities.

"Without further ado," Paris continued from the stage, her voice rising in volume. "I present to you the best rock band in the world. Please welcome, Punch Line!"

"I'm getting the guy on the left, my left. The one with camera...which isn't a camera," Lee said in a rush. "Holly, knock that River Dancer down before he does something. It's go time!"

CHAPTER SEVENTY-SEVEN

Terrace Boxes, Hollywood Bowl, Hollywood, California

"Coming through!" Lee yelled, leaping over rows of the audience. They were all startled by nearly getting knocked in the head by her boots as she jumped down toward the building to the left of the stage.

The fans were all poised and ready for the show about to start, their adrenaline at an all-time high as the lights lowered and the band members soundlessly came onto the stage. Lee knew that she had seconds to get into place before this assassin tried to take his shot at the band. They should've had extra security to check those coming into the venue, but regrets were useless at this point.

The buzz of the audience was growing at an alarming rate. Lee needed to be on top of that building. Once the lights came up, her chance to take this jerk out would be over.

Launching herself off an empty seat in the dark, Lee clung to the side of the building. Her face knocked into the concrete. Her mouth hurt. Her teeth felt loose.

Shaking this off, she threw her leg over the building's eaves, and as she'd had to do on many occasions when taking out waste-of-space lowlifes—to make the world a better place, mind you—Lee rose into position soundlessly.

Right on cue, a guitar played a single note that reverberated through the outdoor amphitheater. The audience erupted with anticipation. A rolling drum beat met the guitar note still echoing in the air.

Lee tensed, and when the lights flashed on the stage, she was ready to kick some ass.

She was in luck. Standing right in front of her with his back to her was a squatty figure dressed all in black. Before Lee made her move, she noticed that Holly had jumped down off the stage onto the short building where the other dark figure was standing. She'd come right at that guy so he saw her coming. They were engaged in a straight-up fistfight. The audience was absorbed in Punch Line's first song and didn't notice.

Unfortunately, someone must have noticed her because some idiot in the crowd pointed up at Lee and yelled. "What are they doing?"

The guy in front of Lee turned, spotted her immediately, and backed away. A mask obscured the guy's face, but she saw a small screwdriver in his hand.

Lee dove for him, but the guy shot a combat spell from the device in his hand and Lee had to jump to the side to avoid being hit. From such close range that could've been deadly. She was about to charge at the guy, but the coward dove off the building on the opposite side from the audience.

Lee glanced to see if the jump would be safe. It would be for her, but it would put her outside the amphitheater in a wooded area where she couldn't do her job. From up high, she watched as the jerk tore through the bushes, darting away. She'd keep an eye out for him if he returned.

With her attention free once more, she jerked her head up and in Holly's direction. The fairy was in the act of delivering a very impressive roundhouse kick to the guy's face. His jaw swung to the side, and he flew off the top of the building and over the side, the same as the guy who'd fled from Lee.

A moment later, over the comms, Holly said, "All is clear and safe here, but someone might want to retrieve the trash I threw on the ground."

"Good work." Lee turned her attention back to the crowd, impressed that the fairies were tougher than she'd thought.

CHAPTER SEVENTY-EIGHT

Backstage, Hollywood Bowl, Hollywood, California

If Paris thought she was paranoid before about someone trying to attack the concert, she knew now that her concerns were well-placed. There were at least two somebodies based on what she'd witnessed from the side stage of the bandshell.

She couldn't believe what she'd seen when the one guy dove off the side of the building after attacking. Even more impressive was the kick that Holly launched at her assailant, sending him over the edge and hopefully to a place where he'd be appre-hended. However, they were already short on staff, so Paris didn't have anyone to send after him right then.

Currently, all her efforts would be on keeping Punch Line safe. Thankfully they were giving a killer performance and not seeming to notice that fights were breaking out on the fringes of the amphitheater all around them.

Paris scanned the crowd, watching as Lee and Holly did the same from their high spots above the audience. If they remained vigilant, they could make it through the show without any prob-lems, Paris hoped. She consoled herself with the idea that maybe those were the only planted attackers. Maybe there would be no other threats.

Because life had to be ironic, the speakers screeched and went dead. The band continued to try to play, but the music on the instruments didn't come through the amplifiers. Something was wrong with the speaker system.

Paris pressed her comms furiously. "Fare, what's going on with the audio? It's cut out."

"I know," he answered over the comms. "I don't know...I meant it's that problem I thought I'd patched earlier."

"What is it?" Paris asked as the audience started to chatter. The band members looked at each other in confusion. Archer glanced to the side stage at Paris, holding up his hands, dumbfounded.

She held up a finger to pause him.

"I think it's some sort of magitech interference," Faraday answered over the comms. "I think...oh, no..."

"What?" Paris barked, panic making her suddenly breathless.

"I think someone's hacked our speakers." Over the comms, she heard Faraday typing furiously. "This would be some crazy powerful magitech."

"Can you fix it?" Paris watched as the crowd grew more agitated as the band remained not playing, their instruments unable to amplify enough for the crowd to hear without speakers.

"I can, but I think there's a bigger problem," Faraday imparted, tension lacing his tone.

"What?" Paris gulped.

A note rang through the speaker.

"It's working," Paris said with relief.

"Punch Line isn't playing that," Faraday stated as another, even more ominous note played over the speakers. "Well, they aren't playing that now..."

"What?" Paris asked again. Then the next note was something familiar. Something she hoped never to hear again.

"That's *Heartbreak View*," she said in a rush.

"Yes, and someone's about to play it for everyone here to hear!" Faraday said in a mad rush.

"Get our speakers back," Paris stated with conviction. "I'll do what I can to stop the song. Work fast. This concert isn't over. It ends with a love song. Not this heartbreak!"

CHAPTER SEVENTY-NINE

Band Shell, Hollywood Bowl, Hollywood, California

AS if she knew exactly what she was doing, Paris strode out onto the stage, straight up to Archer. He still held the microphone and wore a look of pure confusion.

"What's going on?" he asked in a rush over the hum of the audience and the melody chiming to life over the speakers. They were seconds away from feeling pure heartbreak. Over fifteen thousand people would feel complete agony. There would be no amount of potions to fix that.

Paris gave him a look of conviction. "Someone's hacked the speakers so I'm going to fix things with magic until my tech squirrel can fix the audio."

"Should we leave?" Archer asked, his eyes crazed with worry, looking at Ella in the front row.

The song was ramping up over the speakers. The audience was going quiet, ready to listen.

Paris yanked her brand-new wand from its holster. She shook her head at Archer. "No! Get ready to play when I say. We're creating love tonight, one way or another. First, I have to protect you all."

"How?" Archer asked.

However, Paris didn't answer. Instead, she directed all of her magical power through Amantis, realizing that her first time using the wand would be an experiment. One she had to do on a huge stadium of innocent people. She had to do whatever it took to protect hearts.

A green spark like a lone firework shot straight up from the wand's tip as Archer's recorded voice began singing *Heartbreak View*.

That was all anyone heard because a second later, countless green sparks radiated over the Hollywood Bowl like a dome, protecting those inside it. By protecting them, it made them deaf —unable to hear the heartbreak song playing over the speakers.

Paris' arm trembled as the magical spell, powerful and all-encompassing, radiated from her. It was the biggest amount of magic she'd ever performed and never had there been a better reason.

However, as the audience realized they were deaf, panic broke out. Archer yelled, but no words came from his mouth. Paris was deaf too, and she knew the terror that people were experiencing as they tried to talk to their neighbor or to hear anything and didn't. The panic grew like pandemonium. Paris' heart went out to all the people experiencing so many fears at once.

However, she couldn't tell them that she was protecting them from hearing a gut-wrenching song that would tear out their hearts. Even if she could tell them, right then, she had to focus. Her job was to keep the people inside the Hollywood Bowl protected in a dome of deafness.

Sweat poured down Paris' face. Her fingers grew hot from Amantis. Her arm shook violently. There was no way she could keep this up much longer.

The crowd was close to breaking loose too. People got out of their seats and rushed for the exits. They were screaming, but no one could hear them.

Tears pricked Paris' eyes from the pain of the moment and the loss of so much magic. However, she kept her hand in the air, and her wand pointed at the heavens. She'd protect people until they were safe. Or until she passed out.

However, when she felt something tug at her leg, Paris was forced to look down. To her relief, she found Faraday at her boot, giving her an "all's clear" thumbs up.

Paris dropped her arm and the spell with it, making it so everyone in the Hollywood Bowl could hear once more.

People stumbled as the ambient noises returned to their ears and their screams registered. As they realized they could hear once more. These people had been through so much already. It was time to take this show to the next level. And it was time to catch whoever was behind this.

Paris turned to Archer, who was frozen beside her, perplexed by all that had happened.

"You have a new song," she said in a rush. "Play it now! Play it like your life and everyone's heart in this place depends on it."

CHAPTER EIGHTY

Band Shell, Hollywood Bowl, Hollywood, California

As if Archer Finch understood the severity of the moment, he cued his band, and they started with a bang, the guitar hitting a high note first to get the audience's attention.

"Who out there is ready to love someone?" Archer sang into the microphone. "All you have to do is live in a world without sound to appreciate the love that music brings us."

The crowd erupted with deafening applause. Paris backed off the stage, mesmerized by their reaction. The audience seemed to think it was all a part of the show. Some sort of crazy special effects all to bring them a better, more impactful performance.

If Archer didn't have everyone's attention before, he did when he began singing his new love song, his attention directed at the girl in the front row. His eyes seemed to say, "You're the only person in the world for me. You are my world."

He sang the lyrics of his new love ballad.

"I never thought that we would go to lovers from friends."

The crowd was silent, hanging on his every word.

Ella Sparrow was regarding the lead singer with unrelenting love.

Paris felt the emotions building in the air but knew that she had other jobs to attend to soon. She had to protect these people. However, she lingered for one more moment to listen as the crescendo of the chorus hit, and Archer Finch sang words etched on his soul rather than his arm.

"I never thought that we would go to lovers from friends. But now I hope that you will be my song that never ends."

CHAPTER EIGHTY-ONE

Band Shell, Hollywood Bowl, Hollywood, California

Jumping off the side of the stage, Paris put Amantis in its holster in exchange for one of the potions Bep had given her. She'd depleted her reserves, so now was the time to rely on other types of magic, like potions.

Paris scanned the crowd, looking for suspicious figures like the ones in all black that Lee and Holly confronted. Archer was belting out his song now. The audience around Paris was swaying, and unmistakably, she felt love in the air. However, if whoever was behind the heartbreak returned to do more damage, it could all be ruined. Paris couldn't have that. She was going to ensure that this night ended happily.

When she was to the super seats, Paris turned from her high perch and surveyed the amphitheater. She saw the hills around the Hollywood Bowl and the sight constricted her throat.

"Lee, where are you?" she asked in a rush over the comms.

"I'm on the eastern side at the top of the Bowl."

"Look west," Paris stated. "What are those?"

Paris was asking about the strange UFO-like objects flying over the Hollywood Hills toward the amphitheater.

SARAH NOFFKE & MICHAEL ANDERLE

"Looks like drones to me," Lee stated.

"Why?"

"After the stunts I've seen tonight, I'd say to try to poop all over our party."

"Well, what are we going to do about it?" Paris counted at least a dozen.

"Honestly, they outnumber us." Lee sounded defeated. "Who knows what they're carrying? A type of gas to drop. A sonographic pulse. After what I've witnessed tonight, it's hard to say, but I wouldn't underestimate whoever you're up against. They don't want you to succeed."

"As informational as that was, it wasn't helpful," Paris retorted tersely. "Fare? You there?"

Paris watched as the lights on the drones grew closer. They were almost to the Hollywood Bowl. Archer's love song was almost over. Then the audience would see the enemy approaching, and it would be more pandemonium.

"Pare, I see them, but honestly, I don't know how to combat them. There are too many. I'm getting a weird infrared signal that tells me they're carrying some dangerous magitech. Whatever they've got, whatever they're about to drop, we don't want to be here. I say we evacuate."

"Okay." Paris sprinted back to the stage.

The love song was coming to a brilliant and heartfelt end. Then Paris would have to jump on the stage, tell people to get out, and hope they didn't trample each other on the way out. Hopefully, all the good Punch Line had done with their music wasn't about to be undone by this evil force.

Paris' demon blood delivered her to the stage faster than humanly possible. She was about to jump onto it and take the microphone from Archer as he belted out his last note. However, something in Paris' ear made her pause.

"Didn't you say that the Hollywood Bowl is a no-fly zone?" Christine asked over the comms.

Paris froze, looked up, and held her breath. "Yes, why?"

"Because it looks like planes are coming in from either side of the drones, surrounding them," Christine answered over the comm.

"Yeah," Lee stated.

"Those aren't airplanes," Faraday said, and excitement filled his voice.

Walking backward, Paris retreated, looking up at the starry sky. Archer's voice still reverberated in the air and the last notes of his song echoed as the Dragon Elite streaked over the Hollywood Bowl as if they were the finale to the best song of the night —of the decade. Of the century.

Flying in a beautiful display of choreography was Sophia Beaufont on her dragon Lunis and her friends from the Dragon Elite and the Rogue Riders—two groups that had banded together to protect justice, diplomacy, and peace.

Half of the dragons created a beautiful show over the Hollywood Bowl, and the audience stared up in wonder, shock, and amazement. The other half of the dragons attacked the drones, knocking into them, shooting them out of the air with fire, or swatting them into the hills. However, no one but the security team saw that because everyone else was too mesmerized by the dragons circling overhead.

Two dragons—one blue and the other white—flew toward each other. When they were still far enough apart, they opened their mouths and shot fire at each other. However, it didn't hit the other. Instead, their fire connected, radiated off the other, and bounced in the opposite direction, creating a heart of flames in the air over the Hollywood Bowl and its audience—who had seen a show that night unlike any other.

Paris smiled, grateful that her mother called in security backup that night and a fireworks show too. It seemed that after everything, they had a happy ending.

Hopefully, love had sparked for some. If one couple found

happiness from that event, it was enough for Paris. She suspected that there were many full hearts as the crowd stared up at the sky and the fiery heart that burned in the night air over Hollywood, California.

CHAPTER EIGHTY-TWO

Hollywood Bowl, Hollywood, California

"Thanks for everything." Paris shook Archer Finch's hand, giving him a meaningful look.

He shook his head like she was wrong. "I owe you everything. If it weren't for you...well, I wouldn't have what's most important in my life." The lead singer looked fondly across the room to the girl laughing and collecting their stuff. "Ella is the best thing that ever happened to me, and now I'm never going to let her go...in a non-stalker, loving way."

Paris laughed. "I know what you mean. I'm glad you found your way back to each other."

He laughed too. "If by find our way back, you mean that magical fairy godmothers fixed everything and gave us a second chance."

Paris smiled, looking at her team beside her. "We do what we do because it matters."

"And the pay is crazy good," Holly lied.

"Well, I better help the band load up our stuff." Archer smiled at the fairy godmothers.

"Sorry about your gear," Paris said. "My uncle says he'll have it replaced."

"No problem," Archer said. "I've gotten more than my money's worth from this event. Those dragons were a spectacular finale. Any time you need us to play a charity concert for you, we're game."

Paris beamed, waving at the lead singer of Punch Line as he joined Ella and his band, leaving out the back of the Hollywood Bowl.

"I can't believe I didn't throw myself at that man." Holly deflated like she'd been holding her breath the entire time.

"I can't believe that after all this, I never got introduced to King Rudolf Sweetwater," Isha grumbled.

"I promise that you will," Paris consoled, smiling at her team. "Great job, you all. Who wants beers? I'm buying."

"Another time." Lee shook her head. "I'm exhausted and need a foot rub."

"Me too," Christine stated.

"Yeah, after searching this place for those creep trespassers, I'm beat too," Penny added.

"Well, thanks for trying to find them." Paris tried not to allow her disappointment to show. "We'll find out who's behind this."

"Of course, we will," Lee said. "And by we, you mean you. But do call me when you want me to break someone's neck. I'll be there at a moment's notice."

"Thanks." Paris waved at her friends as they retreated for the exit too, leaving her mostly alone backstage.

She was all too aware that Agent Barney Jasper was hanging in the corner of the space, talking to Headmistress Willow and Mae Ling and looking for his opportunity to talk to Paris. The two fairy godmothers waved at Paris as he approached her, as if to politely say their farewells. Everyone was exhausted after the longest night ever.

"Tonight was full of unexpected events," Agent Jasper began, his hands in his pockets.

"For me, it was."

"You think I'm behind this." He called out what she was thinking.

"I don't know what to believe."

Agent Jasper nodded. "I get that we didn't start on the right foot."

"Right foot? You pretty much treated me like a second-class citizen and told me I was worthless from the beginning."

He nodded again. "I know. I'm sorry. I'm used to things running in a certain manner, and I won't say that it's the best. I don't do things the way I should, and tonight has made me realize that. When Saint Valentine came to me and told me that I had a new agent who was a woman, I didn't act maturely about it. I made assumptions about you, thinking you got to where you are because of your name. However…"

He motioned at where Headmistress Willow and Mae Ling talked to him. "Your professors had a lot to tell me about you. I realize now that you didn't get to where you are because of your name. I realize it's who you are. I saw that tonight. You didn't quit even when you could have. When that song started to play, you performed magic unlike I've ever seen and all so you could protect love. It's…well, it's what FGA should be about. It's what we've lost. I hope that if I give you a fresh start, you'll give me a second chance."

At the conclusion to his words, Agent Jasper held out his hand, offering it to Paris.

She considered the guy before her who had seemed way more than just pompous when she first met him. However, she wanted to believe that people could change. Maybe he wasn't the bad guy she thought he was. Maybe he was misguided. That meant she still had a bad guy out there to find.

After making him wait longer than she intended, Paris took

his hand and shook it. "Okay, I look forward to working with you, Agent Jasper."

"Call me Barney," he stated.

"Okay, Barney."

"And Paris?" He gave her an honest look. "I think it's evident now that you have enemies you need to guard against more than ever. I have to protect all my departments but don't think that I'm not supporting your efforts."

"You're playing the political game you mentioned," she guessed.

He nodded. "I have to be discreet. Not all of us can be as bold as you."

Paris nodded. "I came from nothing, so I never mind risking it all."

"I get that. But still, be careful. Know that I'm on your side, even if it might not look like it."

"Politics," she repeated. "So, can you tell me anything about who is behind all this? Do you know?"

"I don't know entirely enough to give you anything of real use," he answered, again trying to be sincere. "Things are very complicated in this arena. However, I can tell you, follow the money. If you follow that trail, you're sure to find out what's going on behind the scenes."

Paris had so many questions, but the time for answers would have to wait. Barney seemed to agree, and she believed he'd told her most of what he knew of use.

With that, the agent of the Basic Love branch for FGA backed up and waved goodbye before leaving her alone standing backstage at the Hollywood Bowl.

CHAPTER EIGHTY-THREE

Little Pleasures Farmhouse, Outskirts of Boulder, Colorado

Nothing felt better to Paris Beaufont than to be lying in Hemingway's arms that night as the fire crackled on the living room hearth.

"You're not tired." Hemingway brushed Paris' hair off her forehead.

"I realize that I should be," she admitted. "It's just that I have so many questions unanswered and so many ideas. Not to mention all the thank you notes I have to write for all the favors I called in."

Hemingway laughed, his soft chuckle the best sound ever. Paris dearly loved the man in her arms. All she wanted was for others to find comfort like what she had when she laid her head on his chest at night, sleeping safely in their farmhouse.

"It sounds like you had an amazing first week at FGA." Hemingway tried to hide his yawn. "I can't believe you threw a concert."

"Yeah, Saint Valentine told Headmistress Willow that the love meter had a huge boost afterward. It was probably the dragons."

"It was the music," Hemingway argued, pulling her closer to

him as they lay on the sofa. "It was you and all that you did to protect love using magic, bravery, and skill. Your new wand seems amazing."

"Amantis is impressive." Paris knew she couldn't have pulled off that deafening spell on so many thousands of people without the incredible wand. "I can't wait to use it again. Oh, and all the potions I never got a chance to play with."

He snickered. "Yes, Bep seems to have loaded you up with some mysterious stuff."

"Everything went okay with the restaurant this week?" Paris asked. "You and Uncle Clark got on all right?"

"Of course," he answered. "You know that you're what got this place going, but we can manage without you...just barely."

"Well, I'm glad and want you to be happy when I'm not here. Not too happy, mind you. Just enough that you're not in pain. But not like giddy or really satisfied. You get the idea."

"Don't worry, Pare. There's no way my life would be complete without you. You're my puzzle piece. I realize I have to share you because you fix so many others' lives so they can be happy too. I'm the luckiest man because I get to be the one who holds you at night and shares my life with you. And see you as no one else does. I'm forever grateful that you're mine."

"I feel the same way, and I'm grateful that I get to come home to you at the end of a day at the office." Paris snuggled into Hemingway's chest, enjoying his warmth and the acceptance she always felt when in his arms. If anything, Paris could bring love to the world because she felt so secure in her life. It hadn't always been that way. Creating a happy life took risk. And bravery. It took singing the sad songs until they turned into happy anthems.

Paris hummed the last song she'd heard Punch Line sing that night with a wide smile on her face.

"What's that?" Hemingway startled awake.

She snuggled into him. "Just singing."

"Oh, I love it when you do."

She lifted her chin, kissed his cheek, and sang to him, "I hope that you will be my song that never ends."

Hemingway squeezed her tightly, smiling with his eyes closed. "Forever and ever, Paris Beaufont. Until my final breath."

"Familia Est Sempiternum," Paris said in a soft whisper, reciting the Beaufont family motto. In Latin it simply meant, "Family is forever." And for the Beaufonts and for Paris and Hemingway, nothing was truer. He was her family. Her forever.

"Familia Est Sempiternum," Hemingway repeated, hugging her into him once more. And a minute or two later, Hemingway fell asleep, his gentle breath better than music to Paris' soul.

CHAPTER EIGHTY-FOUR

Front Porch, Little Pleasures Farmhouse, Outskirts of Boulder, Colorado

After putting Hemingway in bed, Paris snuck back out to the quiet of the front porch, needing a bit longer to unwind and process after the long day.

"I thought you'd end up here." Faraday was sitting in an old rocking chair that made him look ridiculously small due to its size.

She nodded, taking a seat in the other rocker next to him on the oversized wraparound porch. Her hands found the armrests and gripped them, enjoying the way they felt strong in her fingers. "Yeah, I couldn't sleep."

"A lot happened." Faraday flicked his tail.

"You were brilliant, getting the audio back up at the concert after that hack."

"Thanks," Faraday chirped. "I don't know what we would've done if you didn't create that deafening spell. I've seen you do a lot of incredible things, but that one takes the cake. I can only imagine the power you'll have now with Amantis."

"Thanks. I look forward to working with my wand and finding out what I can do with it. More than that, I want to know who's behind all this mess. There were several goons. And drones. Then the magitech that hacked the system."

"I know," Faraday agreed. "It's a lot to sort out, and I have some ideas…"

"Oh?" She was immediately intrigued as she looked out at the starry sky, dark prairie, and mountains in the distance.

"Well, it could be Jackson Zelle, but it could also be Agent Josh Emerald. Those two could also just be jerks the same way Agent Barney Jasper was, so we don't want to convict them."

"The guy who fought Lee had a magical instrument that was a screwdriver like Agent Emerald. And Dwyer said someone from his department asked about magical tattooing ink."

"Oh, believe me, that's compelling evidence," Faraday admitted. "But it's not anything definitive. I think it means we keep an eye on Agent Emerald. And Jackson Zelle. We shouldn't take our eyes off any other potential threats, though. We need more information. We need to fill in this picture. What did Agent Jasper tell you?"

"He said that I needed to follow the money trail."

Faraday nodded. "That's a good strategy because as we've learned, FGA runs on money. It's the motivator. It's the driving force for departments."

"Instead of love," Paris scoffed.

"Look what you did with no money. Think of what you'll keep doing."

"Yeah, and I think there's so much politics that I do have to be careful. I have to play their game until I'm in a better position. Many are watching me. Many want me to fail. I refuse to, but I can't put myself in a position where they can set me up."

"You have your trusty wand that makes you seem like them now."

"Amantis," Paris said proudly. "It's better than anything they have."

"That's because you're better than any of them."

SARAH NOFFKE & MICHAEL ANDERLE

"I'm just me," Paris argued while rocking, enjoying the sound of the crickets in the distance making their music, singing their song.

"Do you want to go in soon?" Faraday asked after a moment.

"Yeah, in a minute. You can go in if you're ready to sleep. I want to sit here a bit longer and think about all the good and true things we can do to make FGA better. To create more love. To help the world."

"How can I sleep when thinking such things is a possibility?" Faraday rocked his chair slightly, but it took more momentum on his part.

Paris grinned fondly at her best friend. "That's how I feel. There are so many things ahead of us."

"Lots of missions."

"Yeah," she admitted.

"Mysteries to unravel."

"Sure."

"Evil to squash," Faraday added.

"Of course."

"There's so much love to create too," he said in between the squeak of his rocking chair.

"Tomorrow, we'll get back to work unraveling, squashing, and creating."

"I can't wait, Pare."

"Me too, Fare."

The two friends fell silent, although their minds were loud with excitement about all the good and true things they would do. They'd already had a big first week at Fairy Godmother Agency, but there were so many more adventures to come. They both knew this was only the beginning of a brand-new chapter in their lives.

Paris Beaufont and Faraday were destined to save the world because they were the stuff of legends. They were the heroes who would sacrifice everything for the most important riches in this world—love.

THE STORY CONTINUES

The story continues with book two, *The Ruthless Negotiator*, available at Amazon.

Claim your copy today!

SARAH'S AUTHOR NOTES

JANUARY 26, 2022

Thank you so much for taking a chance on this new series. Thanks for buying and reviewing the books. For supporting LMBPN and for being awesome!

This first book is about music. I got to thinking that love and music were so intertwined that it made sense for that to be the plot of this book. What if spelled music could break hearts? And were songs about love automatically magical? In the end, a love ballad that isn't spelled is stronger than the cursed tragic song that breaks hearts.

If you're new to my author notes, then you may not realize that I call everyone by nicknames here. I'm Tiny Ninja, named by Mike and the readers. Michael is Bird Killer, named by me and the readers. My boyfriend is the Scotsman, named because that's what he is. My daughter is Mini Me because, okay I'm not explaining that one. You're up to speed now so I will continue.

The Scotsman and I love music. We first bonded over our mutual love of Taylor Swift. And when we first started dating, I might have disclosed that I'd proposed to Gary Lightbody from Snow Patrol at a concert. Gary said no. And the Scotsman has never let me forget that I told him this information. Oh, the things we tell boys before we know they're going to become our one and only. I have regrets.

Anyway, we love music. Craig, aka, the Scotsman, has made me many a Spotify playlist over the years. I make them for him too because what better way to express my love than with other people's words. And back in the day, before we could tell each other how we felt, it was through music that we communicated.

So music is important in love. But I also like to listen to sad music. I know, it sounds weird to punish myself with heart break songs when I'm in a happy relationship. But when writing, it helps me to get inspiration. And I love the poetry and emotions of such songs.

However, the Scotsman has questioned me on whether this is a healthy process. But herein lies the background for this book. Not all songs can be happy and what if the sad ones had the power to actually break up lovers.

So I needed lyrics for both the heart break and love song in the book. Craig, a writer as well, gets full credit for those song lyrics. I love that in the end, the happy one was about music: "I hope that you will be my song that never ends."

Okay, enough of that mushy stuff. Let's talk corporate bull-shit. That's the opposite of love.

When MA and I were coming up with the premise for this series, we decided that FGA would be totally corporate. In my past life, I worked in Corporate America where I wore pant suits and high heels and went to meetings about budget reports. Oh, I think I'm getting hives just talking about it.

Back then, I lived for the weekends. I would sit around with my friends and we would never talk about our jobs. Ever. I can't even tell you what they did for a living. And if I wanted to have no friends, then I'd tell mine that as an Academic Specialist, I assessed student learning outcomes using gradient measures and practical application tests. Again, I think the old rash is coming back...

These days, I don't even know what a weekend is. I work every day and I live to work! And when I sit around with my friends, I can't wait to tell them about what I'm working on. "I've got these new characters and one is obsessed with doing lunges and squats and the other has fake everything. And when they get in trouble, their boss won't let them workout and takes away their hair extensions."

It's really a wonder that I have friends at all...

Anyway, my old corporate bosses would have probably punished me in similar ways. My characters are based on me, although my eyelashes and hair are all mine. But I often reward myself with a one-minute plank in between writing sprints because I'm sick like that.

When I worked at Corporate America, I used to take my breaks to walk the stairs up to the 12th floor and back. Then I'd smoke a cigarette and return to work all breathless. In my defense, I wasn't making enough money to afford a gym membership. It never occurred to me that I could have given up smoking to pay for it.

And look how I've derailed the author notes once again. It's a talent.

Anywho, I really loved the opportunity in this series to revisit the arbitrary bullshit that is corporate politics. One of my favorite parts of writing urban fantasy is turning a known whimsical thing on its head. So we have fairy godmothers who are supposed to be all pretty and happy, but they are managed by a bunch of bureaucratic agents who only care about line items and weekly reports and quarterly meetings. That felt right to me.

Furthermore, I loved the idea of the headquarters for love being in a stuffy skyscraper in Manhattan. That also felt right. Creating FGA Tower was a lot of fun with the magical coffee shop and curry restaurant and shoe shine station. And my daughter Lydia, aka Mini Me, helped with the different floors and departments. What is on the 26th floor? And what's up with the basement? Many mysteries to be revealed.

I'm glad that I can channel the soul crushing experiences of my corporate past into this series. For the outline for this book, I created an organizational chart for all the branches and departments. I even had a big Smart Art graphic! I was really proud of myself when I sent it over to Mike to review.

I'm strangely looking forward to scenes where I get to dip back into my "managerial" lingo. Don't tell anyone but I have a Masters in Management. Yeah, I know, I write urban fantasy… It makes zero sense at all.

But think about how fun it will be when some snotty nosed executive tells Paris that, "At your next 360 degree review we're going to need to focus on optimizing high-level learning. We're going to dive deep into ways to lay the foundation so that we're not reinventing the wheel and ensure that we're leveraging ways to get low-hanging fruit." To that, Paris is going to stick out her tongue and say, "Why don't you optimize this."

We have a lot of fun things in store for this series. Ones that will require me to put back on my managerial hat and also learn about some modern-day business strategies. I'm hoping to bring something really cool and different to this series while also having bad dad jokes and lots of awesome fight scenes.

On that note, I'll turn you over to our esteemed leader. Hey Bird Killer, aren't you glad that we don't have a bunch of corporate bullshit where we work? Could you imagine if we had a really strict HR department? What would they say about the names we call each other?

Much love and Peace,

Tiny Ninja

MICHAEL'S AUTHOR NOTES

FEBRUARY 16, 2022

Thank you for not only reading this series but these author notes here in the back as well. I hope you enjoy this new series by the elegant (if not tall) Tiny Ninja™.

And a word to the wise… She makes up nicknames without the fans' help. Sarah is just using you as a smokescreen to hide behind.

Cause it doesn't take much to hide her. She's small.

Seriously *tiny*.

Later a word about me, but right now a word about…me and corporate @#%@#.

I've never been a huge enterprise employee. However, I've been a consultant or contractor to big companies in multiple industries. I was—in a past life—a software and solutions developer.

I programmed in Microsoft languages and databases. (It sounds better said the other way.)

For those who have not read anything by Sarah, go back before any of the latest stuff and read Sarah "BC" (Before Craig) and realize how nauseatingly in love she is. It's disgusting.

Here, go read this and see if you can make heads or tails of the person writing THESE books (2) and the person who wrote these author notes.

Trust me; it's worth it ;-)

The title (before ads got us in trouble) was *Everybody in LA is an Asshole*. It's BC Sarah. LOL.

http://www.amazon.com/gp/product/B07HFW78NS

I've got to go. These author notes are longer.

Since we are going to put the "About me" at the bottom, I have to go. We REALLY appreciate you reading our books and listening to the two of us cantankerous authors gripe about each other in fun and frivolity.

With no HR department…thank God!

Ok, now a little about me if you haven't met me.

I wrote my first book *Death Becomes Her* (*The Kurtherian Gambit*) in September/October of 2015 and released it November 2, 2015. I wrote and released the next two books that same month and had three released by the end of November 2015.

So, just over six years ago.

Since then, I've written, collaborated, concepted, and/or created hundreds more in all sorts of genres.

My most successful genre is still my first, Paranormal Sci-Fi, followed quickly by Urban Fantasy. I have multiple pen names I produce under.

Some because I can be a bit crude in my humor at times or raw in my cynicism (Michael Todd). I have one I share with Martha Carr (Judith Berens, and another (not disclosed) that we use as a marketing test pen name.

In general, I just love to tell stories, and with success comes the opportunity to mix two things I love in my life.

Business and stories.

I've wanted to be an entrepreneur since I was a teenager. I was a very *unsuccessful* entrepreneur (I tried many times) until my publishing company LMBPN signed one author in 2015.

Me.

I was the president of the company, and I was the first author published. Funny how it worked out that way.

It was late 2016 before we had additional authors join me for publishing. Now we have a few dozen authors, a few hundred audiobooks by LMBPN published, a few hundred more licensed by six audio companies, and about a thousand titles in our company.

It's been a busy six plus years.

Have a great week or weekend! Talk to you in the next story.

Ad Aeternitatem,

Michael Anderle

ABOUT SARAH

Sarah Noffke is a prolific USA Today Best-Selling Author, who writes YA and NA science fiction, fantasy, paranormal and urban fantasy. Most of her stories draw on her experiences living on the West Coast, growing up in Texas or traveling the world.

Her passion for art, culture and literature drives her to create stories that are full of whimsey, humor and philosophy. Her books appeal to readers who enjoy an escape, a bit of magic mixed with science and the unexpected--like a dragon who tells bad jokes and has a video game addiction, but fights for justice.

Noffke's books are top rated and best-sellers on Amazon. Her books are available in paperback, audio and in Spanish, Portuguese, German, Dutch and Italian.

To stay up to date with Sarah, please visit her website and subscribe to her newsletter: www.sarahnoffke.com

For a complete list of books by Sarah and a suggested reading order, please see: www.sarahnoffke.com/reading-guide/

BOOKS BY SARAH NOFFKE

Check out other work by Sarah author here.

Ghost Squadron:

Formation #1:
Kill the bad guys. Save the Galaxy. All in a hard day's work.
After ten years of wandering the outer rim of the galaxy, Eddie Teach is a man without a purpose. He was one of the toughest pilots in the Federation, but now he's just a regular guy, getting into bar fights and making a difference wherever he can. It's not the same as flying a ship and saving colonies, but it'll have to do.

That is, until General Lance Reynolds tracks Eddie down and offers him a job. There are bad people out there, plotting terrible things, killing innocent people, and destroying entire colonies. **Someone has to stop them.**

Eddie, along with the genetically-enhanced combat pilot Julianna Fregin and her trusty E.I. named Pip, must recruit a diverse team of specialists, both human and alien. They'll need to master their new Q-Ship, one of the most powerful strike ships ever constructed. And finally, they'll have to stop a faceless enemy so powerful, it threatens to destroy the entire Federation.

All in a day's work, right?

Experience this exciting military sci-fi saga and the latest addition to the expanded Kurtherian Gambit Universe. If you're a fan of Mass Effect, Firefly, or Star Wars, you'll love this riveting new space opera.

NOTE: If cursing is a problem, then this might not be for you.

Check out the entire series <u>here.</u>

The Precious Galaxy Series:

Corruption #1

A new evil lurks in the darkness.

After an explosion, the crew of a battlecruiser mysteriously disappears.

Bailey and Lewis, complete strangers, find themselves suddenly onboard the damaged ship. Lewis hasn't worked a case in years, not since the final one broke his spirit and his bank account. The last thing Bailey remembers is preparing to take down a fugitive on Onyx Station.

Mysteries are harder to solve when there's no evidence left behind.

Bailey and Lewis don't know how they got onboard *Ricky Bobby* or why. However, they quickly learn that whatever was responsible for the explosion and disappearance of the crew is still on the ship.

Monsters are real and what this one can do changes everything.

The new team bands together to discover what happened and how to fight the monster lurking in the bottom of the battle-cruiser.

Will they find the missing crew? Or will the monster end them all?

The Soul Stone Mage Series:

House of Enchanted #1:

The Kingdom of Virgo has lived in peace for thousands of years...until now.

The humans from Terran have always been real assholes to the witches of Virgo. Now a silent war is brewing, and the timing couldn't be worse. Princess Azure will soon be crowned queen of the Kingdom of Virgo.

In the Dark Forest a powerful potion-maker has been murdered.

Charmsgood was the only wizard who could stop a deadly virus plaguing Virgo. He also knew about the devastation the people from Terran had done to the forest.

Azure must protect her people. Mend the Dark Forest. Create alliances with savage beasts. No biggie, right?

But on coronation day everything changes. Princess Azure isn't who she thought she was and that's a big freaking problem.

Welcome to The Revelations of Oriceran. Check out the entire series here.

The Lucidites Series:

Awoken, #1:

Around the world humans are hallucinating after sleepless nights.

In a sterile, underground institute the forecasters keep reporting the same events.

And in the backwoods of Texas, a sixteen-year-old girl is about to be caught up in a fierce, ethereal battle.

Meet Roya Stark. She drowns every night in her dreams, spends her hours reading classic literature to avoid her family's ridicule, and is prone to premonitions—which are becoming more frequent. And now her dreams are filled with strangers offering to reveal what she has always wanted to know: Who is she? That's the question that haunts her, and she's about to find out. But will Roya live to regret learning the truth?

Stunned, #2
Revived, #3

The Reverians Series:

Defects, #1:
In the happy, clean community of Austin Valley, everything appears to be perfect. Seventeen-year-old Em Fuller, however, fears something is askew. Em is one of the new generation of Dream Travelers. For some reason, the gods have not seen fit to gift all of them with their expected special abilities. Em is a Defect—one of the unfortunate Dream Travelers not gifted with a psychic power. Desperate to do whatever it takes to earn her gift, she endures painful daily injections along with commands from her overbearing, loveless father. One of the few bright spots in her life is the return of a friend she had thought dead—but with his return comes the knowledge of a shocking, unforgivable truth. The society Em thought was protecting her has actually been betraying her, but she has no idea how to break away from its authority without hurting everyone she loves.

Rebels, #2
Warriors, #3

Vagabond Circus Series:

Suspended, #1:
When a stranger joins the cast of Vagabond Circus—a circus that is run by Dream Travelers and features real magic—mysterious events start happening. The once orderly grounds of the circus become riddled with hidden threats. And the ringmaster

realizes not only are his circus and its magic at risk, but also his very life.

Vagabond Circus caters to the skeptics. Without skeptics, it would close its doors. This is because Vagabond Circus runs for two reasons and only two reasons: first and foremost to provide the lost and lonely Dream Travelers a place to be illustrious. And secondly, to show the nonbelievers that there's still magic in the world. If they believe, then they care, and if they care, then they don't destroy. They stop the small abuse that day-by-day breaks down humanity's spirit. If Vagabond Circus makes one skeptic believe in magic, then they halt the cycle, just a little bit. They allow a little more love into this world. That's Dr. Dave Raydon's mission. And that's why this ringmaster recruits. That's why he directs. That's why he puts on a show that makes people question their beliefs. He wants the world to believe in magic once again.

Paralyzed, #2
Released, #3

Ren Series:

Ren: The Man Behind the Monster, #1:
Born with the power to control minds, hypnotize others, and read thoughts, Ren Lewis, is certain of one thing: God made a mistake. No one should be born with so much power. A monster awoke in him the same year he received his gifts. At ten years old. A prepubescent boy with the ability to control others might merely abuse his powers, but Ren allowed it to corrupt him. And since he can have and do anything he wants, Ren should be happy. However, his journey teaches him that harboring so much power doesn't bring happiness, it steals it. Once this realization sets in, Ren makes up his mind to do the one thing that can bring his tortured soul some peace. He must kill the monster.

Note This book is NA and has strong language, violence and sexual references.

Ren: God's Little Monster, #2
Ren: The Monster Inside the Monster, #3
Ren: The Monster's Adventure, #3.5
Ren: The Monster's Death

Olento Research Series:

Alpha Wolf, #1:
Twelve men went missing.

Six months later they awake from drug-induced stupors to find themselves locked in a lab.

And on the night of a new moon, eleven of those men, possessed by new—and inhuman—powers, break out of their prison and race through the streets of Los Angeles until they disappear one by one into the night.

Olento Research wants its experiments back. Its CEO, Mika Lenna, will tear every city apart until he has his werewolves imprisoned once again. He didn't undertake a huge risk just to lose his would-be assassins.

However, the Lucidite Institute's main mission is to save the world from injustices. Now, it's Adelaide's job to find these mutated men and protect them and society, and fast. Already around the nation, wolflike men are being spotted. Attacks on innocent women are happening. And then, Adelaide realizes what her next step must be: She has to find the alpha wolf first. Only once she's located him can she stop whoever is behind this experiment to create wild beasts out of human beings.

Lone Wolf, #2
Rabid Wolf, #3
Bad Wolf, #4

CONNECT WITH THE AUTHORS

Connect with Sarah and sign up for her email list here:

http://www.sarahnoffke.com/connect/

Michael Anderle Social

Website: http://lmbpn.com

Email List: http://lmbpn.com/email/

https://www.facebook.com/LMBPNPublishing

https://twitter.com/MichaelAnderle

https://www.instagram.com/lmbpn_publishing/

https://www.bookbub.com/authors/michael-anderle

BOOKS BY MICHAEL ANDERLE

Sign up for the LMBPN email list to be notified of new releases and special deals!

https://lmbpn.com/email/

For a complete list of books by Michael Anderle, please visit:

www.lmbpn.com/ma-books/